200 Miles to Liberty

Book 4 in the Perilous Miles Series

P.A. Glaspy

COPYRIGHT 2019

All Rights Reserved

P.A. Glaspy

1st Edition

Published by Glaspy Publishing Inc

Other works by P.A. Glaspy

A Powerless World Series:

Before the Power was Gone

When the Power is Gone

When the Peace is Gone

When the Pain is Gone

Perilous Miles Series:

300 Miles

15 Miles from Home

Another 20 Miles

Never miss a launch! Sign up for the newsletter here:

http://paglaspy.com/add-me/

RECAP

300 Miles, Book One in the Perilous Miles series, introduced us to Carly Marshall and her sons, Aaron and Cameron. Her parents, Joel and Lauri Chambers, live close, just a couple of miles away. We meet Elliott Marshall, Aaron and Cameron's paternal grandfather, who lives in the country. We also get a glimpse of Carly's brother, Will, who is on his way home when everything falls apart.

We see them going through their day-to-day lives, unaware that something sinister is being plotted on the other side of the world. Something that will turn their lives upside down.

Book Two, 15 Miles From Home, picks up after the event and follows Will's journey from Interstate 40, where his car stopped running, to his parents' home. He meets Amanda Frye on the road and invites her to come with him, since she lives in Wisconsin and would likely never get there safely, if at all. There's something about her that feels comfortable and right.

Carly isn't handling the situation well and can't keep her mind off the fact that her sons are twenty miles away and she has no way to get to them or that her previous life is gone. A once strong independent woman is becoming a pain in the butt with her whining and crying. Joel and Lauri try to comfort her as they anxiously await the arrival of their son. Joel spends a lot of time helping his neighbors with things as simple as building a fire while trying to get them to understand this isn't just a power outage. His words fall on mostly deaf ears.

We find out who the president of the United States is and his plan for the country after the attack. It's not a good plan — especially for the people of the country. He wants to take away rights and freedoms and doesn't care if anyone agrees with him or not.

Speaker of the House Phil Roman is concerned when the president says he will not be stepping down for the newly elected president in January. He knows this is unconstitutional, but then pretty much everything the president is planning falls into that category as well. In a private meeting with General Charles Everley, United States Army and senior member of the Joint Chiefs, a decision is made to collect the president-elect in New York City and bring him to D.C. General Everley tasks his aide, Major Damon Sorley, with the mission. In a military Humvee and one of very few vehicles that still work, his trip will not be covert. On the contrary, he will be a target for anyone who thinks they can commandeer his transportation. The mission will be dangerous, even more so for a man traveling so many miles alone in a land where desperation leads people to make bad decisions.

In Book Three, Another 20 Miles continues the story with Carly and her family dealing with needy neighbors while trying to figure out how to get to Elliott and the boys. Carly is sullen and moody, lashing out at anyone close to her. Will and Joel, along with Amanda, go to one of Joel's friends who lives nearby, Teddy Patterson, in the hopes of bartering for some of the guns Joel knows he has. They find Teddy in a very poor state and help him get situated. When Teddy finds out they are trying to get to Tipton County, he offers them the miracle they've been looking for — a running vehicle. They figured out the "how". Now they just had to decide the "when".

Elliott is teaching the boys how to manage without electricity. His own neighbors are looking for answers and assistance. They're making preparations for the rest of the family to arrive. They didn't expect the one who showed up.

Damon reached New Jersey and met some Guardsmen and women who volunteered to help him complete his mission. Their trip to New York City was a success, though they ended up leaving a man behind. With the president-elect on board, they returned to the Guard station to spend the night before continuing the journey. Their group increased in size, with the help of a camper, and they headed out together the next morning to complete the mission.

President Olstein consistently attempts to control the military, as well as the people of the country. The Joint Chiefs are stalling, particularly General Everley, because they don't agree with the president's ideas and goals. Everley hasn't told the other Chiefs about the plan to bring President-elect Tanner to D.C. They'll know soon enough.

And now, the continuation of the Perilous Miles series, 200 Miles to Liberty.

Cast of Characters

Carly Marshall - sons Aaron and Cameron
Joel and Lauri Chambers - Carly's parents
Will Chambers - Carly's brother
Amanda Frye - Will's friend, met on the journey in 15 Miles From Home
Elliott Marshall - Carly's father-in-law, the boys' paternal grandfather
Ethan Marshall - Carly's estranged husband

President Barton Olstein - current president
David Strain - newly appointed Chief of Staff to the president
Phil Roman - Speaker of the House
General Charles Everley - senior member and Chairman of the Joint Chiefs
Vanessa Jackson - former Chief of Staff for President Olstein, fired

Major Damon Sorley - General Charles Everley's aide
Captain Chris "Hutch" Hutchinson - senior officer of the New Jersey National Guard base
Other members at the Guard base - First Sergeant Marco Perez, Corporal Elizabeth "Liz" Thompson, Sergeant Darrell Light, Staff Sergeant Kevin Blake, and Lieutenant Stacy Manning

President-elect David Tanner - wife Melanie, son Brock
Jason Stephens - Secret Service Agent

The rest of the Joint Chiefs
General Angie Bales
General Carl McKenna
General Anton Drysdale
General Keith Weston
Admiral Arthur Stephens

Other Persons of Interest
Roger Harrison - wife Cindy; Elliott's next-door neighbors
Taylor Livingston - wife Wendy, kids Heather, Grayson,
and Derek; live on the other side of Roger

Chapter 1

Damon, along with the Guardsmen and the Tanner family, were making slow progress. The route Darrell suggested was indeed lacking in people. Miles of fields and the occasional farmhouse were the whole of South Middlebush Road. The trip down Jacques Lane would be the same. However, the travel was tedious. The two feet of snow that had fallen the previous day had drifted to four feet or more in some spots on the open roads. More than once they had to stop and dig their way out of a drift. Though the temperature was about zero — a guess since there was no weather app available to tell them — the diggers worked up a sweat. They rotated out every ten minutes or so to keep everyone fresh. A good-sized drift could take them an hour to clear the part of the road they were on and far enough in front of them to be able to get moving again.

"Whoever thought to bring those snow shovels is a genius," Damon remarked to Hutch as they stood guard.

"That ... would be ... me," Darrell said, huffing the words out as he scooped then tossed a shovel full of snow over his shoulder. "Kind of ... wishing ... we'd packed ... a snow blower ... now."

"I second that!" Marco called from the other side of the camper.

"It's going to take a long time to get to D.C. at this rate," Hutch said. "We've been on the road for hours and only gotten a short way down this road. It's about two hundred miles to Washington. When the storm got into this farmland area, there was nothing to block the snow blowing across these open fields. There's no telling how much longer it's going to take to get to the end of Middlebush."

Damon nodded. "Yep, but we don't have much choice, unless you think we should turn around and try the interstate."

Hutch was scanning the area. "I don't even know why we're standing guard. There isn't even a cow around here, much less people." Turning to Damon, he said, "If my calculations are right, we are only about a half mile from Jacques Lane. That's another mile and a half of open road lined with fields. Once we turn onto Canal, the snow shouldn't be as deep. There's a line of trees between the river and road. The direction the wind was blowing, the road should have gotten some protection from the drifts through there. We'll be on that one for a while. Once we get to Kingston, we're probably going to have to decide whether to try to stay on back roads or head for I-95."

Stacy walked up to the two men. "Can I make a suggestion, Cap?"

"Absolutely, Manning. We are wide open to that."

"I think we'd make better time if we stay on this until it runs into Highway One. We'll go through some 'burbs in Kendall Park, but after that, there will just be spots with a few houses and lots of trees on both sides of the highway. It runs through Princeton, which should be pretty deserted since the students were already gone. We can stay on Highway 1 all the way to 295. Really, Kendall Park would probably be the highest threat area between here and there."

Damon went to the passenger side door of the Humvee. He reached inside and pulled the maps out of his bag. Laying them on the hood, the three checked the route together.

"Yes, it would definitely get us headed in the right direction. But we are going to have quite a few more miles of open road, aka deep snow, first. We're looking at another two and a half to three miles of it going that way."

Hutch was using his finger as a calculator from the map legend's distance meter.

Damon studied the map and replied, "True, but it looks like it will cut our mileage down by a third. I think we should try it."

Hutch nodded. Stepping back and looking toward the camper, he called out, "Keep shoveling, guys. We're going to be doing this for a few more miles. The good news is you're excused from PT today!"

Amidst the groans, a sound started growing from the group that was shoveling. In a deep baritone voice, Darrell was singing.

"Hi ho, hi ho, it's off to work we go ..."

The whistling picked up as if on cue.

The Tanner family was inside the camper snuggled under some blankets they had found in a storage compartment under a seat. Hutch had offered to light the heater, as the propane tank had fuel. Mr. Tanner declined. Agent Jason Stephens was standing guard outside the door.

"I guess if you and your people can work outside in this weather to get us to Washington, we can handle a little cold in here."

Brock was between his parents and appeared to have nodded off. Melanie looked at her husband.

"David, I'm scared. Are we going to be in any danger when we get there?"

"What kind of problems do you think we'd have, Mel?"

She looked down at her son who had laid his head in her lap. She replied softly, "If Olstein says he's not stepping down for you to be inaugurated, how can you make him?"

"Once I'm sworn in, he has to vacate the White House. He no longer has any authority there."

3

With a troubled look, she continued. "What if he finds a way to keep you from being sworn in?"

"That would be an attempted coup; and since the Joint Chiefs — or at least one of them — sent someone to fetch me, I don't think they'll let that happen."

Melanie laid her head on his shoulder. "I hope you're right. I feel like we left the frying pan and are headed toward the fire."

There was a knock on the camper door and Damon leaned in. "We're ready to try to get moving again, Sir. If you and your family would please move to the Humvee, we can get underway."

Tanner stood up. "Of course, Major. Honey, do you want me to carry him?" he said, looking back to his wife.

She was already gently shaking her son. "No, he can walk. Come on, sweetie. Time to go."

Brock moaned as he opened his eyes. "Can't I stay here and sleep?"

Melanie addressed Damon. "Would that be alright, Major? Could we stay in here?"

Damon shook his head. "No, ma'am, I'm sorry, but we can't do that. If something were to happen and we lost the trailer, we'd lose you as well. I need you all in the Humvee with me."

"He's right, Mel. Come on, son. Let's go." Tanner reached his hand out toward his son. Brock took his father's hand and let him help him up.

Damon stepped back as Agent Stephens held his hand out to Mrs. Tanner. "Ma'am, watch your step."

Melanie took his hand and stepped out of the camper. Tanner followed, then turned to make sure his son got out without slipping. They moved together to the vehicle. Once they were settled inside, Hutch called out to the ones shoveling snow.

"Okay, dwarves, let's get going!"

4

The men and women under his command laughed as they loaded into the camper, tapping the shovels on the side to get the caked-on snow off. Marco turned to Darrell at the doorway.

"Hey! We should give each other names, like the seven dwarves!"

Pushing him in, Darrell replied, "You can be Dopey. Move it!"

Leaning his shovel against the stove, Marco grumbled, "Well I guess we know who Grumpy is."

It took them several hours to get the next mile done. Hutch, behind the wheel, suddenly came to a stop. Damon had been studying a map and looked up to see why they were no longer moving.

"What's up, Hutch? Did you see something?"

Hutch was peering through the windshield. "It looks like there's something up ahead in the road, close to those houses. I can't make out what it is though. And I don't want to get too close until we know."

Damon pulled a pair of binoculars out of his pack and looked ahead. "Yep, looks like a roadblock has been set up with sawhorses. I see two men, one with a hunting rifle, the other has a shotgun. They haven't brought them to bear on us. Just looking this way, watching."

Darrell and Stacy had climbed out of the camper and jogged up to the passenger door. Damon put the window down.

"What's up, Cap? More snow removal?" Stacy asked. When she saw where the occupants of the Humvee were looking, she turned her head. "Ah, I see now. Want us to go see what their deal is?"

"Yes, and take Perez. We only see two guys so maybe if they're outnumbered, they'll be less likely to engage."

"Copy that."

Darrell was already on his way back to the camper. He pulled the door open and said, "Come on, Dopey, let's go. We got some real soldiering to do."

Marco jumped out of the camper with his pack and rifle slung over his shoulder. "Woohoo! I'll take anything that isn't shoveling snow!"

As they got to the passenger door, Damon stepped out and addressed the three. "Keep your eyes peeled, guys. They don't look hostile but looks can be deceiving."

"Oh man, don't I know it," Marco replied with a grin. "Friday night, I was at this club and this chick —"

"Can it, Perez!" Hutch barked. "Get serious! If you get shot, I'm going to kick your ass!"

His smile immediately disappeared. "Sorry, Cap. We've got this." Marco turned to his fellow Guardsmen. "Ready?"

Darrell nodded and set out. "Yep. Let's go introduce ourselves to the neighbors."

The three headed toward the makeshift roadblock. Damon and Hutch climbed back in the Humvee.

"He's a good kid, hell of a soldier, he's just a little … flighty," Hutch said to no one in particular. Turning to face Damon, he asked, "Do you think they'll be okay?"

"Were they trained right?" Damon responded.

"Hell yes!" Hutch cried out.

Smiling, Damon raised the binoculars back up, watching them as they went. "Then they'll be fine."

The three Guardsmen watched the two apparent civilians as they made their approach. The two being watched eyed them warily but didn't move to raise their guns. When the three were about a hundred yards away, one of the men raised a hand and called out, "That's far enough. State your business."

Manning, as ranking member of the small squad, took a step forward and replied, "We're New Jersey National

Guard on our way to Washington D.C. We just want to pass through."

Two more men appeared from a small stand of trees to their left. "Shit," Darrell said under his breath. All three of them tightened their grip on their weapons and let their thumbs rest on the safety.

The man who addressed them continued. "What's the big hurry to get to D.C.? It's not like they have power. Or do they?"

"No, I'm sure they don't. We're under orders from the Chief of Staff of the Army to —"

"How'd you get orders?" the man asked, interrupting her. "No power, no phones, no faxes, no radios, no way to communicate. How do we even know you're really National Guard? You could have picked those uniforms up anywhere."

"We have ID we'd be happy to show you." Stacy started to reach for her wallet.

"Stop! No sudden moves! Come forward slowly and keep those rifles pointed down. We'll do the same as long as you do."

Stacy looked to the man on either side of her as they had both stepped up to flank her and gave them a quick nod. They advanced slowly together, rifles pointed toward the ground, thumbs still resting on the safeties. Two of the men at the barrier started toward them when they got close.

"That's good right there. Now, let's see that ID, nice and slow."

The three soldiers pulled their wallets out and flipped them open to show their photo IDs. The man who had been doing all the talking looked them over then looked at Stacy. "I guess you're legit. It's alright, fellas," he called out over his shoulder. Reaching a hand toward her, he went on. "I'm Barry. Barry Broome. So, how *did* you get the orders? Maybe in that nice operational Humvee back there?"

Sensing possible danger, Stacy shook his hand and replied coolly, "Yes, they were delivered in person. We really need to get through here. Why do you have the road blocked anyway? You're not robbers, are you?" Her thumb went instinctively back to the safety of her rifle.

The man chuckled. "No, we haven't robbed anybody, though some of us have been robbed. We set up security points here, at Claremont Road and down Claremont to Mattawang Drive. We've got about fifty homes in this area and a pretty close community. Some boys from Kendall Park thought we'd be easy targets for smash and grabs. They busted into a few places on Arrow Head Lane before we could get security organized."

"Seems like you've got that handled," Stacy commented, relaxing a bit.

"Like I said, we're a close community. Block parties, neighborhood watch; many of us have lived here for years. We've pooled our resources of food. Well, most of us. There're quite a few folks in here with pools, so we'll have water for a while. We've also moved families in with others to share work and save having to try to heat so many homes. The ones with wood-burning fireplaces are packed and stacked. We're just hoping we can ride it out together until we get help from the government. What are they doing about this, do you know?"

Stacy shook her head. "No, we haven't heard anything about that. The man who came in the Humvee left D.C. early Sunday morning. You said most of you were working together. Why not all?"

Barry shrugged. "Some are scared no help is coming and don't want to share the food they have. No biggie. It's their choice. So, what's so important in D.C.?"

"I'm sorry, I can't say anymore. The orders are classified. We need to be on our way though."

"Right, right. Go ahead and send one of your guys back and tell them to come forward. We'll let you pass. Speaking of pass, you'll need this to get through the other side without any problems." He handed her an index card with the word "Pass" written on it with his signature. "Just hand it to the guys at Claremont Road and tell them Barry said *Christmas is coming.* That's the pass code for today."

Stacy took the card and looked at Barry with renewed admiration. "That's pretty tight security. Where'd you learn how to do that?"

He smiled and replied, "United States Marines, Ma'am. Gunnery Sergeant Broome, retired."

She returned the smile. "Thank you, Gunny. Semper Fi." She turned to head back toward the Humvee.

"Be safe, Lieutenant."

Once they passed the next checkpoint, where the sentries' alarm at the sight of their rig gave way to surprise at the valid pass and code, they didn't have any problems continuing down South Middlebush. There were houses here and there, but most of them weren't facing the road. They got to a section that was tree-lined on both sides and Hutch stopped again. Everyone got out and stretched their legs while Damon and the Guardsmen talked.

"We're coming up on Kendall Park. From here to Highway One, it's pretty densely populated. We could run into all kinds of trouble." Hutch was talking while Damon studied the maps.

Looking up from them, Damon replied, "Let's put someone in the turret. Hopefully that will deter any carjacking wannabes."

"Agreed. Light, you get in the turret in the Humvee. Perez, I want you on top of the camper. We won't be going fast enough for you to come off. Manning, you and Thompson be ready to pop screens out of the windows back there so you can get your rifle barrels out. I hope we don't have to shoot, but I want everyone to have a clear line of sight if we do. Damon, you drive, I'll ride shotgun."

"Do you really think all this is necessary, Major?" Tanner asked. "Surely they wouldn't attack or try to commandeer a military vehicle."

"Yes, Sir, they would. It happened to me on the way up. It's two days later. It's going to be worse now."

Tanner shook his head. "How desperate they must be to attempt something like that."

Damon shrugged and said, "What would you do to try to take care of your family, Sir?"

Tanner replied, "Anything. Everything."

"Exactly. Just like them. Let's get ready."

Chapter 2

"Ethan?" The surprise in Joel's voice was mirrored across the faces of his family.

Amanda leaned over to Will and whispered, "Who's Ethan?"

Will replied in a louder than needed tone, "The sperm donor for my nephews. No one that matters."

Carly looked at Elliott. "What is he doing here? He's not staying."

"Carly, this is Elliott's house. You don't have the right to say who stays here," Lauri said quietly.

"Fine. If he's staying, we're leaving." She turned on Ethan. "I guess I should have figured you'd do something like this. The world goes to shit and you're looking for someone to take care of you, right? Figured your dad would know how to make it through so you'd come here. It's so like you to show up on someone's doorstep, expecting them to help you —"

"Aren't you doing the same thing, Carly? You came here looking for a place to stay, too!" Ethan barked at her.

"*We* were invited!" she screamed back at him. "Since no one has heard from you in *years*, I'm pretty sure *you* weren't!"

"Carly, Ethan, please stop," Elliott said. "We all need to sit down and talk this over calmly. Let's all go inside. We can work this out."

"There's nothing to work out, Elliott. If he stays, we're leaving. Boys, get your things."

"And go where, Carly?" Joel said. "We have nowhere to go."

"We'll go back home. We can figure out how to get water. That's all we needed, right? We had food, heat ... we just needed water. We could get it from the pond."

"We can't go back, Car," Will replied. "It's going to get bad there, really bad. All of my visions involved city streets and neighborhoods like ours. We have to stay away from anything like that."

"Well, I can't stay here with him. I won't." She crossed her arms and glared at Ethan. A thought crossed her mind and she asked Elliott, "How long has he been here anyway?"

"Since Sunday night. He was already on his way here before the pulse hit. He walked five miles from where his car stopped."

Will laughed. "It took you all day to walk five miles? I walked fifteen that day and still got home before dark. Still underachieving, I see."

"Lay off him, alright?" Cameron shouted. "He's dying!"

The stunned silence that followed was deafening. Ethan looked at his youngest son with a small, grateful smile as the rest of the group's faces held varying degrees of shock.

"Bullshit," Carly finally said. "That's just his latest lie to get what he wants, and that lie is so you, Ethan." The hatred was pouring off of her in waves. "How sad that you would treat your father that way, though. Make him think you're dying —"

"It's the truth, Carly. I have pancreatic cancer, like my mom had. I've only got a few weeks left."

Carly stared at him then. She could see that his face looked sunken in, how his clothes hung on his body. She let her arms fall to her sides.

"Well, I'm sorry to hear that, Ethan. No matter how much I despise you, I wouldn't have wished that on you."

12

Ethan nodded but didn't reply. Elliott spoke up. "Can we just go inside? I'd like us all to sit down and talk this over. We can unload your things in a little while." He looked at Carly in particular. She rolled her eyes.

"Fine. Let's go in. I need to pee anyway."

They filed into the house. Amanda and Will were bringing up the rear. She leaned over to him.

"Exciting family you have here."

He shook his head. "You have no idea."

Once they were inside and settled around the table with hot drinks, Joel shared his story of how things were going downhill quickly in their neighborhood. Elliott nodded, telling them about his own neighbors visiting and how ill-prepared they were, especially for people who lived outside the city. Will told of his trek home and meeting Amanda on the way and the other stranded people looking for someone to help them as they couldn't understand what had happened. Ethan's story was short, since his walk was along Portersville Road, which was mostly farmland. Carly was staring daggers at Ethan the whole time. It didn't go unnoticed — by anyone.

Finally, Ethan barked out, "Enough already! Go ahead, Carly! Get it off your chest so we can move on and figure out where to go from here."

She jumped at the raised voice directed at her. "Don't yell at me! I haven't seen you for ten years. Forgive me for being in shock over you sitting here across the table from me."

"Sorry, but I'm pretty sure there's knife wounds in my face from the looks you're giving me."

Cameron snickered and Amanda hid a grin behind a manufactured cough at Ethan's retort. Carly gave Cameron the "mom" look, and he quickly averted his gaze to the cup of hot chocolate sitting in front of him.

13

"Aaron, Cameron, I think you should go in the other room while the grownups are talking." She looked at each of her sons in turn. Cameron started to stand but Aaron stayed where he was.

"I'll be eighteen in a few days, Mom. Cam isn't a little kid anymore either. You can't shield us from what's happening, and you can't leave us out of anything. Pap told us that we're going to have to grow up and work together, protect each other, and learn how to get by in this new now. If you and Dad need to —"

"*Dad?* Did you just call him *Dad?* You don't have a dad! He may be your father, but he is not a dad! A dad is there for you whenever you need them. He teaches you how to do things. He goes to your football games and piano recitals. Ethan gave up the right to be called *Dad* when he left us — when he left *you!*" Ten years of pain and resentment were spewing forth in Carly's words.

Aaron nodded slowly as he replied, "Yep, you're right, Mom. He threw us away. And I agree one hundred percent with what you said. The thing is, he can't take back what he did. He can't undo the past, and he doesn't have much future left. So, I'm giving him the chance to do as much good as he can in the few weeks he has. It's mostly for Pap's sake, to be honest. But a little bit for me, too."

Carly sat staring at her oldest son. She looked from him to Ethan and back to Aaron. She opened her mouth, as if to speak, then closed her lips into a thin line when Lauri reached over and laid a hand on her forearm. After a moment, she said, "Fine. Call him whatever you want to. Just don't expect me to like it." With that, she got up from the table and went into the living room.

Everyone sat in silence as they watched her leave. Finally, Elliott said, "We might have to rethink the sleeping arrangements with two more than I was planning when everything went down, but we should be able to work it

14

out. We'll put the boys and Will in the third bedroom. We've already put the bunk beds back together."

"And, apparently, I get to sleep on the floor," Cameron interjected. "Sometimes being the youngest ain't all it's cracked up to be."

There were grins and giggles around the table as Elliott went on.

"You'll survive, Cam. Carly and Amanda can have the second bedroom, but they'll have to share the bed. That leaves Joel and Lauri in my room, and Ethan and I will take the couch and recliner in the living room."

Lauri was poised to speak as soon as she heard her name and jumped in when Elliott paused. "Absolutely not! We will not put you out of your own bed, Elliott. I won't hear of it!"

Aaron turned to his grandfather with a smirk. "Told ya so, Pap."

Elliott leaned back in his chair and crossed his arms over his chest. "My house. My way. End of discussion."

Lauri was still shaking her head. "No! It isn't right. I can't —"

"Thank you, Elliott. We truly appreciate it," Joel said, cutting his wife off. When it seemed Lauri would continue, Joel held his hand up and said, "Not now, honey. We've got more important things to talk about."

"What could possibly be more important than Elliott giving up his bed to us?" she cried.

Slipping his coat back on, Joel replied, "Figuring out where we're going to put everything we brought. Boys, let's get the car unloaded. It may take us until dark with all the clothes your mother brought."

They unloaded bags for an hour. When they finally got down to what was on the bottom, Elliott's eyebrows shot up.

15

"Where in the world did you get all these guns and ammo, Joel? I know you didn't have them already."

As they carried everything inside, Joel told him about Teddy. Elliott nodded solemnly and replied, "I guess there will be a lot of folks like that. No way to get the medical supplies they need for treatments and such." Checking that Ethan wasn't around, he lowered his voice and went on. "I'm afraid we may have a bad situation with Ethan real soon. He tries to hide it, but I see the pain in his eyes. He smokes marijuana for it, and he says it helps, but it won't help at the end. They had my wife, Judy, almost in a coma with morphine, and she was still in agony. It's going to be rough on everybody. You can't hide that in a house this size."

Joel stopped and turned to Elliott. "We'll deal with it. We may have to send the boys out on chores or something if it gets too bad. It's hard enough on them not having seen him for all these years. To watch him die now may be too much for them to handle."

"It may be too much for me, too," Elliott said, with a tear slipping down his face.

Laying his arm across Elliott's shoulder, Joel replied, "We'll be here to help you through it, old friend."

Elliott smiled and wiped the tear from his chin. "Thank you, buddy. Now let's get this loot inside and see what you brought."

The bags of clothes and linens had been spread throughout the bedrooms. The bags of guns had been deposited in the living room floor. Cameron was down there with them peering into the duffel bags. When his grandfathers came into the room, he looked up at them, eyes wide.

"Pap! Look at all this! I thought *you* had a lot of guns. This is enough for an army!"

Carly walked in from the bedroom just then. "Cameron Elliott Marshall! What do you think you're doing? Get away from those guns this instant!"

Cameron jumped at his mother's raised voice. Aaron, who was sitting on the couch behind his brother, leaned over and whispered in his ear, "She used all three names. You're in big trouble, bro."

Cameron jabbed his brother in the shin with his elbow. Turning his attention to Carly, he said, "Geez, Mom, we've already learned about guns. We've taken them apart and cleaned them. Pap took us plinking and it was awesome!"

"Plinking?" Carly asked with a confused look.

"Target practice," Elliott replied. "They're both good shots and are *still learning* about guns." He stared pointedly at Cameron. Cameron looked down at his hands.

"Well, I'm still not comfortable with them handling guns. Surely out here in the country we don't have to worry about people attacking us or trying to steal our stuff."

Elliott shook his head. "We may not have as many people around as you did in town, but we still have people who weren't prepared for this. We can help anybody who needs water; but beyond that, we may be tightening our own belts before we can plant in the spring. We won't be able to share our food, and we probably have more than most people out here. Plus, I'd bet good money folks in town will start making their way out of the city when it gets really bad."

"It's already really bad, Elliott. They've looted the stores, and a cashier was killed at Kroger! I mean, how much worse can it get?"

"Are you forgetting those guys on the road, Carly? What do you think they would have done to us, especially you and me and even your mom if we hadn't been able to defend ourselves?" Amanda interjected.

Carly seemed to consider what Amanda had said. When she realized what Amanda was referring to, she exclaimed, "Ew! Gross! No way! I'd never do that!"

Amanda cocked her head to the side. "How would you have stopped it?"

"Well, I ..." she hesitated to look for the right answer. "I don't know, but I'd do something. I wouldn't just lie there while —"

"Back to my question. How would you — no, how *could* you stop it? You aren't strong enough to fight off an attack by a guy, Carly. I'm sorry you have such a fear and aversion to guns; but unless you want to be raped or murdered, or both, you'd better get past it. Quick."

Amanda leaned over and looked into the bag sitting beside Cameron. She pulled out a pistol, checked to see that it was unloaded, and held it out to Carly. Carly looked at the gun then Amanda. "I'm sure I don't need to carry one of those things in the house. I don't even know how to shoot it."

Elliott pulled his pistol out of his pocket and held it up for her to see. "I've been carrying one since the day it happened. Everybody should be armed, especially if they go outside. We'll take care of teaching you how to shoot tomorrow."

"It's a lot of fun, Mom! You'll like it!" Cameron added with enthusiasm.

Carly declined the offer of the pistol from Amanda and stuck her hands in her pockets. "I doubt that."

With a grin, Amanda leaned over and whispered, "I've heard shooting a gun releases the same endorphins as having sex."

Eyebrows raised, Carly replied in a hushed tone. "Okay, I might have to give it a try."

Chapter 3

President Olstein opened the door to the conference room. His eyes grew wide when he found it empty.

"Where is everyone? I didn't tell anyone they could leave!" His exclamations were directed at no one in particular but it didn't matter. There was no one there to hear them. He stormed back out into the hall. "David!"

His newly appointed chief of staff, David Strain, stepped out of his office. "Yes, Mister President?"

Olstein gestured to the empty room. "Where are the Joint Chiefs? I didn't give them permission to leave!"

David walked over and looked into the empty room. "I'm not sure, Sir. I wasn't here when they left."

"Well, find them! Get them back here *now*! They need to hear my orders and start abiding by them ASAP!"

"Yes, Sir, I'll try."

"Don't try — do it! You tell them their Commander-in-Chief *ordered* them to get back here immediately!"

"Yes, Sir. Oh, here are the copies you asked for." David handed him the pages, then turned and hurried down the hall.

The president went into the conference room and took a seat at the head of the empty table. The wait staff had cleared the breakfast food and dishes from the room, leaving a large coffee urn and several pitchers of ice water. Olstein sat grumbling about insubordination and dereliction of duty as he read through the updated edicts he had written. Smiling to himself, he laid the paper down and went to get a cup of coffee. Adding cream and sugar to the cup, he turned back to the vacant room as he stirred the mixture.

"There's going to be quite a few changes around here. I can't wait to see their faces when they hear what I have in store."

David had made his way to Speaker Phil Roman's office. The walk wouldn't have been long under normal circumstances; but with no equipment or workers clearing sidewalks and streets, it took well over an hour to walk the approximately two and a half miles. He could have gotten someone to drive him there in one of the Humvees, or even driven himself, but he needed the time to think. Since he had typed up the executive orders for the president, he knew what was in them. He knew the chaos that was about to ensue. He knew they were wrong and completely unconstitutional. He knew the man had to be stopped. He just didn't know how. He hoped the other men did.

After kicking snow from his boots and knocking larger clumps from his pants legs, he entered the Longworth House Office Building. He was struck by how quiet the building was. Even though Congress had adjourned for the year, there were usually people scurrying around the building — interns, clerks, maintenance, housekeeping — year-round. The lack of people gave the building an ominous feeling, like that of a crypt. He thought how poignant that analogy was. If the president got his way, the Republic was in a death spiral.

He made his way to the Speaker's office and knocked on the door. "Come in!" he heard from the other side. He opened the door to find Phil Roman packing clothes and personal items into a sports bag on the sofa. He looked up and smiled at David.

"David! Good to see you. Although the look on your face says this isn't a social call, not that we have time for those kinds of things now. Is something wrong?"

20

David walked over and sat on the sofa beside the bag.

"Sir, we have a problem."

Phil stopped his packing and gave David his full attention. "Sounds serious. What's up?"

David waited for Phil to pull up a chair. When he was settled, David began.

"President Olstein has written a number of executive orders; and, honestly, I think every single one is unconstitutional."

David's eyebrows raised. "How many?"

"Half a dozen."

"What?"

David looked down at his hands. "The number isn't the worst of it. It's the contents."

"Which are?"

David pulled a folded piece of paper out of his pocket. "He instructed me to find everyone who was in the meeting this morning and tell them to get back immediately. He said to tell you all that he ordered you to get back ASAP." He handed the paper to the Speaker.

Phil read the content of the page, and a myriad of emotions crossed his face. Shock became amazement, which then morphed into anger. He looked at David and, without saying a word, stood up and walked to his desk. He picked up the satphone and punched in a number.

"Charles. You need to get over here. Now."

General Everley must have been succinct, because Phil set the phone back on his desk after just a moment. "David, we're working on something that will change the future for all of us in a good way. I can't tell you what it is yet. That's for the best. Plausible deniability for you is a good thing. You should go back to the president. Tell him you found me, and I told you I would be there in about an hour. Tell him I spoke to General Everley while you were here, and he'll take care of contacting the rest of the Joint Chiefs.

21

We'll see you later. Thank you for sharing this with me, David."

David stood and put his coat back on. "You won't let him know I shared that with you, right, Sir? I'm sorry to say that I have nothing at my apartment to eat. I never cook and always eat out. If I'm going to live — that is, not starve to death — I need to be able to stay at the White House. I'm ashamed but not crazy enough to think I can make it anywhere else."

Phil shook his head. "It will be our secret. And don't be ashamed. That bag sitting there is my clothes and toiletries that I'll be taking with me when I go back. General Everley and I are both moving into the barracks section. There's food, running water, electricity ... at least for a while. There's no shame in doing what you have to do to survive, David."

David let a small smile come over his face. "Thank you, Sir. I'll see you in a bit then."

Phil walked him to the door, shook David's hand and closed the door behind him. To the now empty room he said, "It'll be a little longer than that."

Ten minutes later, General Charles Everley burst through the door of Phil Roman's office. He found Phil sitting on the sofa beside a duffel bag staring at a piece of paper. "What's going on?" he exclaimed.

Phil indicated the chair across from him. "You'd better sit down."

Charles sat and addressed Phil. "Okay, I'm sitting. What's wrong?"

Phil handed him the paper. As the general read, his eyes grew bigger and his face started turning red. When he reached the end, he looked up at the Speaker of the House, the man who quite possibly was next in line to be president if something happened before Tanner arrived.

"This is insane! I told Arthur Stephens on day one Olstein had lost it. This proves it! He doesn't have the power or the authority to do most of the things listed here and shouldn't do the rest. He has to be stopped. Immediately!"

Phil nodded slowly. "Yes. I was really hoping we could hold him at bay until Tanner is sworn in, but I don't think we have that luxury now. He's bound and determined to seize control of everything he can with no remorse for what the consequences may be, especially to the American people. We do need to come up with a plan and it needs to happen fast. We'll need the rest of the Joint Chiefs to be on board. Do you think that will be a problem?"

"Are you kidding? This one is enough to get them on board!" He pointed to a section on the page.

Executive Order 148921: Effective immediately, in the absence of the Secretary of Defense, the Joint Chiefs of Staff will no longer command the troops of the United States. That responsibility will rest solely with the President of the United States. As well, the Joint Chiefs will no longer be asked to advise the President on any matters, military or otherwise. They are excused from their duties.

"*Excused*? Is that supposed to be like an honorable discharge? He does *not* have the right to do that! Hell yes, they'll be on board!" He pulled the satphone out of his coat pocket and punched in a number.

"This is Everley. Collect the rest of the Chiefs and meet me in Speaker Roman's office right now!" He didn't wait for an answer, clicking the phone off at his last word. Turning his attention back to the damning missive, he shook his head. "Well, we have no choice now. We're going to have to remove him from office."

"Well, we can't impeach him. Congress isn't here. There's no way to bring articles of impeachment to a vote. You know what that means, right?" Roman was looking pointedly at Everley.

"Yes. The one thing I was trying to avoid. It will have to be a coup."

Phil shook his head and said, "I hate that he's making us go there, but we cannot let him trash every aspect of our Republic in his attempts to *help*. If we let him start down that path, there will be no way to stop him. That saying 'Absolute power corrupts absolutely' describes the situation we'd be in rather quickly if he isn't stopped. We need to make a solid plan, and there can't be any room for error. We'll only get one shot at this. Once we show our hand, if we don't follow through, we won't have another chance."

Charles had pulled out a pen and was making notes on the back of the paper. "Way ahead of you, Phil. Don't worry. We'll get it in one."

David walked back to the White House filled with trepidation, yet hopeful that he had done the right thing. He knew the president's plan was wrong — wrong for the country and its possible future, bleak as it seemed at the moment. He knew it was unlawful; but with most of the government home for the holiday, the legal routes to stop him were pretty much unavailable. Yet, he had to be stopped. The fate of the nation depended on it.

He entered the bunker and found many more soldiers and Secret Service agents there than when he had left. He stopped a Marine walking down the corridor in battle gear and carrying his rifle.

"Sergeant, what's going on? Has something happened?"

24

The Marine paused long enough to reply, "I'm not sure, sir. All I know is the president called for all available military personnel to gear up and assemble at once in the barracks."

"No one knows what for?" David asked, nervous curiosity apparent in his voice.

"Well, we heard there's going to be a major change in the leadership of the military. No idea what that means. Excuse me, sir, but I need to get down there." The sergeant hurried away.

David's hand went to his mouth as he said aloud, "Dear God, it's starting already!"

Chapter 4

The area they entered had hundreds, if not thousands, of apartments and condominiums. With an average of two people per unit, that put the possible population in that one confined location in the tens of thousands. There were apartment buildings on both sides of South Middlebush, and just past the first facilities, was a housing community with hundreds of houses in it. The travelers weren't prepared for what they found.

To their right, an entire set of apartment buildings had burned to the ground. They could only assume that the wind pushing the winter storm through the day before had fueled the fires that burned unfettered. There was a smoky haze over the area; the acrid smells of burned wood, plastic, and possibly human flesh hung heavily in the air. Melanie placed a gloved hand over her nose and mouth.

"Wow. Can you even imagine the heat that came off that blaze?" Hutch commented, peering through the side window as they passed the skeletal remains of the complex. "There's no snow on the ground over there. It melted it — and we had a lot of snow!"

"Heads up!" Darrell shouted from above. "Civilians at the next cross street."

Everyone inside the Humvee looked out the front. There was a large open area between the road and the apartments to their left. There were people outside, despite the bitter cold, with fires burning in large steel drums set closer to the road than the complex, probably to keep what happened on the other side of the street from happening on their side. At the sound of a running vehicle, all heads snapped around to stare at what the previous week would have barely garnered their attention yet had now become a bizarre sight. Some of them started slowly toward the Humvee, while others were backing away. When they didn't slow down, one of the women in the group started shouting in their direction.

"Hey! We need help! You could haul a lot of people in that camper! Take us somewhere so we can get some food!"

Her words were followed by a chorus of, "Help us!" and "Don't just leave us here!" along with increasing expletives hurled at them as they continued down the road without stopping. Suddenly, a barrage of bottles and rocks were being thrown at the vehicle and the camper. The occupants inside flinched, even though the projectiles couldn't get to them. One hit the driver side window and made Hutch jump.

"Son of a bitch!" he exclaimed as he involuntarily jerked the wheel. The movement was enough to cause the camper to fishtail slightly. Tipping the side view mirror up so he could see the top of the camper, he saw Marco sliding toward the edge. "Light! Get eyes on Perez!"

Darrell peered around the hatch door to see Marco sliding toward the edge, trying to brace his left foot against a tiny ledge along the top of the camper, while maintaining control of his weapon with one hand, and scrabbling for purchase on the smooth top with the other. Just when he thought Marco was going over the side, he halted his progress with his other foot and the butt of his gun, which he was holding with both hands.

"Perez! Sitrep!" Darrell yelled.

Marco was cautiously repositioning himself, moving back to the center of the camper top. When he was situated and stable, he replied, "All good! Man, that was close!"

Darrell gave him a thumbs up and turned back to the front. "He's good, Cap," he said down into the Humvee. He turned his attention back to the people outside. They were

27

still moving toward the street, getting closer and louder. They had come to within fifty feet of the vehicle.

"Light, I think you need to get their attention. Chamber a new round."

"You've got it," Darrell replied. The sound of the action on the rifle expelling a bullet and seating a new one in its place created the desired effect. The growing mob stopped in their tracks, eyes shooting daggers at the man and his gun but, obviously, not taking the chance to find out for sure whether or not he was willing to carry out the implied threat.

"Relay this message to them: We know you need help. The entire country does. This is not a search and rescue mission. We are on our way to Washington to see what we can do to help. The best thing you can do for yourselves is pool your resources and try to hold on until someone gets here with supplies. Now please step back. We don't want to hurt anyone." Damon recited the words from notes he had scribbled hastily in a notebook. Darrell repeated them to the agitated group outside.

"We're already hurting, man!" came a male voice from the crowd. "We weren't ready for this! My family is almost out of food, so what resources do I have to pool with anyone else? I've got four kids who are going to be hungry tomorrow!"

From inside the Humvee, Melanie said softly, "Oh my. Those poor children. How can they be out of food already? It's only been a few days."

David Tanner looked at his wife. "Many families live paycheck to paycheck, sweetheart. Depending on when he gets paid, it's a very real possibility. Plus, Christmas is almost here, and I'm sure folks like him have cut corners on some things to get gifts for their kids. There are probably millions of families just like his out there in the same situation."

"This couldn't have come at a worse time," Melanie replied.

"I'm pretty sure that was the plan," Damon interjected from the front seat. "The middle of a nationwide winter storm, the week before the biggest holiday of the year, most of Congress out of town already … it's not a coincidence."

"It's a cowardly, heinous act, and I hope the president is putting a plan together to retaliate," Tanner said.

"I don't think that's in the works, Sir," Damon replied. "Not right now anyway."

"Well, it will be in about thirty days, Major. Count on it."

Hutch cut in. "I'm going to try to get a little more speed here so we can get out of this area as fast as possible. Light, tell Perez to get ready."

Darrell leaned back so he could see Marco again. "Perez, hang on!" Marco gave him a quick nod and braced himself as best he could.

At the sound of the engine's increase in RPMs, the crowd started toward them again, voices raised in anger and desperation.

"Please don't leave us here to die!" one woman shouted.

"You can't just abandon us like this!" yelled another. "You're supposed to help people!"

Darrell raised his rifle and pointed it in the general direction of the crowd. "Stay back! Do not approach the vehicle!"

While most of the crowd complied, one man rushed out to stand in front of the Humvee. "You're not just going to drive away! You'll have to run me over. I'll probably die soon anyway, so this is as good a time as any!"

Darrell turned to point his weapon toward the man blocking the road. The man's face changed from a look of determination to one of concern. Darrell called down

29

toward the interior, loud enough for the crowd to hear. "Orders, Cap?"

"Fire a warning shot toward the ground beside him. Let him know that's the only one he'll get." Hutch had slowed slightly but had not come to a stop.

Darrell did as he was told. When the gun went off, the man jumped instinctively away from the projectile, which moved him out of their way. There were screams from the crowd as they all moved away from the road. Marco set his sight on the person closest to them in the group. The man regained his composure and started back to where he had been. Darrell expelled the spent casing and chambered another. He took aim at the man again.

"That was your only warning, sir. Please stay back!" he said in a raised, authoritative voice.

The man's face was filled with rage as he yelled, "What gives you the right to use that ride? It's government property! The government works for us! Everything is fair game now. Survival of the fittest. There's more of us than there are of you! How are you going to stop all of us?"

At his words, Marco rapped on the roof of the camper twice. Two rifle barrels appeared, one from a side window and the other from the front. The back hatch on the Humvee opened and a third became visible. Hutch rolled his window down part way to reveal himself pointing his pistol at the crowd. Damon was leaning out the other side with his own sidearm trained on the belligerent man.

The sight of all the weapons had the crowd moving back quickly, the man in the road included. Hutch took advantage of the opportunity and pressed the accelerator. As they passed the crowd, the man who had tried to bar their way ran beside them as he yelled out a final time.

"You'll all go to hell for this!"

Hutch murmured from behind the wheel. "I sure hope he's wrong about that."

Long before sunrise, the Chairman was up and busy going through intelligence reports. A knock at the door hours later was not enough to take his eyes off what he was reading.

"Come!" he barked, as he continued to scan the documents, a smile growing on his lips.

One of his aides came into the room, closing the door behind him. He bowed timidly and said, "I have more news, Excellency."

The Chairman looked up at that and motioned impatiently with his hand. "Well, bring it to me!"

The aide hurried over and handed the folder to the Chairman. Taking it, the Chairman dismissed the man with another wave of his hand and sat down at his desk. He opened it and quickly started skimming through the contents.

"Ha ha! It is working!" he exclaimed to the empty room. He pressed the intercom button on his phone.

"Yes, Excellency?" A female voice rose from the speaker.

"Get the council together immediately! I want everyone here in one hour!" Not waiting for a reply, he disconnected the conversation.

He continued going through the reports, jotting notes as he went. He was startled when the intercom delivered the female voice again.

"The council is here and waiting for you in the conference room, Excellency."

Looking at the clock on his desk, he saw that almost an hour had passed. He had been so engrossed in what he was reading he hadn't realized that much time had gone by. He quickly gathered all the information together and headed for the conference room.

The assembled council members rose from their seats as he entered. "Be seated," he said as took his place at the head of the table. Once the men were sitting down, he began.

"The reports I am receiving from news agencies and from radio transmissions around the world confirm that the United States is in turmoil. The people are already acting like wild animals, pillaging, stealing, and killing each other. The government is all but abolished, while their weak president tries to control an out-of-control populace. I believe we can speed up our timeline for invasion. I want our troops ready to deploy in ninety days. Is there any reason that cannot be done?"

The council members looked at each other but none replied. The Chairman waited for someone to speak. Finally, one of his generals rose from his chair.

"It will be done, Excellency. We will see to it."

The Chairman smiled. "Very good. We will be growing something different this spring. We will plant the seeds to start the growth of our new power in America!"

Chapter 5

Elliott and Lauri had been standing in the kitchen arguing for at least thirty minutes. All eyes were on them.

"I'm not saying you can't help with the cooking and cleaning, Lauri. I'm just saying you don't have to do all of it." The exasperation in Elliott's tone was not missed by anyone watching the interaction.

Hands on her hips, Lauri replied, "And I'm just saying there isn't much outside I can do for this family with my knees in the shape they're in. These are things I *can* do. Everyone is going to have to do their part. This is the part I am able to do and it's something I'm good at." Her hands left her hips as she crossed her arms with a flourish. Elliott shook his head.

"Fine. And you're right — everyone is going to have to do their part and pull their weight for us to survive. In fact, maybe we should write down everything that needs to get done every day and assign chores to everybody."

"I think Uncle Will would be great at pumping water!" Cameron offered.

Elliott raised his eyebrows at his youngest grandson. "Which would leave you more time for chopping and hauling wood, Cam. Oh, and milking the goat. Good idea."

Cameron opened his mouth to speak, hesitated, then closed it into a firm line. Aaron snickered, Ethan chuckled, and everyone else besides Elliott had a confused look on their face.

"Not sure what private joke y'all have going on there, but Cameron milking a goat is something I'd love to see!" Will said, eliciting laughter from everyone except Cameron. "I'd be more than happy to pump water, but that wouldn't take up a whole day. I think a chore list is a great plan. I have absolutely no idea what it takes to get by without electricity or grow food, outside of what I've seen Mom do in the backyard. What else can we do to help, Elliott?"

"We'll get all that sorted out in the next couple of days. There's not near as much to do in the winter as there is in the spring, summer, and fall. We will need to do some hunting real soon to beef up our food stores. We can pressure can the meat, which we'll probably start doing tomorrow with what's in the freezer. It already feels like it's warming up outside, so we need to work on that stuff first. I see a lot of soups and stews in our immediate future. We can spend the rest of the day getting everything you brought with you stored away. We'll get the chore list put together this evening. In the meantime, let's —"

A knock at the front door interrupted Elliott. All heads turned toward the living room. Elliott held a hand up for quiet and started toward the sound. Ethan followed, as did Joel. Everyone else drifted to the doorway between the two rooms.

Elliott looked through the peephole then opened the door. Taylor was standing there with what was apparently his wife and kids. Taylor smiled at the men standing in the doorway.

"Hi Elliott! I was hoping we could get some more water from your well. Oh, by the way, this is my wife, Wendy, and my kids, Heather, Grayson, and Derek. Kids, say hello to Mr. Marshall."

There was a chorus of "Hellos" from the kids. Elliott stepped out onto the porch, followed by Ethan and Joel, who closed the door behind him. He pointed out to the pump in the yard.

"You're welcome to pump up as much water as you can carry, Taylor. If you need any help working the pump, just let us know." He started to turn back toward the house when Taylor spoke again.

"Um, I was wondering if we could talk to you about something else, Elliott."

"What's up, Taylor?" Elliott asked with a slight hesitation.

"Well, we're not really set up for a situation like this. We have a fireplace but not a lot of wood for it. I was going to get a buddy of mine to bring me some next week. He cuts and sells firewood on the side. I don't have a chainsaw or an ax, just a small hatchet. You know we don't have water. Our food will only last us about a week, two tops, and that would be a stretch. I'm not sure how we're going to get through this." Taylor paused, as if waiting for something.

"I'm really sorry, Taylor. I might have an old ax you could use; it will probably need to be sharpened. As I said, you're welcome to the water any time." Elliott didn't go on.

"I … um … was wondering if maybe me and my family could stay here with you? You have a big house, and we could all stay in one bedroom. We'd help out with things that needed to be done … I don't really know what that would be, but I can do anything I put my mind to. You only have to show me how to do something once and I've got it down. I really need to find a better place for my kids. Your house is toasty warm, you have plenty of water, food …" He left the sentence hanging, looking expectantly at the three men.

Elliott shook his head. "I'm sorry, son, but we have a houseful. We don't have room for anyone else."

"But there are only four of you!" Taylor exclaimed. He stared at Joel. "Wait, you weren't here earlier. Where did you come from?"

"That's none of your business," Elliott said in a low, menacing tone. "You should get your water and go on home now."

"Five then! Five of you and five of us. Ten people can get a lot more done than five. We can help each other!" Taylor's voice was taking on a desperate sound.

"We have a lot more than five people here now. We can't take you in."

Taylor stepped toward Elliott as if to grasp his arm. Elliott stepped out of his reach and stuck his hand in his pocket. Taylor stopped and said pleadingly, "What are we supposed to do? How are we supposed to survive? I can't sit and watch my kids starve or freeze to death!"

Sadly, Elliott replied, "I don't know, Taylor. Maybe you could hunt for deer or rabbits, squirrels, or raccoons. There's plenty of wildlife around here."

"I know nothing about hunting! I don't even own a gun! What am I going to do, chase them down?" he cried, sarcasm dripping with every word. "I guess since you have everything you need to survive you don't care what happens to anyone else. Nice attitude toward your fellow man. Come on, kids. Let's get our water and go."

The three men watched in silence as the small family headed toward the hand pump on the well. Seeing the pain in his friend's eyes, Joel stepped up beside Elliott and spoke in a low voice.

"It's a hard thing to do, not helping others when they ask for it. We had to do it before we left home. It doesn't feel very Christian-like, but you can't help everyone, especially in a situation like the one we have found ourselves in. At some point, you have to decide whether you're going to help a lot of people for a short time or take care of your family for as long as possible. This is not going to be over anytime soon. We have nine people here who are going to need to eat and have a roof over their

36

heads. Is there any food to spare? Not that I'm saying you should give any of it away."

Still watching the Livingston family, Elliott replied, "No, there isn't. We may have to ration ourselves before spring. I wish I had been more prepared. Even with the things I've done — extra flour and sugar, lots of toilet paper, jugs for water — it's nowhere near enough for this situation. Honestly, I don't think I ever really believed anything like this would happen. I just felt a little better having the extras."

"Well, I'm truly thankful you have what you do, old friend. I don't know where we'd be without you and this place. I only wish we could have brought food with us. I'm thinking that will be our main focus, outside of staying warm. I really wish I could have brought the generator. That would have been a big help, I think."

They watched as Taylor and his family started back down the driveway. Taylor turned back and shot them a hateful look then continued on his way. Elliott and Joel headed back toward the house. Elliott seemed lost in thought and suddenly stopped in his tracks.

"You know, I've got an old generator out in the barn. The engine went bad on it and I never got it replaced. I wonder if we could do something with that."

Joel's eyes lit up. "It's worth taking a look at it. Let's check it out."

The two men walked around the side of the house toward the barn. Looking down at the slush on the ground, Elliott commented, "Yep, it's definitely melting. The stuff we have out on the back porch in coolers we're going to be needing to cook soon."

They went to the barn and opened the door to go in. Flossie bleated at them, as if she were delivering a reprimand to the men for disturbing the quiet atmosphere. Ignoring the petulant goat, Elliott led the way to a stall in the back that held multiple items covered with an old tarp. Peering into the dim area, Joel said, "Looks like more than an old generator under there."

"Yeah, I've got a few other things here. Projects I started and didn't finish, pieces and parts I thought might be useful someday, that kind of thing."

Elliott pulled the tarp off the equipment causing a cloud of dust to be released in the stall. He waved a hand to clear the air in front of his face then leaned over a work bench. Joel ventured further in and peered over his shoulder.

"I forgot I even had this old thing!" he exclaimed as he pointed to one. "That's an old belt-driven water pump I found at a junkyard. Had an idea to rig up a solar set up for it to use if the power went out. I didn't pay hardly anything for it, but I never got around to getting the solar panels. Maybe we should see if we can find some. We might still be able to hook something up to the well. Here's the generator."

Joel squatted down beside the machine Elliott was pointing to and looked it over. Years of dust had given it a brown hue. Rubbing a finger across the top of the frame, he found red underneath. He spied an old rag on the bench above and pulled it down. Dust motes danced in the light filtering in between the slats of the barn wall as he wiped the generator off to get a better look at it.

"Well, it's certainly an older model. It doesn't even have an electronic display, just a voltage gauge. My guess is if we clean it up and figure out how to power it, we might be able to use it."

"Yeah, but what can we use in place of the engine?" Elliott asked.

Joel looked at the generator, then the old water pump, and finally turned to look at the tractor sitting in the middle of the barn. He turned back to Elliott with a huge grin and replied, "I've got an idea."

Chapter 6

While waiting for the rest of the Joint Chiefs to arrive, Everley and Roman started working on their plan of action. They had notes strewn around the office. With no heat in the building, the room was frigid, but both men had slipped off their overcoats and jackets. Whether caused by the physical activity in the office or their elevated states of agitation, they were comfortable without them.

Phil was studying a sheet full of scribbling. "What's the timeframe, Charles? How long will it take once we put everything in motion?"

Everley looked up from his papers. "It will be immediate. There can be no hesitation or cessation once we start the operation. After we place the president in custody, you will step in to run things until Tanner is sworn in. As far as when? That ball is in Olstein's court, but I don't think it will be very long. When the rest of the Joint Chiefs see this," he said, holding up the missive delivered by David Strain, "they won't stand for it. Make no mistake: the president is declaring war on all of us."

A knock on the door turned their attention to it. "Come in," Phil said.

The Joint Chiefs filed in, faces a mixture of curiosity and apprehension. Standing awkwardly in a semi-circle with her two fellow chiefs in attendance, Air Force General Angie Bales addressed the two men. General Bales was the first female chief in history.

"I can only guess this has something to do with the president ... again."

Everley nodded. "Everyone, take a seat." Phil was gathering the randomly strewn papers from the sofa and armchairs as the generals came over and sat down.

"Angie, I gotta say again how glad I am you just happened to be in town when this happened," Everley said. "We've got everyone but Admiral Stephens and General Weston, and we're going to need all hands now. Phil, you're up." Everley sat on the arm of the sofa as all eyes turned to the Speaker.

Phil looked down at the list of executive orders and took a deep breath. "The president has been quite busy this morning. He has demanded we return to the bunker immediately so that he can inform us of his new EOs. I have a copy of them here."

General Carl McKenna laughed. "He's acting like a child. I think we should just ignore him and wait out his little temper tantrum as long as possible. His plans are ridiculous. No one is going to give up their food or gas, and they most certainly are not giving up their guns. No guns, no way to defend themselves and keep their food and gas."

"I wish we could do that, General. As you know, that was the original plan: to procrastinate as long as possible on carrying out his orders or demands or whatever you want to call them. However, that is no longer an option. These new orders will tell you why." Phil began reading the list.

"Executive Order 148917: Effective immediately, no new president will be sworn into office for the foreseeable future. The current President, Barton Olstein, will remain in office for the duration of this catastrophic event as the country will need as much stability as possible in our present state to persevere. A regime change is not prudent at this time."

"Okay, he starts out with an unconstitutional edict. He can't do that. Nowhere is it written he has the power to proclaim himself as permanent ruler," Angie stated. "He can be removed from office under the Twenty-fifth Amendment for that statement alone, because he has obviously lost his mind!"

"That would seem to be the best course of action; but with no vice-president here to replace him, the job would then fall to me," Phil replied. "Here's where it gets sticky. I would have been one of the two people who would have been notified of his inability to lead the country. You can see that it could definitely be construed as a conflict of interest in the eyes of the American people."

"We're going to have a lot to discuss, but let's hear everything first," Charles interjected. The Speaker continued.

"Executive Order 148918: Effective immediately, the United States is under martial law. All state and local law enforcement will fall under the direction of the President, who will command the National Guard forces. State governors will no longer command and give direct orders to the National Guard of their respective state. All orders and assignments will come from the President."

Phil paused to see if anyone wanted to discuss it. The shaking heads and the looks of astonishment on the faces of the Joint Chiefs told him to go on.

"Executive Order 148919: Effective immediately, the Second Amendment has been repealed. Private gun ownership is now illegal. The National Guard will be deployed on search and secure missions among the citizens of the United States to gather all guns held by anyone other than military or law enforcement. As such, the Fourth Amendment is repealed as well. All residents of the United States will surrender their guns or face severe consequences."

General McKenna snorted. "Oh, a twofer! Two amendments killed with one EO! I'm surprised he didn't just repeal the whole Constitution!"

"Executive Order 148920: Effective immediately, hoarding of supplies such as food and water is forbidden. Each family may keep three days' worth of these items. Anything over that will be confiscated by the National Guard and delivered to FEMA camps, which will be set up in each state capital and any large city over one million people. The resources will be distributed equally and fairly from there."

"Fair to whom? Definitely not the people who planned for something like this," Angie said. "How in God's name do you take food from people who have it and will need it to feed their families in the coming months? How is that right?"

Phil answered her. "I believe his rationalization is 'the needs of the many outweigh the needs of the few', which he has been touting for years as the way of our country's future. That we are all responsible for our fellow man and we must all sacrifice so that everyone is treated fairly."

"I'm pretty sure that's going to go over like a lead balloon and will get good men and women killed in the process." Angie leaned back indicating she had said her piece.

"Executive Order 148921: Effective immediately, in the absence of the Secretary of Defense, the Joint Chiefs of Staff will no longer command the troops of the United States. That responsibility will rest solely with the President of the United States. As well, the Joint Chiefs will

no longer be asked to advise the President on any matters, military or otherwise. They are excused from their duties."

The room erupted in shouting as the Joint Chiefs leapt to their feet in anger.

"He can't do that! He can't just dismiss us like students in a class!" Carl raged. "He has to be stopped!"

"Read them the last line, Phil," Charles said quietly.

"Anyone who does not comply with the above orders will be arrested and executed for treason. Signed, Barton Olstein, President and Supreme Commander of the Republic"

No one spoke at first. Then Carl started laughing. "Are you effing kidding me? Supreme Commander? He has gone off the deep end. What are we going to do about this? What can we do?"

Phil smiled. "I'm glad you asked. Charles and I are working on a plan."

~~~~~~

After hearing about the mission to retrieve the president-elect and what they planned to do in the interim, the Joint Chiefs were all in.

"What do you need us to do?" Carl asked eagerly.

"Well, for starters, you're going to have to corral the Marines in the bunker. They need to know they take their orders from you, not Olstein. Grab a couple of sergeants to detain him when the time comes. I guarantee you he won't go willingly."

"What about me?" Angie queried. "Not really a lot of Air Force personnel there. At least, I wouldn't think so."

43

"That's okay. With Stephens gone, I want you to take over the radio operations with the Navy. You'll relay the new information as soon as Olstein is secure."

"Where is Arthur anyway? I haven't seen him since the first day." It was the first time General Anton Drysdale had addressed the group aloud.

"Art chose to get out while he could. He has a brother in East Tennessee with land and supplies to make a go of it. I don't blame him. If I'd had someplace like that to go, I probably would have skinned out, too. It's going to be tough for a while. He was well past retirement. I wished him good luck. I hope he made it."

Drysdale looked confused by what he'd just heard. "Huh. I find that a little strange."

"Why is that?" Everley shot back. "You think he and his wife don't deserve to find a safe place to hunker down and wait this out? Jean, his wife, isn't in the best health. I'm sure he just wanted to get her away from the madness that may already be enveloping the city streets."

"That's not what I was talking about. I don't blame them a bit either. I just mean I find it strange that they left without their son."

Now it was Everley's turn to look confused. "Which one? I thought all of their kids were in other parts of the country."

"They are, but one of them was just a few hours away. His name is Jason. He's in the Secret Service and he's assigned to David Tanner right now."

"Then he's on his way here," Charles replied. "Sorley told me one of them had demanded he come along. He said his name was Stephens. I just didn't put two and two together."

"I don't think they were close. Jason's wife is a lobbyist and there were more than a few heated discussions between her and Art about how the lobbyists are ruining the country with their interference in the election process. I think Jason just found it easier to stay away." Anton had a sad look on his face. "It was hard on both of them, but Jean took it the hardest. She begged Jason to stop by, even if it was only for a few minutes every so often, but he wouldn't. He said he needed to support his wife. She finally stopped asking. Tough spot."

"I had no idea. Outside of Jean, Arthur never really talked about his family," Angie added.

Charles shrugged and said, "Well, that's a discussion for another time. Right now, we need to get our plans finalized. This has to happen today. Let's get busy."

~~~~~~

"I've called you all here to inform you of some immediate changes in the structure of your chain of command," Olstein began. "The crisis our country is facing calls for drastic measures to ensure the majority of the populace is provided for in terms of their basic needs: food, water, shelter, and security. To that end, I have written a few executive orders to be put in place immediately. They are as follows ..." the president proceeded to recite the EOs he had written. There were murmurings among the assembled troops and Secret Service personnel. Olstein became agitated.

"I see there is some discussion going on. Please share with everyone!" he snapped at the crowd. After a moment, a lieutenant spoke up.

"Mister President, I don't think you have the authority to do that."

"Well, I think I do. Our country is in complete turmoil, and we need to get control of the situation! We can't have people running around with guns threatening other people or robbing them. There are a number of people out there who have much more food than others. That isn't right! We should all be helping each other to get through this. Those with an abundance of food will need to donate that to help the greater good."

"But, if you take their guns and their food, at that point, aren't *you* robbing *them*, Sir?" came a voice from the crowd. The attendees in the room were talking louder now.

Olstein's face was turning a darker shade of crimson with each passing moment. "I don't think you understand the gravity of the situation, people! We need everyone to pitch in here! You all will be responsible for gathering the supplies. This is not a request! This is an order from your Commander-in-Chief!"

"Gathering? Don't you mean commandeering? No, Sir, I can't, in good conscience, do that," one of the soldiers responded from the group. "I didn't enlist to steal from or hurt law-abiding Americans who have done nothing wrong." He turned around and started for the door. Several others in attendance followed him.

"How dare you walk out on me! You took an oath to obey my orders! Security! Stop them!"

The lieutenant who had spoken earlier was among the group who were leaving. She stopped, turned back to Olstein, and replied, "We also took an oath to support and defend the Constitution against all enemies, foreign and domestic. You aren't doing that, Mister President, so your orders are null and void." With that, she continued on toward the door. The remaining troops followed, leaving Olstein fuming with rage. He turned on the Secret Service agents standing behind him.

"Why didn't you stop them? I gave you an order! I want them all arrested!"

Agent Walters looked calmly at the president and replied, "Our job is to protect you, Sir. They posed no threat to you, so we had no reason to intervene. They're

46

following their oath and doing what they think is right. That's not a reason to arrest them."

"If I order you to arrest them, that's all the reason you need! Why is no one following my orders?" Olstein fumed.

"I'm sorry, Sir, but I can't detain people who have done nothing wrong. I think we should get you back to your quarters now, Mister President."

Olstein stomped off toward his office. Under his breath, he mumbled, "I need to find new people who will do what I say without question. There's going to be some changes around here very soon."

Chapter 7

Damon and crew were progressing slowly, but steadily, down South Middlebush Road. The decision made earlier to keep the rifles visible seemed to be working as a deterrent to the people outside who saw them. Shouted questions came from the side of the road, along with shaken fists and rude gestures, but no one approached them again. Nearing Highway 27, the housing complexes fell away, but a new problem surfaced. Damon tapped Hutch on the arm and pointed in front of them.

"That's gonna be a problem." Hutch nodded slowly in agreement. Where South Middlebush crossed the highway, a multi-car pileup was blocking the intersection.

"I'm open to suggestions here," Hutch said. "I don't see us pushing our way through this with a camper attached to the Humvee."

Damon had donned a hat and was slipping on a pair of gloves. "I'm gonna get out and see if I can come up with an alternate route. Hold tight for a minute." He grabbed his rifle and stepped out into the snow.

"Roger that. Light, keep him in your sights," Hutch replied.

"On it, Cap." Darrell watched as Damon stepped out and surveyed the area. To their right was a small strip mall, doors and windows already broken in. A liquor store and candy shop were especially hard hit. On the left was a physical therapy rehab center. Damon walked around the front of the Humvee and on toward the highway. Watching for any potential threats, he stepped out onto the highway and looked in both directions. Landscaped shrubs and trees adorned the corners, making it impossible for them to try to go around the problem. Scanning the surroundings, his eyes lit up at something. He hurried back to the Humvee and went to the driver side door.

Hutch rolled the window down and said, "Well, have you solved the puzzle?"

Grinning, Damon replied, "I think so. If you turn left here at the entrance to the rehab center, it loops back around to the highway. Then we can go through the parking lot of that Japanese restaurant over there." He pointed to the building across the street. "We can get back on track from there, although it looks like the street changes names to Sand Hills Road. After that, we need to get our speed up again and make sure everybody is ready, because we'll be going to the heart of Kendall Park then. Lots of houses, which equals lots of people, between here and Highway 1."

"Okay, go ahead and climb in and let's get moving." Hutch put the Humvee in gear and looked expectantly at Damon.

"I think I'm gonna walk alongside until we get to the highway. My legs could use the stretch." Damon took another look around then motioned for Hutch to come with him into the parking lot. Hutch turned the rig and followed him.

The snow had drifted at the parking lot entrance, but the building had provided a buffer for the rest of the lot. Damon was scanning the building, the doors and windows in front surprisingly unscathed, and the parking lot on the other side. Not seeing anything that caused him concern, he turned back to face the Humvee.

"I think it's clear," he called out. "Just keep coming —" His remark was cut short when a bullet hissed past his head.

"Shooter!" Darrell yelled. "Perez, help me find him, but stay low!"

Damon dropped onto his belly in the snow. He heard another shot and the sound of a round hitting metal. He immediately rolled until the Humvee was in front of him. He rose to a crouching position then stood a bit straighter until he could see inside the vehicle. Jason had closed the back hatch and had the Tanners bent over so that they were shielded by the seat backs. Stacy and Liz had popped out of the camper and taken up positions between it and the Humvee, one on each side. Darrell and Marco were both scanning the strip mall on the other side of the street, as that's where it appeared the shot had come from.

"Anybody got eyes on the shooter?" Hutch called out from inside the Humvee.

"Nothing yet, Cap," Marco responded. "Hold on! I've got something — one o'clock!"

Damon moved to the driver side of the hood and looked through the scope of his rifle. Though it was hard to see within the dimly lit interior of the former liquor store, he was able to make out two heads attached to two bodies with handguns pointed their direction. He rapped lightly on the hood to get the attention of the occupants. Hutch and Jason both turned his way to see him pointing at his eyes with two fingers and then holding two up indicating he had seen two people.

"Sorely has eyes on two, Light," Hutch said aloud for Darrell's benefit. "Confirm."

"Confirmed. I only see two in the liquor store." Darrell continued to scan the area around the liquor store. "Wait — two more next door at the gym!"

Stacy, who was behind the passenger side of the vehicle, spoke. "Another two on foot taking cover behind a car in the parking lot. Rules of engagement, Sir?"

"Don't fire unless fired upon. When that happens, don't miss," Hutch said resolutely.

"Copy that. Perez, Thompson, if they shoot, we shoot back!" she called to Liz and Marco.

"Got it," Liz replied.

"Roger!" Marco answered as well.

The team waited to see what the attackers' next move would be. They didn't have to wait long. One of the men in the parking lot yelled out, "Nobody needs to get hurt! You all just step on out of that vehicle and walk away! We just want the ride!"

"Never gonna happen!" Damon retorted. "This vehicle is owned by the United States government, and we are on official business. Have your men come out and lay down their weapons, or we will be forced to fire upon you!"

"Ha! Come and take them! We ain't laying down a damn thing!" the man retorted.

"Light, pick one in the gym. Relay to Perez to pick one in the liquor store, and Manning to target one of the two on her side. Thompson is backup for that side." Hutch spoke calmly as he checked his rifle and his vest. Turning toward the back, he said, "Stephens, I'm going out to assist. The Tanners are yours. Sir, Ma'am." He addressed them each in turn, then slid over and climbed out on the passenger side. He crouched down, shut the door, and ran the best that he could to join Damon up front. Once there, he acquired the two in the parking lot. "Manning, I've got your six," he called out. She gave a quick nod to acknowledge him but never took her eyes off her target.

"Well, this is unexpected," Hutch said to Damon. "Any ideas on how to proceed?"

"I have a feeling somebody is going to get hurt or die here." Damon made the statement with a hint of sadness in his voice. "Let's make sure it's not any of our people."

"Roger that."

The man from the parking lot shouted again. "Best I can tell there isn't any United States government anymore! It's every man for himself now. From what I can see, we've got a pretty even matchup here! What do ya say we see who's the better shot!"

As he said the last word, he took aim with an AR-style rifle and fired on Stacy's position. Stacy jumped and ducked back to the front of the camper, even though the bullet was high over her head.

"Manning! Status!" Hutch yelled.

"All good! My granny can shoot better than that asshole and she's almost blind!" she shouted loud enough for the would-be carjackers to hear. Her fellow Guardsmen made a point of laughing uproariously so the sound carried across the street.

Voice filled with rage, the man bellowed, "I'll show you some shootin', bitch!" He pointed the rifle at Stacy again. A shot rang out, but it wasn't from his gun. The man dropped his gun and grabbed his jacket pulling it open to reveal a stain of crimson blood that was expanding across his chest. He dropped to his knees then fell face first into the snow at his feet. His buddy started to leave his position and apparently thought better of it, staying behind the SUV he was using for cover.

"Threat neutralized!" Marco called out.

"Who else wants to die today?" Damon shouted across the street. "We're trained soldiers! We don't miss!"

One of the men came running out of the gym toward the man lying on the ground. "John? Johnny! No!" He slipped in the snow, got up, and hurried to his fallen comrade. After turning him over, the look on his face told Damon's crew what they already knew.

"You murdered my brother, you assholes! You're supposed to protect us not kill us!"

"Then lay down your weapons and come out with your hands up like I told you to do from the beginning! No one else has to die!" Damon waited; body tensed ready for action; his finger off the trigger but hovering near it. The whole team seemed to be anxious, poised to act if the situation called for it.

The man made his choice. "I'll see you in hell first, you son of a bitch!"

The action of raising his pistol to aim their way was enough for Stacy to take aim and fire at him. The bullet hit him in the chest, and he dropped to the ground beside his brother. With two of their people down, the other four appeared in the parking lot unarmed, arms raised.

"Hands behind your head and get down on your knees!" Damon's voice held no hesitation and left no room for misinterpretation. The men complied.

"Manning, Thompson — keep your eyes peeled on the parking lot. Light, Perez — you watch the buildings." Hutch issued the orders as he and Damon started toward their attackers. They walked slowly, checking the area, looking for threats or anything out of place. They approached the men kneeling in the snow. Three of them wouldn't meet their gaze. The fourth glared up at them.

"Do you have something you want to say?" Hutch asked, addressing the belligerent-looking man.

"Zeke was right. You're the National Guard, aren't you? You're supposed to protect us, help us! You killed two men!" The man spat the words at them in a venomous tone.

"Those two men were shooting at us," Hutch replied calmly. "When someone shoots at us, we shoot back. We gave you the choice to walk away with everybody alive. You chose poorly."

"Well, what are we supposed to do? We're almost out of food. None of our cars or trucks run. The water will stop flowing any day now. We've got no way to heat our houses. We're either going to freeze, starve, or die of dehydration!"

"So, you felt that trying to carjack a bunch of soldiers was your only recourse?" Damon asked. "Not real smart on your part. Where are your weapons?"

The man jerked his head toward the building. "Ours are inside. Leon's is over there by the two men you murdered."

The insinuation was not lost on them, but Hutch and Damon ignored it. Damon replied, "Here's what's going to happen. We're going to get back in our vehicle and get going. We have a lot of miles to cover to get back to D.C. You boys are going to stay right here until we can't see you anymore. If you move from this spot while you are still within our sight, the man on top of the camper will make the body count go up. Do you understand?"

All four men nodded. The other three still had not spoken a word. The fourth asked in a pleading tone, "Isn't anyone coming to help us?"

"I don't know," Damon said. "I'm sorry I can't tell you something different, but I honestly don't know what's going to happen. I do think you should choose another way to try to get your hands on supplies, though. This one is pretty dangerous, as you can see. The next person you try to steal from may not be nice enough to leave any of you alive. Good luck, guys."

Hutch and Damon turned to head back across the street. Hutch called out loud enough for the men behind him to hear, "Perez, anybody moves, you shoot. Understood?"

"Yes, sir!" Marco replied sharply.

As they walked, Hutch said under his breath, "They didn't train us for this."

Damon nodded. "There is no training for a situation where we are forced to fire upon American citizens. That's not what we're supposed to do. Yet, here we are, doing it."

"This is turning into a pretty sucky day," Hutch added.

Damon replied, "Agreed. And there's still some of it left."

Chapter 8

"Okay, run that by me one more time, Joel." Elliott had a confused look on his face.

Excitedly, Joel explained his plan. "You have everything we need here to power this generator with the tractor. We use the power takeoff shaft to turn the big pulley from the water pump. It uses the belt to turn the small pulley which powers the generator! I may need to scavenge some parts from other equipment here to mount everything up, but I think it can be done. Do you know what the PTO speed is relative to the tractor engine's RPM?"

"I think the specs were five hundred forty PTO RPMs at like twenty-six hundred engine RPMs."

"So, that's real close to a five-to-one ratio. Close enough for this setup. The pulleys are twelve inches on the big one and about two on the little one. That's a six-to-one ratio. If the tractor engine idles at around one thousand RPMs, that means the PTO is turning at about two hundred. That gives us approximately twelve hundred RPMs at the small pulley on idle. I think we're going to need more than that to get the right frequency; but without testing equipment, we may just have to wing it. If we can run the tractor at idle, it will use much less fuel; but I think we're going to need about eighteen hundred RPMs to reach one hundred and ten volts. The voltmeter on the front will tell us what we need once we get it going."

Elliott was starting to get excited himself. "You mean we could actually run power to the house with this setup?"

Grinning, Joel nodded. "Yep. Nothing too heavy — no HVAC or water heater, pretty much nothing with a heating element. But lights, fridge, freezer — I think that's totally doable."

"What about the well?"

Joel's forehead wrinkled. "That's two hundred and twenty volt. I don't know if we can generate that kind of power. It won't hurt to try. You said it was an artesian well, right?"

"Yep. Great water, great pressure. Only takes one pump, maybe two, to get it going. It was coming up out of the hole pretty good when they hit it."

"Well, it must be a non-flowing one or it would be bubbling out of the ground all the time. Maybe we could come up with a solar system to run the pump, if we can get our hands on some solar panels."

"Sounds like a scavenger hunt to me," Elliott chuckled. "Wow, this will definitely change things for us, Joel! If we can run the fridge and the freezer, that opens up all kinds of options for food storage."

"Yes, it does. We may not be able to keep the fridge cold enough. Those doors let a lot of air in and out when you open them. It takes a refrigerator like eight to twelve hours to get to the set temp. The freezer is easier. It's a chest type, so when you open the door, the warmer air of the room doesn't drop down into it, because hot air rises and the colder air in the freezer doesn't rise out. We should be able to run the generator for an hour, then off for two, to keep the freezer stuff frozen. We can cover it in blankets or sleeping bags when it's off. That will help hold the cold in. How full is the freezer?"

"Almost to the top. I bagged a deer a couple of weeks ago, and there's flour and meal in there as well. Lots of meats and some vegetables. The bottom is lined with gallon jugs of water."

Joel smiled and nodded. "Excellent. That's one we won't have to worry about then. It could probably go forty-eight hours without anything thawing if it was kept closed at full capacity. We're past that now, but, hopefully, we can salvage any meat that's starting to thaw. We'll try to keep the fridge cold as well, but we may need to coordinate running the generator with eating times when it would be opened more. Let's get to scavenging!"

Most of the family joined them for the construction of the generator. Aaron and Cameron were in awe as they watched their grandfathers build it. Ethan and Will assisted with tool requests. Amanda was talking softly to Flossie and rubbing her neck. Lauri and Carly had stayed in the house to work on supper.

When everything was ready, Joel said, "Well, only one way to see if it's going to work. Let's take it for a test drive."

Elliott climbed on and fired up the tractor. The generator started running, and a group shout went up. Joel squatted down by the front of the generator to check the voltmeter.

"Yep, that's what I expected. We're getting about eighty to ninety volts at idle. Give it a little gas, Elliott."

Elliott pushed the throttle slowly, and the engine revved up. Joel watched as the voltmeter started climbing. When it got to one hundred and twenty volts, Joel called out, "Right there! What's your RPM?"

Elliott looked at the gauge. "Seventeen fifty, give or take."

Standing and arching his back, Joel replied, "That's about what I figured it would be. Well, we can still do it, but we're limited to whatever fuel you have."

Elliott turned the tractor off and climbed down. He pointed to a fifty-five-gallon drum not far from him. "That one's full. I've got another one out back that's probably half that. We've got a little for now."

"Well, all that's left is to get the power from the generator into the house. Do you have a cord for the generator, Elliott?"

"I think so. Let me see what's over there." Elliott went back to the corner and rummaged through some items. He held up a twenty-five-foot long heavy-duty power cord. "Here we go!" He handed the cord to Joel.

Joel took the cord, looked it over and smiled. "Perfect. Now, I'm going to have to ask you to make a sacrifice, buddy."

Elliott's eyebrows raised as he replied, "Um, okay. What do you need? Blood? A pinky finger?"

Everyone laughed as Joel said, "No! Nothing that drastic or painful. I just need to cut the plug off your dryer cord."

"Is that all? If it gets juice to the house, you can have the whole dryer!" Elliott started for the door of the barn. Joel and the rest followed, still chuckling over the interaction.

When they got back to the house, Elliott went straight to the laundry room. He pulled the dryer away from the wall. "Do you need me to take the back off and detach the cord?" he asked, looking at Joel who was standing in the doorway.

Joel shook his head. "Nah, it's going to be ruined when I get done with it. Just cut it off. Leave me a couple of feet of cord to work with."

Elliott cut the dryer cord close to the back of the machine. He handed it up to Joel and came out from behind the dryer. He started to push it back to the wall, but Joel stopped him.

"We're going to need that outlet. Just leave the dryer where it is for now."

Lauri walked out to the laundry room, drying her hands on a dishtowel. "What are you boys up to?"

58

Joel turned to his wife with a twinkle in his eye. "We're going to make electricity."

Carly bounded over. "Oh my God! Are you serious? We're going to have power again? I'm so glad I brought my cell phone and my tablet. I can charge them up and maybe we can get on the Internet and find out what the hell is going on!"

"It doesn't work that way, honey," Joel said, shaking his head. "The pulse fried their circuitry. Those devices won't work again, ever."

"What? No cell phones anymore?" Carly exclaimed wide-eyed.

"No, not until new ones can be made anyway. But cell phones are way down on the priority list right now for what we need to live." Joel was using a pair of wire strippers Elliott had given him to expose the wires inside the cord as he talked.

"Maybe low on *your* priority list," Carly mumbled. "Some of us had a life that was pretty awesome. Everything is just a big bag of suck now."

"What is *wrong* with you?" Amanda's loud exclamation caught everyone by surprise and made Carly jump. "You have been nothing but catty, whiny, snarky, and mean since I met you! It's like you blame everyone around you because this happened! None of these people caused this. None of them can fix it. Life is as good or as bad you make it. My mom is a thousand miles away dealing with this alone. I may never see her again! She could be dead because some asshole wanted the food she had in the house, and I will probably never know. You have your family here with you. Do you ever stop to think about anyone but yourself? I'm sick of your bitching and moaning about every little thing! I think it's about time you pull up your big girl panties and start acting like a grownup instead of a bratty, petulant child. Excuse me!" Amanda brushed past Ethan and went outside.

Everyone stared at the closed door she had exited, shocked at the outburst from a person they had just met. Cameron broke the silence.

"Wow. She's got a set of lungs on her."

Carly spluttered, "Well, that is about the rudest anyone has ever been to me! Will, I know you like her, but I don't think I can stay in the same house with her. I don't think this is going to work —"

"Think again," Will replied. "Everything she said is true. Rather than acting like the strong woman I've always believed you to be, you have been behaving like a spoiled teenager. No offense, guys." He looked at Aaron and Cameron, who were both in shock over the whole situation. "For a single mom who put herself through school while raising two boys and working, I expected more. Our world is changed, likely forever, but at least for the foreseeable future. I, for one, do not want to spend it listening to you complain about it. This is it. This is what we've got. Deal with it. And for everyone's sake, grow up, Carly." Will went out the door as well.

Silence ensued again. Finally, Joel spoke. "Well now, that needed saying. I really do like that Amanda. Come on, Elliott, let's go make a cord to get some power in here."

Joel and Elliott left the room with the rest of the menfolk following. Carly was standing in the middle of the kitchen, still shocked by the interactions with her brother and Amanda. She turned to her mother. Before she could say anything, Lauri spoke.

"Amanda is right, honey. Your behavior has been horrendous. We all love you and didn't want to hurt your feelings. Your father and I talked about it more than once. We honestly thought you would get over it at some point and get on board. I admit, it's been hard for me to accept, too. But we have to accept it and make the most of it. Amanda was absolutely right. We are blessed to be together. We have a place to live that is better than where we were, providing warmth and safety. We can build a new life, but we have to work as a team. I know how strong you are. I know you can do this and be a vital part of this family. But you need to deal with *this* life and stop pining over your former life. It's gone, probably for good. Now, let's get back to supper."

Carly walked slowly over to where Lauri was standing. Quietly she said, "I'm sorry, Mom. I guess I was taking it out on everybody else. It's just so ... surreal, you know?"

Lauri hugged her and replied, "I know, honey. It's going to be alright. We'll figure it all out. I do think it would be a good idea for you to extend that apology to the rest of the family. Later tonight sounds good."

"Yeah, Lord knows there won't be anything else to do besides talk."

"Carly ..."

"Sorry."

Chapter 9

President Olstein slammed his office door closed behind him.

"How dare they walk out on me! I think everyone in Washington has lost their minds, because no one is listening to me!" He slammed the papers he had been carrying down on the desk then, in a fit of rage, he swept his arm across the top knocking everything onto the floor. He grabbed a glass pyramid off the credenza and threw it violently across the room. It shattered, making a very loud noise, which had Agent Walters bursting through the door.

"What's happening, Sir? Are you alright?" he asked, scanning the room for potential danger.

"I'm fine! Get out!" Olstein screeched at the head of his security detail. Walters gave him a curt nod and left, closing the door as he did. The president stared at the mess he had created. He waded through the rubble on the floor, opened the door, and bellowed into the hall, "Strain! Get your ass in here!"

David hurried down the hall and stood in the open doorway looking down at the mess strewn across the carpet. Finally, he said, "Yes, Mister President?"

"Where are they?"

"They, Sir? Oh, you mean the Speaker and the Joint Chiefs. Speaker Roman said he would be here shortly." He waited for the president's reply, fidgeting nervously with the pen and notepad in his hand.

"How shortly?"

"Well, he didn't give an exact time frame, Sir."

Olstein rolled his eyes. "Of course he didn't. He wants me sitting around here with my thumb up my ass waiting for him! If I could, I'd fire him, too. Maybe I'll write an order giving myself the power to do that, too."

"Oh, I'm sure that's not what they were thinking when I saw them, Mister President."

"They? Who else was there?" the president snapped.

"Um … well, he wasn't there … not right away, but …" David stammered, trying to find the right words — the ones that wouldn't upset the man any more than he already was. His attempt was in vain.

"Spit it out, dammit! Who else?" The vein on the side of Olstein's temple was bulging with pent-up anger.

"Speaker Roman called General Everley and asked him to come over before I left." David hoped it would end there. It didn't.

"Why would he do that? Why would they need to meet before coming here?" Olstein looked at David with a confused expression.

David replied hesitantly, "I don't really know, Sir. Perhaps they were going to ride together or something. If there's nothing else, I should probably go check to see if the conference room is ready. I'll let you know as soon as they arrive, Mister President."

Olstein waved his hand toward the door. "No, go ahead. But I want to know the *second* they get here."

David nodded and shut the door. He closed his eyes and thought, *I hope they get here soon. I have a feeling this is going to be a really bad day.*

~~~~~

The four Chiefs and Speaker Roman arrived at the White House just before dark. A city that was normally bathed in light after sunset looked foreign without it. They exited the Humvee and grabbed their duffel bags from the back, having returned to the Pentagon for the other Chiefs to grab some clothes and personal items. The military members were dressed in fatigues while Phil wore a sweatshirt and jeans. They weren't dressed to impress — they were dressed to work.

Charles addressed the group in the waning light. "If anyone asks, we're here at the president's request. Carl, you head immediately to the barracks in the bunker and gather your men. I don't think the Secret Service agents will try to stop us, but if they do, your orders are to restrain and detain. We don't want any casualties if at all possible. I think they'll be on board when they see we have no intention of harming him.

"Angie, you get to the radio operations room. Let them know that in Admiral Stephens' absence, you will be taking over their assignments. Find out if Olstein has issued any orders we don't know about regarding our deployed troops and if he has tasked them with sending out any messages. If he hasn't gotten that far yet, it's all good. If he has, have them immediately contact anyone they have at his behest and belay those orders until we have control of the president. Anton, you're with me and Phil. Alright, let's get this over with."

They made their way to a side entrance. The two Marines stationed there snapped to attention and saluted. The Chiefs returned it. One of the Marines opened the door and held it as the Chiefs and the Speaker entered. "Thank you, Corporal," Phil said as he passed the young woman. She gave him a small smile, nodded, then closed the door behind them and returned to her post. They broke out flashlights and made their way down the empty hall toward the stairwell that would take them down to the bunker.

"It's so eerie without people ... well, everywhere. I've never been here that there wasn't somebody around." Angie spoke barely above a whisper.

"There's no reason to be up here," Phil replied. "Nothing works. It's actually easier from a security standpoint because every exterior door is manned and there is only one way in or out of the bunker now — the stairs. The elevator doesn't work either. There are two flights of stairs, one at each end, but those are easily guarded as well. All the action is below ground, along with the provisions."

They continued to the door leading to the stairwell. A sole Marine sergeant stood sentry. He snapped to attention at their approach.

"At ease, Sergeant," Everley said. The Marine relaxed his stance a bit and opened the door for them. They made their way down the stairs in silence, all apparently lost in their own thoughts. What they were about to do was unheard of in America, yet they deemed it necessary to save the Republic. The founding fathers fought and died to free the country from a tyrannical ruler. Now it was their responsibility to prevent such a thing from happening again.

The door at the bottom of the stairs was manned by a Secret Service agent. He turned quickly at the sound of the handle being engaged but relaxed when he saw the group. Addressing General Everley, he said, "The president is waiting for you. Shall I tell him you've arrived?"

Charles replied quickly, "No, we'll let him know ourselves in a few minutes after we get settled. We want to drop our things in the barracks."

The agent nodded and resumed his duties. The group continued down the hall to the barracks area. When they arrived, a number of soldiers hurried over to them.

"Sirs, Ma'am, did you hear what the president wants us to do?" one of the young men asked.

General McKenna stepped forward. "Yes, we heard. I need to see all of you back here," he said as he started toward a rear corner of the area. The soldiers followed without question.

"Angie, head down to the radio room. Make sure Olstein doesn't see you." Charles dropped his duffel on an empty bunk. "We'll let you know when it's over."

"On my way. Good luck, fellas," she said as she turned toward the doorway.

Anton, Charles, and Phil made their way back to the spot where Carl was addressing the troops. They could tell by their demeanor that the young men and women were apprehensive about what he was saying.

"… and we're going to do this in a way no one gets hurt. We don't want anyone injured or killed. Understood?"

A chorus of tentative, yet affirmative, responses came from the group.

"Good. Any questions?"

A young female corporal raised her hand. "Sir, is this legal? I mean, I know what the president wants to do isn't, not according to the Constitution anyway. But is what you want us to do any less … well, wrong?"

Carl crossed his arms over his chest. "What's your name, Corporal?"

"Salvia, Sir. Kelly Salvia."

"What was the first promise you swore when you took your oath, Salvia?"

"To support and defend the Constitution, Sir."

He waited a moment. When she didn't go on, he prompted her, "And what's the rest of that line?"

"Against all enemies, foreign and domestic, Sir."

"So, if we stand by and let the president issue unconstitutional executive orders, then we are not, in fact, upholding our oaths. Correct?"

She nodded. "Yes, Sir!"

Carl looked around at the group of twenty or so young men and women. "I'm not going to order you to assist in

66

this operation. It is far outside of anything we have trained you to do, mostly because we never envisioned a situation like this. I will tell you that the success of this mission is imperative if we are to save our country's freedom from an internal attack at the highest level of government. We cannot let President Olstein enact the changes he wants to make. If he starts down that path, it will be the end of our country's freedom. With that said, anyone who wants to join us please take one step forward."

The entire group of enlisted men and women stepped toward him. With a smile, he said, "Thank you. Let's get ready."

Carl walked over to Anton, Charles, and Phil. "Okay, you've got troops. When do we do this?"

"Now. I'm going to call the Secret Service agent by the stairwell door in here. Phil, you're on." Everley walked over to the door and called out, "Excuse me, agent? I'm sorry, I didn't catch your name. Could you assist us for a moment?"

The agent looked at him and responded, "It's Masters, Sir, and I can't leave my post unguarded."

"Oh, we'll put someone on in your place. Salvia? Please take Agent Masters' post for a few minutes."

"Yes, Sir!" The corporal hurried out to the spot where the agent was standing. The agent hesitated a moment then went to the door where Everley stood.

"What do you need, Sir?" he asked calmly.

"Actually, I was the one who wanted to speak with you, Agent Masters. Please, come in and sit for a moment." Phil was standing beside a table and pulled a chair out indicating the agent should sit there. Masters hesitated again then went further into the room. He took the seat and looked expectantly at the Speaker. Phil sat across from him.

"What's your first name?" he asked the agent.

"John," Masters replied succinctly.

"John, are you aware of the new executive orders President Olstein intends to enact?"

Masters eyed Phil, then let his gaze travel up to Charles, Carl, and Anton, who were standing behind him. "Yes, Sir, he shared them will all of us a little while ago."

Phil nodded slowly. "And what do you think about them?"

John leaned back a bit in his chair. "Off the record?"

Anton and Charles looked at each other with raised eyebrows. Phil smiled at John. "Absolutely."

"I think it's complete bullshit," John said. "You can't just go around issuing edicts that are against the Constitution. I don't care who you are. He tried to get us to arrest those soldiers over there," he indicated the troops watching the interaction, "because they wouldn't bow down to his insanity. I mean, seriously, who the hell does he think he is?"

"That's something we intend to rectify, John." Phil watched him closely. Carl looked back toward the corner and gave the men and women there an almost imperceptible nod. They started making their way over, spreading out so that some of them appeared to be heading for the door, while others were ambling towards bunks. All of them were positioning themselves around the room.

"How? How are you going to stop him when most of the government is at home dealing with God knows what?"

Phil took a deep breath and replied, "We're going to have to remove the president from office. We have no intention of harming him or anyone else. But we can't sit by and let him turn this country into some kind of dictatorship. We must do whatever we can to keep our country free."

John looked confused now. "Again, how? Congress is gone — well, everyone besides you. You can't impeach him. The only way ..." His confusion cleared and changed to shock. "A coup! You're going to remove him from office, right?"

"Yes. Unfortunately, we have no other option at this point. We are not asking you to assist, John. We're just suggesting you don't interfere. We will confine him to quarters for the time being. I will act in his stead for the next thirty days until David Tanner gets here to be sworn in."

"Tanner is in New York. No way he has a working vehicle, and he sure as hell can't walk that far."

"We have already secured Mr. Tanner, and he is in route to D.C. as we speak. As I said, we are doing everything in our power to stop President Olstein from making a terrible situation worse. So, my question to you, John, is will you try to stop us?"

The soldiers had formed a loose half circle behind Agent Masters. No one knew how he would react nor whether they would have to restrain or disarm him. The anticipation hung heavy in the room.

He smiled, stood up, and extended his hand toward Phil. "Just let me know what I can do to help. It would be my pleasure to serve on your security detail, Mister President."

Chapter 10

The sun was dropping in the sky as Damon and crew made their way through Kendall Park. Outside of a few gawkers and people shouting questions at them, they didn't experience any more trouble. Perhaps the people had heard the gunfire from their previous altercation at the strip mall. Sound travels farther when there is no ambient noise from electrically powered transformers or running vehicles. Or maybe they were just moving indoors, as the temperature was definitely falling. Whatever the reason, the travelers were all happy to see the signs for Highway 1. When they got on the highway, they could see that there had been at least one vehicle through there since the snow had ceased, as visible tire tracks attested.

They got past a couple of residential areas and stopped. Everyone got out to stretch their legs and Marco climbed down from the roof of the camper. He bent over, stretched, arched his back, and stretched again.

"Man, that was tougher than I thought it would be! There's no traction up there!"

Damon and Hutch were looking at a map spread out on the hood. "I think we'll bring you back inside for now, Perez," Hutch commented. "Looks like we'll be out of the residential areas for a while. I'm hoping Princeton is pretty dead, with everyone already gone home for the holiday. Are you planning to stop for the night, Sorley?"

Damon shook his head. "I'd rather keep going. We have enough people so we can rotate out drivers. I think we'll be better off driving through the night. Hopefully, most people will be indoors trying to stay warm and sleeping. We're way behind where I wanted to be by now. If we continue on, we should be in D.C. before morning."

"Works for me," Hutch replied. Looking back toward the rest of the team, he said, "Let's get some food and water passed out. It's going to be a long night. Somebody see if they can heat water on the stove back there. Coffee would be amazing right now."

"On it, Cap," Stacy said as she was going up the steps into the camper. Liz had gone in and come back out with a box of MREs she was passing out. Jason and Darrell were standing watch front and back. Melanie leaned over to David and whispered something in his ear. David nodded and looked to Damon.

"Major, would it be possible for my wife to use the facilities inside? I'm not sure what, if anything, needs to be done for that to be feasible. Don't these things have to be winterized or something?"

Hutch spoke up. "If I may, Sir, it should have anti-freeze in the plumbing. It won't hurt anything for her to use the bathroom. I'd suggest not putting any paper in. Just flush it when she's done. Um, well ... as long as it's just urine." His cheeks took on a tinge of pink as he did his best not to look at Mrs. Tanner. "Just pour a bottle of water in after you flush."

She smiled and said, "Yes, that's all, Captain. Thank you." Agent Stephens took her arm and led her to the camper door. He stood outside and waited for her return.

Stacy leaned out the door. "I found a coffee maker and coffee in here. Just a few more minutes."

Hutch gave her a nod then went back to studying the map with Damon. "So, what's the route you are proposing we take?"

Damon ran his finger along the highways as he spoke. "We'll stay on Highway 1 until we hit 295. That will get us around Trenton. We'll follow that highway until we can get on the Jersey Turnpike, probably from Mt. Holly Road.

Satellite imagery shows that to be a commercial area so, hopefully, no residents out and about."

"Why the turnpike instead of 295 all the way down?" Hutch asked.

"The turnpike goes through fewer residential sections and has less exits, thus fewer potential spots for an ambush. I came up that way and it was fairly quiet."

"Okay, but remember you came through there two days ago when no one had figured out what was going on yet. It may be a whole different scenario now."

"Agreed. I think we should have your men and women try to get some rest back there. Have two on sentry and two sleeping. Two hours on, two hours off. That will give everyone a break and keep them fresh."

"Sounds like a plan," Hutch replied. "When will you be taking your two hours?"

Damon smiled and said, "When we complete this mission."

~~~~~

After they had eaten and gotten some hot coffee in them, there was a renewed sense of urgency among the team. They all wanted to get going. Marco and Darrell were extremely happy to be inside the camper for a change and offered to take the first watch while the girls slept. Stacy and Liz didn't argue with them.

As they approached Princeton, they could see no lights and nobody out on the streets. While Princeton University itself was across the lake, there were campus facilities around the highway they were traveling as well. The sun was setting, and it was apparent no one wanted to be out after dark. An area that was usually teeming with people, even with the holiday approaching, now looked like an eerie winter ghost town.

Being on a highway, there weren't many residential complexes right on the thoroughfare. Most of the houses were on streets off of the highway which meant it wasn't as likely that people would be able to get outside and to them before the Humvee had already passed their road. But they didn't see anyone even attempting to come out. The houses they could see were shut up tight, curtains drawn, and not a sliver of light to be seen.

"This is downright creepy," Hutch said from the passenger seat. He and Damon had swapped for a while. "It looks completely dead out there."

"My guess is something has the people too scared to venture out, especially at night." Damon made the comment as he peered through the last dregs of daylight. Finally conceding defeat, he turned on the headlights. The road ahead was now bathed in light. He glanced over at Hutch and added, "Or someone. Those guys we ran into back there aren't the only bad guys out now."

"You're probably right. It's hard to believe everything has gone downhill so fast. I mean, it's only been two days." Hutch was shaking his head.

"Yes, but people aren't stupid. They know it's going to be a lot longer than two days until things get back to normal — if they ever do. No one is working, which includes police, firefighters, EMTs, doctors, or nurses, for all intents and purposes. Everything they use to do their jobs is fried. Squad cars, fire engines, ambulances, monitoring and testing machines — hell, lights and electricity, period. There's going to have to be some serious restructuring of how we do everything until we get the power back on." Damon had rattled all of that off without having to stop and consider his words.

Hutch looked at him a bit awestruck. "Have you been practicing that spiel?"

Damon chuckled. "I had a lot of time to think on the drive up here. It's not like there was anything on the radio."

Just then, Damon's phone rang. Hutch pulled it out of Damon's bag on the floor and held it out to him, but Damon shook his head. "You're going to have to talk to him. I don't need to be distracted at all right now. Who knows what might be in the middle of the road up ahead?"

Hutch flipped the phone open. "Captain Hutchinson speaking." He put the phone on speaker and held it out between himself and Damon.

"Where's Major Sorley?" General Everley's voice boomed from the phone.

"I'm here, Sir. We've got you on speaker since I'm driving."

"Oh. I actually want to speak to Mr. Tanner. Is he there with you?" Hutch took the phone off speaker and passed it back to David.

"Yes, I'm here, General, and you are no longer on speaker. How are things going there?"

They could not hear the other side of the conversation. Damon glanced up into the rear-view mirror and saw Tanner's face go from shock to anger to resolve.

"The decision has already been made for us to drive straight through. I will let the men know that it is imperative we get there as soon as possible. Please let me know how things go there, General. Once everything is in place, I'd like to talk to Speaker Roman as well." He nodded at something Everley said, then ended with, "We'll talk again soon." He closed the phone and handed it back to Hutch, who could tell Tanner had a concerned look on his face.

"Everything alright, Sir?" Hutch asked as he took the phone and put it back in Damon's bag.

Tanner shook his head. "No, everything is most certainly not alright, Captain. We need to get to Washington as fast as humanly possible."

Damon looked up into the rear-view mirror. "Has something happened, Sir?"

"Yes. President Olstein is trying to institute a bunch of executive orders that are unconstitutional; some even border on treasonous."

"Well, I knew he was talking about doing things like that. That's why General Everley sent me to get you," Damon said. "He's actually going through with it?"

"It would seem so. Stopping the inauguration, repealing the Second Amendment, calling for the use of the military to enforce that, as well as the confiscation of weapons and supplies, dismissing the Joint Chiefs, and worst of all naming himself Supreme Commander over everything. He has to be stopped."

Hutch's mouth dropped open. "He is actually trying to dismiss the Chiefs? Why would he do that?"

"From what General Everley told me, he wants all the troops recalled to enforce his confiscation orders here. They have been stalling, hoping they could wait him out until I was sworn in. He's forcing their hand." Tanner's look said there was more to be told but he didn't go on. Damon pushed the issue.

"Forcing their hand? To do what, Sir?" he asked.

Tanner hesitated, then replied, "To do something that has never been done in the history of our country. To perform a task that will forever change the face of our nation yet is necessary to keep the country and its government structure intact. To carry out a plan that will shock the world."

The weight of his comments hung heavily within the vehicle. Everyone sat in nervous anticipation of his next words.

"They're going to initiate a coup. They'll take Olstein into custody and seat Speaker Roman as acting president until my swearing in next month."

No one spoke. No one knew what to say. This action was unprecedented in America. No sitting president had ever been deposed. From the rear of the Humvee, Agent Jason Stephens spoke.

"As the son of one of the Chiefs, I don't think he left them much choice. He can't dismiss them. He knows nothing about warfare. He needs them. They're doing the right thing."

Tanner turned to look at Jason. "Wait — you're Admiral Stephens' son? Why didn't I know this? Why didn't you tell me?"

Jason shrugged. "We are what they call estranged. He and my wife don't get along — at all. And I don't use my father's name to garner favor. I do what I do on my own."

Tanner nodded with a smile. "I understand, and I respect that. I'm sure your father will be happy to see you, especially under the circumstances."

Jason turned back to peer out the windows of the vehicle. "We'll see."

Chapter 11

Just seeing the lights come on changed everyone's demeanor. Smiles and laughter filled the house as they ate supper. Carly had hurried to plug her cell phone charger into an outlet as soon as she saw there was power and tried to turn her phone on. Nothing happened. She huffed as she unplugged it and came back to set it on the kitchen table beside her. Joel smiled at his daughter.

"I told you it wouldn't work, Carly. There are delicate electronic components inside your phone that wouldn't make it through a pulse. Besides, I'm pretty sure the cell towers are fried just like everything else so you couldn't call anybody anyway. Plus, no one else's phone works either. You need to just put that thing away. I doubt it will ever work again, but I could be wrong. Go stick it in a drawer or something."

Carly picked up the phone and charger and walked dejectedly to the bedroom she was sharing with Amanda. Lauri looked around the room and smiled.

"It really is wonderful to see the lights on again. It makes it feel a little less like the end of the world, doesn't it?"

Joel nodded. "Yes, it does, but we'll only be able to run them for maybe an hour or so at night. We need to use the generator to power the freezer and the fridge more than anything. I really wish we had some solar panels. That fuel never runs out. I wonder if there are any in the area."

"There's a solar farm up on I-40 about 30 miles from here," Elliott said. "If we can get there in that Scout, we could probably get set up for power to the house and the pump. We'd have to see if we could find some controllers that weren't hooked up when the pulse went off. They may have some there we could scavenge. Then we just need a bunch of car or boat batteries to send the power to."

"I didn't know you knew anything about solar power setups, Dad," Ethan remarked.

"Well, I've read about a few things you could do for alternative power, I just never put any of it to use. I'm sure wishing I had now."

"Yes, hindsight is pretty much worthless at this point," Joel said with a chuckle. "But if we can round up some supplies, we might be able to set this place up to be much more comfortable. It's not an emergency — not yet, anyway — but we can start working on ideas like that to put into place soon."

Carly came back into the kitchen and stood in the doorway. She cleared her throat to get everyone's attention. All eyes at the table turned to her.

"I need to say something. I'm sorry I've been such a hateful bitch since this whole thing started. Life without electricity and all the awesome electronic gadgets it powered blows. But taking it out on all of you isn't helping the situation, and it sure won't fix it. I'm going to try to act better. Just don't expect everything to change right away. I'm still not happy about any of this, but I'm going to work on it. Okay, that's all I had." She went back and sat down at her plate to finish eating.

Amanda grinned at her from across the table. "We'll get through this, Carly. What do you say tomorrow we go out to Elliott's range and I teach you how to shoot?"

Carly shrugged as she chewed her food. "I guess that's a good place to start. It would make a lot more sense to carry a loaded gun than an empty one, which is what I'm doing now."

Cameron looked at his mother wide-eyed. "You've been carrying a gun, Mom?"

78

"Don't get excited, Cam. It doesn't have any bullets in it, and I wouldn't know what to do with it if it did."

"Which is what we're going to remedy tomorrow," Amanda added. "Speaking of which, I'd like to get a better look at what we got from Teddy. We basically just threw stuff in the bag, and the guys did most of that. I want to know what kind of goodies we brought with us." She rubbed her hands together, apparently anticipating something good.

"Me, too!" Cameron exclaimed, jumping up from his seat so quickly he jostled the table. Everyone reached instinctively for their glasses.

"Cameron!" Lauri admonished. "Calm down! There's no need to upend the table."

"Sorry, Nana. May I be excused?"

"I'm pretty sure you're supposed to be getting water heated for dish washing," Elliott said.

"Oh, Carly and I will take care of that, Elliott," Lauri replied as she stood up with her plate. "I think that's the least we can do after you've opened your home to us for sanctuary." Everyone else at the table stood as well and started carrying their dishes to the sink. Elliott turned back to speak.

"I don't want you thinking I expect you to do all the cooking and cleaning, Lauri. There's plenty of folks around here to help out with chores."

"And from what I can tell there will be plenty of chores to do for everyone. I told you this is how I can contribute. This is what I want to do. Let me handle the household. You and Joel can take care of the rest." She walked to the sink and took a pot from the counter. Filling it with water, she set it on the stove and turned the burner on. Turning back around, she found everyone watching her. "What are you all doing standing around here? Aren't there some chores that need to be done before bedtime?"

79

Cameron hurried over and grabbed his coat off a hook. "C'mon, Aaron. Let's get the wood brought in for the night. Who's getting the eggs and the milk? The sooner we get this stuff done, the sooner we can check out the arsenal!"

Elliott laughed at his grandson's enthusiasm. "Ethan and I will get the animals put up. Joel, you and Will can come along if you'd like. It's best if everybody knows what the process is for securing the barn."

"I'll help with the kitchen, too, Lauri," Amanda added. "I bet the three of us can knock it out quick."

"Make sure you get everything put in the refrigerator first," Joel said as he put his coat on. "And try to do it all at once. We'll leave the generator running for about an hour to get it as cold as we can. I don't know how well the fridge is going to do with running just a few hours a day, but I guess we'll find out. The good thing is it's still cold enough outside we could utilize that if we have to."

Elliott picked up a large flashlight as he turned the doorknob. "Back in a bit, ladies."

Carly and Amanda worked on clearing the table while Lauri got the sinks ready for washing dishes. Amanda spoke without looking up.

"Carly, about earlier … I —"

"No, it's fine. You were right," Carly replied sheepishly. "I was taking my self-pity out on everyone else. I lost a lot when the power went down, but, as you pointed out, I still have a lot to be thankful for. You were the only one who called me out on it. We're good. You don't need to apologize."

Amanda grinned at her. "Um, I wasn't going to apologize. I was just going to say I hoped you wouldn't hold it against me and kick me to the floor tonight. Although, I haven't shared a bed with anyone since my last

80

boyfriend, which was a few years ago, so I may be a cover hog, snorer, or both."

Carly laughed at loud. "Well, there I go being all self-centered again. But, I'm right there with you. I haven't shared a bed with anyone since Ethan, which was ten years ago, so I have no idea how I sleep either. We may end up in a fight after all!"

They both giggled and Lauri came over to join them. "I'm glad you girls are getting along. You may have noticed that the females are sparser here than the menfolk so we need to stick together."

"I'm trying, Mom. Not about getting along with Amanda, but about not being such a brat. I'm still pissed it happened, but I guess we have no choice but to deal with it. And Amanda, I *am* sorry you can't get to your mom. I'll tell you what — I'll share mine." She looked from Amanda to Lauri. "She has a big heart and I think there's room for all of us in there."

"She already has a place in it," Lauri said with a smile. "Everyone under this roof does — including Ethan."

"Yeah, well, I'm not ready to go that far," Carly retorted.

"I understand, honey, but keep in mind if it weren't for him you wouldn't have Aaron and Cameron. He is as much a part of their DNA as you are. We all make poor choices at some time in our lives. Should we not forgive each other and try to live the best life we can going forward, especially at a time like this? Ethan doesn't have much longer. It's never too late to ask for forgiveness, and it's never a bad thing to give it."

Carly considered what her mother had said. "I guess you're right, Mom. I'll work on it. No promises though."

"That's all I ask, sweetie. Now, let's get these dishes washed and get some coffee going."

"I can't believe he wouldn't let us stay there!" Taylor slammed the water jugs on the kitchen counter in anger, causing his children to jump in fright. "I bet there wasn't anyone else there either. I bet he lied so he wouldn't have to share with us!"

In a quiet tone, Wendy said, "Tay, please calm down. You're scaring the kids."

He turned on her. "Good! They should be scared. We're as good as dead!"

At that, Derek, the youngest, started crying. "I don't want to die, Mommy!"

Wendy scooped the six-year-old into her arms and glared at her husband. "Happy now?" She turned and went into the den to sit by the meager fire in the fireplace. She sat down on the chair closest to it and wrapped herself and her child up in a blanket. Rocking him gently, she cooed in his ear, "You're not going to die, baby, none of us are. Daddy's just upset. Everything will be alright."

Taylor was pacing between the kitchen and the den. His other two children were sitting on the edge of the sofa as if in anticipation of another outburst from their father. Taylor stopped and looked at his family who were all watching him. He pasted a smile on his face and walked over and kissed Wendy and Derek each on the forehead. He then went and did the same to Heather and Grayson. Reaching behind them, he took an afghan off the back of the couch and draped it over their shoulders. He squatted down in front of them.

"I'm sorry I yelled. Mommy is right. No one's going to die. Daddy will take care of it." He stood up and turned to look at Wendy. A short jerk of his head told her he wanted to talk to her away from the children. Setting her son on the chair and wrapping the blanket around him, she stood and

82

followed her husband into their bedroom. She walked in and shut the door quietly.

Turning to face him, she crossed her arms over her chest and hissed, "Aren't things bad enough without you freaking out, especially in front of the kids? Melting down is not your best option right now, Taylor. It doesn't help. At all."

"I said I was sorry! I'm going to do whatever I have to do to take care of this family, no matter what it takes."

"What do you mean by that?" Wendy asked warily.

Voice full of resolve, Taylor replied, "Exactly what I said. Whatever it takes."

Chapter 12

"That's right, James. We are on a standby order effective immediately. No troop movement until further notification." Angie was speaking to one of the highest-ranking officers of the Marines stationed in South Korea. "If you would, please pass that information along from your position. You actually have more available staff than we do for the task."

She listened for another moment then said, "Thank you for your help, James. Please let me know when everyone has been notified. Stay safe."

She handed the headset back to the petty officer who had made the call. "Let me know when you hear back from him. I appreciate your prompt attention to the matter, Jessica, as well as your discretion. Thank you."

The young lady smiled at her and replied, "My pleasure, Ma'am. I'll come find you after I speak with him again."

Angie went to the door and opened it a crack — just enough so that she could see out into the hall. Finding it clear, she stepped out and quietly closed the door behind her. As she was making her way back toward the barracks area, she ran into Speaker Roman and the other Joint Chiefs who were leading a small group of Marines and one lone Secret Service agent. The group stopped at her approach.

"How did it go, Angie?" Charles asked.

"Just fine. All deployed troops are on standby until they hear from us." She indicated the group behind him with an inclination of her head. "I see you've been busy as well."

Smiling, Everley replied, "Yes. We aren't the only ones who aren't okay with the proposed changes from our current president. We're on our way there now. I think you should come along with us to show a united front."

"Lead the way," she said as she fell in with the rest of the group.

Whether it was the sound of so many booted feet making their way down the hall or just a feeling that something was different, David Strain was standing in the doorway of the conference room when the Joint Chiefs got there. His eyes grew wide as he took in the company of men and women. Phil went to him and laid a hand on his arm.

"You should probably stay here for now, David," he said calmly. "This should all be over soon. Actually, I have an even better idea. Do you know where Vanessa went when she left? Do you think she went home?"

Stammering, David replied, "Um … I don't … I'm not sure, Sir. She was here when everything went down. I think she lives outside of D.C., so I don't imagine she tried to get home. What's going on? I was supposed to tell President Olstein when you arrived."

"Do you know if she has any friends or family nearby?" Phil asked, ignoring the follow-up question.

"I think her sister lives just a few blocks from here. Why?"

"Great, then I have a task for you. See if you can find the address. Check her personal information we have on file. Then get one of the Humvees and go over there. If we can find her, I'd like to have her back here as soon as possible."

Confused, David asked, "Sir, what are you doing? The president —"

"We're on our way to see him right now so there's no need for you to go tell him we're here," Everley said.

"Things are about to get very busy for all of us, David," Phil went on. "It is imperative that you get Vanessa back here quickly. Nothing personal against you, but she is an invaluable asset for dealing with what the coming days will bring. You will, of course, stay on and assist. Do you have a problem with that?"

David shook his head and with a touch of gratitude in his tone replied, "No, Sir, not at all. In fact, I'll be relieved to not have to fill in for her. She's a lot better at this stuff than I am. I'll get going right away."

Phil took his hand and shook it firmly. "Thank you, David. We'll get through this together."

David started for his office to grab his coat. He stopped and turned back to the group. "What if the president calls for me and I'm not here?" he asked in a voice laced with concern.

Everley spoke up. "We'll tell him you're in the restroom. Don't worry — we'll take care of it."

David gave them a nod and hurried off to his office to get his things. Phil looked at Charles. "You ready?"

"It's now or never," Charles said. "Let's get this over with."

President Olstein was sitting at his desk, empty of any clutter since his temper tantrum, scowling at the door.

"How damn long does it take to come when your commanding officer orders you to?" he shouted to the otherwise empty room. "The sooner I get rid of those Chiefs, the sooner these troops will understand this is the way it is now and obey *my* orders!"

As if in answer to his question, there was a knock at the door. "Come in!"

General Everley opened the door and stepped inside the room with no regard for the papers strewn across the floor. He was followed by the other Joint Chiefs, then Speaker Roman. Agent Masters pulled the door closed behind them and remained out in the hall.

"We're supposed to be meeting in the conference room." Olstein stood as he said, "Let's head down there and —"

Everley interrupted him. "Here is fine. Sit down, Mister President."

Surprised at the gruffness in the general's tone, Olstein replied smugly, "Excuse me? Are you giving me an order, General? I think you might be confused as to who is in charge here."

"No, I know fully well who is in charge, Barton, and it isn't you," Charles said with his own smug smile. "Not anymore."

Olstein's face turned red as anger took over. "What? What are you … how *dare* you speak to me like that! I most certainly *am* in charge! I'm the Commander in Chief! I control all of you! I —"

Charles walked around the desk and stood toe to toe with the president. In a low, threatening voice, he growled, "Like I said. Not anymore. Now *sit!*" The last word was punctuated with a shove that put Olstein back in his chair.

"Oh! And now you're assaulting me! Help! I need help in here! I'm being attacked!" He was yelling out for his Secret Service detail to come to his aid. Every head turned toward the door. When no one came in after a few seconds, they all looked back at the president.

"No one is coming to help you, Olstein, because they all know what you're trying to do is wrong," Charles said. "We're here to correct that."

"You have no authority anymore! I wrote an executive order dismissing you — all of you!" he screeched, taking in the rest of the Chiefs. His gaze landed on Speaker Roman. "I suppose you think you have a say-so in any of this? You're nothing without the rest of Congress to back you up!"

"*We're* backing him up," Carl McKenna said, stepping forward. The others stepped up to stand beside him. "We won't stand by and let you tear this country further apart than it already is. We won't tuck our tails and hide because *you* think you can get rid of us with some ridiculous EO you've written. You've gone too far, Olstein, and we're here to put a stop to it."

"That's *President* Olstein, and you can't stop anything! You don't have the authority! *I* have the authority! *I* have the power! *I'm* in control of this country — along with everything and everyone in it!" His eyes were bulging with rage, and spittle flew into the air with every emphasized word.

"Again ... not anymore." Charles cleared his throat. "As senior Chief, I am placing you, Barton Olstein, under arrest for treason."

"You can't do that! You don't have the authority —"

"I have as much authority to do this as you have to write ridiculous, unconstitutional EOs. Aside from your treasonous acts, I am declaring you unfit to fulfill your duties as president of the United States."

"This is preposterous! You are all guilty of treason! I'll see you hang for this!"

"Not likely," Anton said. He walked to the office door, opened it, and called out, "Marines, with me. Take Mr. Olstein into custody and confine him to his quarters."

"I'll see to it that he gets there," Carl added. The troops who had been waiting outside stepped forward to block the doorway. Two came inside and went to either side of Olstein, each taking him by the arm. He tried to jerk away from them, but they held fast.

"Get your hands off me! You can't do this! There's no one to take my place! The vice-president isn't here. Who —" He stopped as the reality set in. Fixing Phil with a hateful glare, he yelled, "Aha! *Now* I understand! It's you!

You think you can just waltz in here and take over! Well, this explains a lot! I suppose you think you'll get to stay in office until everything straightens out, which is probably never!"

Phil looked at the president with pity. "No, Barton. I have no intention of staying in the position any longer than is absolutely necessary. I'll just fill in for the next thirty days until the new president can be sworn in."

Olstein barked out a laugh. "New president? You mean Tanner? He's in New York City. That place is probably a war zone by now. How could he get here without a car? If he's even still alive, which I doubt. It's impossible."

"Actually, it's quite possible," Charles replied. "He's already on his way here."

"Bullshit! There's no way. Cars don't run. I'm guessing planes aren't flying and they just got hammered with about two feet of snow and no way to clear the roads if they did have a car that ran — which I highly doubt. It's not like he has hardened storage sites. And how would you know anyway? None of the phones work. Dream on, *General*."

Charles grinned as he said, "I know because I sent someone to get him as soon as I heard the outlandish ideas you had come up with Sunday, not the least of which was not stepping down for the incoming president. We've been working on this for days. We were going to just ride it out until the inauguration, but you forced our hand. You'll spend the rest of your term under guard. If things do get back to normal, we'll see about bringing formal changes against you then. For now, we're just getting you out of this office to protect the country from your delusions and to save you from yourself."

He took a step back and the Marines all but dragged Olstein out. He was screaming at the top of his lungs for someone to stop them, but the Secret Service agents stood stoically at their posts as he passed. Agent Masters had apparently been successful in his mission to warn them all of what was coming and gotten their approval of the move. The Chiefs watched the spectacle from the doorway of the current Oval Office. Phil addressed Masters.

"Thank you for your part in making this as painless as possible, if not completely peaceful," he said. "Would you and Agent Walker please join us inside?"

They all went into the office, sliding papers and debris out of their way. "I would like the two of you to stand as witnesses so there can be no accusation that what was done was not completely above board." Phil then looked at the Chiefs. "Thank you for doing something I know you were loath to do yet had to be done. We couldn't let him destroy what's left of the country. General Bale, would you do the honors?"

Angie stepped forward with a smile and a Bible in her hand. No one knew she had asked the radio operator where she could find one. The young lady produced it from the backpack at her feet.

"I keep it with me always, Ma'am," she had said. "You never know when you might need the comfort of the Good Book in your day."

"That may be every day for a while, Ensign," Angie replied, and promised to return it to her when they were finished.

Charles chuckled. "I should have known you'd be ready no matter the circumstances."

She inclined her head to him then turned to face the Speaker. Holding the Bible in front of her she waited for Phil to place his hand on it then said, "Repeat after me. I do solemnly swear that I will faithfully execute the office of President of the United States …"

Chapter 13

Interstate 295 had plenty of abandoned cars. Hutch had taken over driving again and remarked that he felt like he was running the gauntlet trying to keep from hitting any of them. Had it just been the Humvee it would have been easier, and they could have even used the large vehicle to push their way through. But with the camper behind them, he had to work his way around instead. While the Humvee held the road pretty well, the same couldn't be said for the trailer it was towing. Even in the pitch black of a moonless night, the taillights reflecting off the front told him there was a lot of movement.

"Man, that camper is not doing well on some of these drifts. I hope those guys are holding on back there." He was watching it in the mirror while trying to keep his eyes on the road.

"You think we should stop and check on them?" Damon asked, voice tinged with concern.

"Not until we get past the river. That's why it's so high here. Not a lot of trees to block the wind blowing across that cold water." He paused a moment, then added, "What the hell —"

They had just passed the Scenic Overlook and were approaching the bridge over Crosswicks Creek which flows into the Delaware River. Hutch let the Humvee come to a stop but left it running.

"That's going to be a problem," he said, looking toward the bridge.

In the beam of the headlights, they could see all four lanes were blocked with a multi-car pileup. There was no way around, and guardrails on both sides prevented them from easily accessing the oncoming lanes, which looked clear from their position; but they couldn't see very far.

Damon's face screwed up in frustration. "Yes, it is. I guess we can check on those guys in the camper after all."

They both climbed out of the vehicle as the Guardsmen exited the camper to see what was going on. Darrell and Stacy donned night vision goggles and took up security positions behind the rig as Liz and Marco went to talk to their captain.

"Hoo-eey, that's a mess right there, Cap," Marco commented as he reached them and saw the problem. "We started the day shoveling, and it looks like we're going to finish it pushing cars."

"Well, I don't know about those cars, but mine won't shift without the key turned on," Liz replied. "How are we going to get them in neutral to move them? Most of them look pretty new."

Marco smiled at her. "Magic."

The four of them walked over to the closest car. Marco checked and found the door unlocked. He climbed into the driver seat and pulled out his pocketknife.

"The reason you can't shift without the key on in newer cars is they have something called a brake transmission shift interlock, or BTSI. Works great as long as there's power to the car, but if your battery is dead and your car is inside your garage, you have to get it out so you can get it jumped off." He stuck the tip of his knife under a small plastic piece by the gear shift. Popping it off revealed a button. "This is the shift lock release. You press and hold this button, and you can shift it." He performed the action as he described it to them and, after placing the car in neutral, looked up at them with a toothy grin. "See? Magic!"

Liz smirked as she replied, "Show-off."

"What? Can I help it if I'm handsome *and* handy?" Marco waggled his eyebrows at her as he climbed out of the car.

Taking his place in the driver seat, Liz rolled her eyes and said, "Fine, handyman. I'll steer; you push."

Marco and Hutch went to the front of the car and pushed it backward. Liz steered it to the emergency lane on the right. She got out, shut the door, looked at the pileup, and said, "Great. Only six more to go."

Once the cars were moved out of the way and everyone was loaded back up, they were able to cross the bridge, though the going was slow, as they had to weave amongst the other dead vehicles. Everyone in the Humvee breathed a collective sigh of relief when the bridge turned back into just a highway. Interstate 295 turned out to be a good choice of routes, because it went from commercial to rural farmlands with very few houses. It also looked as if one of the farmers had some old equipment, since portions of the road were actually plowed.

"God bless the farmers!" Damon called out as he picked up speed on the mostly clear road. There was a feeling of hope inside the military vehicle with the ability to move at a faster pace. The Tanners whispered excitedly amongst themselves and even Agent Stephens cracked a smile. They made the ten miles to Mt. Holly Road in less than thirty minutes.

Another two miles and they were turning onto the ramp that led to the turnpike. As with all toll roads, the first thing they came to was a toll booth. The ones Damon had encountered on the way up to New York had been desolate, looking abandoned and quickly forgotten in a world where most cars didn't run. At first glance, this one was the same, except for the fact that there seemed to be a dead car in every lane. Damon slowed to a stop.

"There's something not quite right about this," he said as he looked the situation over.

Hutch nodded. "Agreed. What are the odds that there was a car in every lane at five in the morning on a Sunday?"

"I think we better check this out." Damon was climbing out of the driver side as he spoke.

Hutch opened his door. "Yep. I'll get the crew." He started toward the camper. The ping of bullets hitting his door had him diving back inside. Damon did the same.

"Ambush!" Damon yelled toward the back right before his door closed. They slammed and locked the doors, then readied their rifles as Damon turned off the headlights and both men donned night vision goggles. Agent Stephens pushed the Tanners into the floorboard. In the side-view mirror, Hutch saw his people exiting the camper and taking up positions behind the Humvee. Marco ran to the back and scurried up the ladder to take a position on top. Darrell opened the rear door of the Humvee and climbed in. Raising the hatch, he waited a moment to see if the attackers would fire at it then stood up with his rifle trained toward the toll booth. He ducked back inside when a shot sailed past his head.

"Definitely a setup!" he proclaimed to the occupants of the Humvee. Pulling his pack to him, he retrieved a small telescoping inspection mirror and raised it into the opening. Hutch and Damon were peering ahead through the windshield.

"I count five shooters, one in each lane behind a car, and the fifth behind the booth. Confirm!" Hutch said.

Darrell scanned the area with the mirror. "Confirmed. I'm not seeing anybody else, but that doesn't mean there aren't more hidden from sight." Rising slightly so that his voice carried outside, he said, "Perez! Eyes on how many?"

Marco had been scanning the area through his rifle scope. "I count five." Just then, a shot grazed the edge of the camper top. He flattened himself across the center.

"We don't want to hurt anybody!" a voice called from the darkness behind the toll booth. "We just want whatever guns and supplies you have and that rig! Everybody get out nice and slow and step away from the Hummer!"

Damon rolled his window down about a quarter of the way and replied through the opening, "We can't do that. This is a United States Army vehicle and we are under orders. We're going to need you to move one of those vehicles out of the way, lay down your weapons, and come toward us with your hands in the air."

"And it's a Humvee, moron! Hummers are privately owned vehicles!" Marco added. Stacy and Liz tried to hide their giggles from below his position.

Those outside could hear the man laughing. "There ain't any army anymore! Hell, there probably ain't a United States either! And I don't care what it's called! We're taking it. We can do it easy, or we can do it hard. Your choice!"

"Perez, give the man our answer. Don't kill anybody … yet." Hutch directed his voice toward the open hatch, hoping it was loud enough that the would-be carjackers could hear it.

With night vision, Marco could easily make out the men. He chose the one closest to the speaker. The bullet shattered the back window of the vehicle he was crouched behind. All of them quickly ducked out of sight. Darrell took the opportunity to pop back up through the roof hatch and line up on the side of the toll booth the spokesman was hiding behind. Hutch rolled his window down all the way and leaned out with his rifle.

Damon called out to the men. "I guess we choose hard!"

Darrell called out everyone's targets. "Manning, you take the first lane; Perez, you take second. Cap will get the third, and Thompson, you've got the outside. I'm on the loudmouth! When they shoot, return fire!"

When the first shot came toward them, they all fired at once toward their assigned targets. The sound was deafening with so many rifles going off at once in such a small area. Mrs. Tanner covered her ears as Mr. Tanner covered his son's, and they all tried to get as low to the floor as they could. Agent Stephens crouched behind them, sidearm pointed in the direction of the threat in case anyone got through the barrage. No one tried. Yelps and screams filled the night, adding to the cacophony. The attackers returned a few shots, but it didn't last long. Deer rifles couldn't compete with night vision and automatic weapon equipped soldiers.

"We give up! We're coming out! Don't shoot!" This came from a voice they hadn't heard before.

Hutch took off his goggles, stepped out, and closed the door, rifle trained in the direction from which the voice had come. "No weapons, hands in the air! Nice and slow! Team, ditch the night vision. Major, light 'em up!"

The Guardsmen quickly removed their own goggles so they wouldn't be blinded when Damon turned the headlights back on. As the lights pierced the dark, the former attackers flinched in the stark brightness, shielding their eyes with their raised hands. When they were about fifty feet from the Humvee, Hutch yelled, "That's far enough! On your knees! Hands behind your head!"

Damon had gotten out as well and switched to his pistol. Doing a quick head count, he said, "There were five of you. Where's the other guy?"

The one who had just spoken replied, "I think he's dead. He's lying on the ground back there." He indicated the toll booth with his head.

Liz and Stacy had moved to the front as well, weapons aimed at the kneeling men. "Thompson, you and Manning go check the other one," Hutch ordered. "And be careful!"

"On it, Cap," Liz answered. The two women headed toward the toll booth.

They were spaced about fifteen feet apart from each other, positioning themselves so they could approach the small building from both sides. Liz was on the right, heading for the spot between the innermost car and the booth. Stacy was following the empty lane that would have been used by traffic heading off the turnpike. Liz had her rail-mounted flashlight on, pointed toward the space she was about to enter. She was panning the light from side to side looking for the missing man when the shot was fired.

The bullet hit her in the chest, knocking her backward. She lay on the ground, a look of surprise on her face. The man, who had been crouched down behind the booth, laughed then coughed, choking on his own blood, which spewed from his mouth into the air.

"Damn government toadies! Riding around like a bunch of hot shots all warm and fed while we're out here starving and freezing to death! What gives you the right to live better than us? At least I get to take one of you self-righteous assholes with me!"

As Hutch, who had rushed to her side, was helping Liz get up from the frozen street while trying to cover her at the same time, Stacy came up behind the man and put the muzzle of her rifle against his head. In a quiet voice, she said, "She's wearing Kevlar. You're not. Lucky for you, you're already dead or I'd finish the job. What gives you the right to take what other people own? When did it become okay for one man to steal from another at gunpoint or to kill someone to get their stuff, not even knowing what they do or don't have? Don't bother answering. I can't stand a thief. Just lay there and die, asshole."

At her words, the man gave one last gurgled cough and fell over on his side. With her boot, Stacy rolled him over onto his back. His eyes were open, staring lifelessly into the night.

She headed back to her team with a grim smile. "I love it when the trash takes itself out."

Chapter 14

Amanda was sitting on the floor with Cameron as they removed the firearms in the bag one by one. Aaron watched over his little brother's shoulder. Cameron would take one out, eyes wide as he looked it over, with the occasional commentary — "Oh, this one is bad ass ... er, as heck!" — then hand it over to Amanda, who was sorting them into groups.

"What are the different piles for, Amanda?" Aaron asked as he took in her actions.

"I'm sorting them by caliber." She pointed to one stack of pistols. "All of these shoot forty-five caliber bullets. If we keep them with that size of ammo, we won't be shuffling through the whole pack looking for what bullets go in which gun."

"That's smart. Which one is the best one?"

She turned to him and smiled. "The one you shoot the best is the right one for you. There's no perfect fit for everybody. Maybe tomorrow we can take some out to this range I heard about and find out which one fits you."

Cameron pulled a black box out of the bag. "Look, this one is still in the box. I wonder why?"

"Let me see that, Cam," Amanda said as she reached for it. She took the box and read the cover. "Kahr Arms. I've heard of them. They're out of Massachusetts, I think. Good quality American-made guns. That's always a good thing." She opened the box to find the paperwork still inside, along with an unmarked white envelope. A seal on the flap had the number "899" on it. She slipped a finger inside the flap and found a card. It read *Certificate of Authenticity, TIG 2018 Special Edition.* The boys looked on as she opened the bi-fold card. Her eyes grew big as she read it.

"Oh wow. This is a limited edition. Only a thousand made. This one is eight ninety-nine. Listen to this: *This is to certify that this Model ST9093TIG is the John "Tig" Tiegen Special Edition for supporting Beyond the Battlefield, The Tiegen Foundation.* That's so awesome!"

She passed the card to Aaron so everyone could see it and lifted the gray foam to reveal a black pistol with coating on the body that looked like snakeskin. She pulled it out of the foam bed and looked it over.

"Hello, pretty." Cameron craned his neck her direction to see the pistol.

On top of the slide was the emblem for Beyond the Battlefield, as well as Tig's logo. On the right side, his signature was etched into the front edge of the slide, along with "899 of 1000". It had one single stack magazine that held eight bullets inside the gun, with a second in the box. Amanda pulled the slide back, locking it open, and peered down the barrel.

"Teddy said he'd shot them all, but it doesn't look like this one has ever been fired. I intend to remedy that tomorrow. It needs to feel loved and appreciated." She released the slide and let it snap closed.

"But if it's a collector's item, won't it retain its value better if you don't use it?" Lauri asked. "That's probably why it's still in the box."

"I don't think there's going to be a big call for guns just to look at anymore," Elliott remarked. "If there aren't any being made anytime soon, they may become a new form of currency. The ammo surely will. Can I take a look at that, Amanda?"

She held the gun out to him. As he reached for it, she snatched it back and said, "Don't go falling for it, Elliott. I'm claiming this one for myself."

100

Elliott laughed. "Not to worry. I just want to check it out."

She grinned and handed the pistol to him. He looked it over and gave a low whistle. "This is nice. Looks like Tig was a Marine, too. It says *Semper Fi* under his signature. You gotta respect him giving back to his brothers. I bet this will be a fine shooter." He held the gun back out to Amanda.

She took it and replied, "I can't wait to find out. First thing in the morning I want to see this range of yours."

It's a date," he said with a nod.

"Woo hoo! Pap's got a date!" Cameron called out. "Watch out, Uncle Will. I think he's after your girl."

Will blushed, but Amanda glared at Cameron. "Are you trying to start trouble, buster? I'm pretty sure we can leave you behind when we go shoot tomorrow. That could happen, couldn't it, Elliott?"

Elliott had a stern expression on his face. "Yes, it could."

Everyone else in the room was trying to hide grins and smirks, including Amanda. Everyone but Cameron. He exclaimed, "I was just joking! I'm sorry! Please don't leave me out of shooting practice!"

Elliott scowled at the boy for another moment, then started cackling. "Gotcha!"

The room erupted in laughter as Cameron's face went from fear to surprise to glee. "Whew! That was close! You had me going there, Pap!"

They had reached the bottom of the bag when Cameron pulled out an AK-47. Eyes as big as saucers, he said in a hushed tone, "Whoa! What is *this*?"

"Mine," Elliott stated. "Gimme that."

"Nice," Amanda commented as Cameron handed the rifle to his grandfather.

"Are there any seven six two cartridges in that ammo pile, Amanda?" Elliott asked as he inspected the gun.

She picked up a plastic ammo can. "This is full of them."

"Good deal. This was a wonderful thing your friend did, Joel. He may have saved some lives," Elliott added as he stood the rifle against his chair.

"I just wish I could have saved his," Joel replied in a voice laced with sadness and regret. "How many lives will be lost because there's no services for medical supplies and prescriptions? How many people will linger and die in pain — no, agony — because of a decision obviously made by one lunatic to cripple this country?"

Ethan got up without a word and headed for the kitchen. When he heard the back door close, Joel turned to Elliott wide-eyed. "Oh, Elliott. I'm so sorry. I didn't even think about —"

Elliott held up a hand cutting Joel off. "Don't worry about it. He knows it's coming. We kind of know what to expect after we went through it with his mother. No morphine will be available for him, though. It will be rough, that's for sure. We'll just have to get through it. The timing is bad for this thing and being able to get Ethan some relief."

"What do you mean, Elliott?" Lauri asked.

"Well, my granny taught me about a plant you could use for pain relief. It's called wild lettuce. It lessens pain similar to the way morphine does. It grows all over in the fields. I use it from time to time myself, and it definitely helps take the edge off when you're hurting. I've got a little bit dried out hanging in the barn that we can use to make him a tea. It will help some, but I don't think it's enough to get him to the end." Elliott's voice caught and he stopped, turned his head away, and wiped a tear from his eye. The room was filled with an ominous silence.

102

With a sniffle of his own, Cameron said, "Just tell us what we need to do, Pap … you know, to help him. I don't want to watch my dad suffer."

Elliott cut his eyes to Carly, who visibly bit her lip at her son's use of the term "dad". She returned his gaze and gave him a small smile rather than speaking the cutting retort that was apparently on the tip of her tongue. He smiled back with an acknowledging nod of his head.

"He's got his own alternative for now. I'll take stock of the herbs I have hanging in the barn tomorrow to see what I can put together. I think we need to start settling down for the night. I don't know about the rest of you but I'm beat."

Elliott stood up from his chair just as Ethan was coming in the back door. He closed the door softly and hurried into the living room.

In a soft voice barely above a whisper, he said, "Dad, there's someone outside."

~~~~~~

Elliott and Ethan went out the front door, while Amanda and Joel went out back. With no electrical sounds, it was eerily quiet, and the lack of exterior lighting left the outside world pitch black with a new moon.

"I heard like a shuffling sound. It's hard to describe," Ethan whispered.

"Where did it sound like it was coming from?" Elliott replied just as quietly.

"Kind of on the side of the house by the driveway. It didn't sound like walking, exactly … more like dragging."

Elliott turned the small flashlight on he had brought with him and started toward the driveway. After just a few steps, he heard a noise. He turned the light toward the sound.

103

"A coon! And he's got that ornery chicken that never wants to come in at night!"

Sliding the thin flashlight alongside the pump so he could see, Elliott raised his shotgun and was about to shoot the nuisance predator when he caught a movement from the corner of his eye. A large German shepherd rushed in and grabbed the raccoon, shaking it fiercely. The raccoon shrieked, filling the night with its distress call. Joel and Amanda came running from the backyard.

"Don't get too close!" Elliott called out to them. "If that dog lets go, that critter might get you!"

Amanda had the newly acquired Tig, which she had chosen to call the new pistol, pointed at the fighting animals. The dog was growling and still shaking the raccoon violently, while the raccoon was making a racket none of them had ever heard before. The noise was so loud it brought the rest of the family to the front door.

"What in the world is going on out there, Elliott?" Lauri called from the doorway.

"Y'all stay inside. We've got a mess out here."

Cameron was standing on his tiptoes trying to see around his grandmother. "What is it, Pap? It sounds like something's fighting!"

"It is, Cam. A dog and a coon." Elliott was holding the flashlight high to cast more light. "I think the dog's winning."

"A real raccoon? I wanna see! Let me out, Nana, please?" he said as he tried to squeeze past her. Carly grabbed the back of his shirt and pulled him back into the house.

"Did you hear what Pap said? He said to stay inside! It's dangerous out there! They're wild animals, probably rabid ..."

"*Mom*, dogs *aren't* wild animals," Cameron said in a slightly condescending tone. "Just because you don't like them —"

"Who said I don't like dogs? I like them fine … as long as they are someone else's, not shedding hair on the furniture, or leaving muddy footprints on the carpet — or worse stuff."

"Well, I love dogs, and Pap's the only one who has had any in this family, and he hasn't had one since Rufus died last year," Cameron said, a sad note to his voice. "Maybe we can keep this one if it wins the fight."

As if in response to Cameron's wish, the noise outside ceased. The dog walked over to Ethan and sat looking at him expectantly, tail swishing through the snow.

"Holy shit!" Ethan exclaimed. "That's Lexi! She's my buddy Dwayne's dog, the one I was staying with in Brighton. She took a liking to me. She must have followed me here." He squatted down in front of her. "Let me borrow your flashlight, Dad. I want to check her over and see if she's hurt."

Elliott held the flashlight above them. "Go ahead and check her over. I'll hold the light." Turning toward the house, he called out, "It's over. You can come out now if you want to."

Cameron pushed past everyone else and hurried over to the scene. The raccoon was dead, its neck broken by the violent shaking from Lexi. The chicken lay not far away, headless. Cameron held his own flashlight and inspected the carnage.

"What happened to the chicken's head?" he asked no one in particular.

"Coons do that," Elliott replied. "I'm not sure why, but they eat the heads off chickens. I'm guessing this one was a momma and was taking the rest back to her babies."

"Gross. But kind of cool," Cameron replied.

"How's the dog, son?" Elliott asked, turning his attention back to the living animal.

"I think she's okay. A few scratches but nothing that needs stitches or anything. I can't believe she followed me!"

"I thought you were driving at first," Aaron remarked. "How did she follow you in a car?"

"I was driving, but the roads were bad, so I was going really slow. It was dark with the cloud cover, so I didn't see her. I'm surprised she didn't come up to me once I started walking, but maybe she didn't want me to send her back home. She's wicked smart. Aren't you, Lexi girl?" he said to the dog as he scratched between her ears. "I swear she can understand everything you say to her. Dwayne was kind of an asshole to her, and I think she likes me better anyway. Well, I guess her showing up here proves it."

Cameron hurried over to see the dog. "Can I pet her?"

"Let her come to you. Call her," Ethan replied. "She needs to get to know you and trust you."

"Hey, Lexi! Hey, girl! Come here," Cameron said in the dog's direction.

Lexi turned at the sound of her name and cocked her head to the side, looking the boy over. She looked back to Ethan.

"It's okay, girl. Go ahead," he told her in a firm voice.

She got up and walked over to Cameron. He reached toward her and she stopped.

"Hold your hand out and let her smell you first," Elliott said. "She'll do the rest."

Cameron did as his grandfather had instructed. Lexi leaned forward and sniffed his hand. Finding him acceptable, she moved closer sliding her head under his hand. Cameron grinned and rubbed the soft fur on top of her head.

106

"How'd you know that, Pap? You don't know this dog, do you?" Cameron asked in awe.

Elliott smiled at him. "No, I don't know that dog, but I know dogs. Their noses tell them lots of things about people and places. They can sense fear and danger, and they're usually a pretty good judge of a person's character."

"Can we keep her? I mean, she obviously wants to be here with Dad."

Elliott turned back to his son. "I think he's right about that. Is she an inside dog or an outside dog?"

"Inside, definitely. Dwayne left her out in his backyard for days on end before I got there. She'd howl to come in, and that just pissed him off. But she's house-trained and you can see she's pretty clean, especially after walking all the way here. I cleaned her up and took her to the vet to get checked out after I moved in with him. The vet said she's in perfect health. I'll take care of her, Dad. She's a great watchdog."

"I'll help!" Cameron chimed in.

"Well, I reckon we could use a dog around here for critter control and security." Elliott leaned down and scratched between her ears. "Welcome to the family, Lexi."

Standing on the front porch, Carly rolled her eyes and turned toward the door. "Great. I can't *wait* to have all of my clothes covered in dog hair."

Will commented as she walked past him, "If that's the worst thing you have to deal with in the days ahead, count your blessings, Car. There may come a time when that dog being here saves the life of someone you love."

She stopped and smirked at her brother. "I thought that's what all the guns were for. Surely, we're safe with Elliott and your girlfriend, Amanda Annie Oakley, on our side."

"Have you already forgotten what it was like at home? What we went through to get here?"

"No, but we're in the country now. There aren't as many people out here. I'm sure we're safe now."

Will shook his head and replied sadly, "I don't think so, sis. I'm afraid it's coming."

Carly cocked her head at her brother. "What's coming?"

"Hell."

Chapter 15

"This is outrageous! It's against the law! It's mutiny! You'll all be executed for treason!" Olstein was pacing his quarters and ranting like a mad man. "I'm the president! You can't just remove the president from office! I haven't been impeached! I haven't done anything that warrants being impeached! I want to talk to Everley! *Now!*" The last word was emphasized by the sound of a fist hitting the door. Agent Warren, who was standing guard, didn't even flinch. He had heard the sounds of the room being trashed for thirty minutes.

Charles was walking up as the tirade ended. He gave a nod to Agent Warren who turned and opened the door. Olstein was standing in the opening, eyes wild with rage.

"You wanted to see me, Barton?" he said calmly. Looking around the mess, he added, "Love what you've done with the place, but you might want to rethink destroying everything. We won't be able to replace furnishings like these for years."

"I demand you release me *immediately!* You can't do this! It's against the Constitution!"

Charles laughed out loud. "Since when do you give a rat's ass about the Constitution? *You* were trying to shred it and throw it away! *We* just followed your lead. Sucks when it's *you* affected by someone else's decisions, doesn't it?"

Olstein started back peddling. "Well … um … perhaps I was a bit hasty with some of the changes I wanted to make. We can talk about it. Let's just sit down together —"

Charles was shaking his head. "You made your intentions quite apparent with all those BS executive orders you were planning to implement. You didn't want our input. You wanted to be a king or something. This is still

America, Barton. Crippled, pained, and slightly broken, maybe. Definitely in need of help. None of that negates the Constitution. Not one of those things is cause to turn aside everything this country was founded on for your ideas of the security and structure needed to get us back on track. I don't care what you, or any previous administration, think is an acceptable way for the government to act at a time like this. We don't steal from one man to give to another. We aren't a communist or socialist country. We aren't Robin Hood, stealing from the rich to give to the poor. It may seem harsh, but the people who have supplies should not be expected to take care of the ones who didn't plan for something like this. As their leaders, we should do whatever we can to help those people who weren't prepared, but not to the extent that we expect other citizens to shoulder a burden that is ours to bear."

Olstein's voice became a whine. "But there was no way to plan for something like this! We didn't know this was going to happen. We couldn't have predicted it!"

Charles crossed his arms over his chest and replied, "You were warned — we all were. The EMP commission, the preppers ... hell, the prepper fiction authors who wrote story after story about it. We — and I'm including myself, the rest of the Joint Chiefs, this administration, and a number of others before it — we all laughed it off and called them crazy, tinfoil-hat-wearing, paranoid extremists. We were so full of ourselves we didn't believe anyone would have the balls to attack us on our own soil. We sent Japan home with its tail tucked between its legs after their attack on Pearl Harbor when we dropped the bomb on Hiroshima and thought no one else would try attacking us. We thought we were the ruling power of this world because of our military defenses. Looks like we were wrong."

Olstein sat down hard on the disheveled bed. "This isn't my fault! Why am I being held a prisoner because of what that little weasel in North Korea did?"

Charles leaned over so that he was eye to eye with Olstein. "Because you were planning to make it worse. It's one thing to fight an enemy who has attacked us. It's another to make enemies of law-abiding citizens whose only crime, in your eyes at least, was being better prepared than their government."

Olstein leaned away from the formidable general and said, "How long do you plan on keeping me in here? I have rights, too, you know!"

"Until the new president gets here. He'll decide what to do with you."

"I thought Roman was already here. That's who you planned to put in place, right?"

"He is, and he's been sworn in. That's not who I was referring to. I meant David Tanner." Charles paused and waited for his reaction. It was almost immediate.

"Tanner? You still think he's going to make it back here?" Olstein barked out, laughing. "I'd be surprised if they made it out of New York City alive."

Charles smiled. "He's well on his way. I talked to my aide just a few minutes ago. I estimate he will arrive tomorrow."

Olstein's eyes were wide as saucers. "I can't believe you did all this behind my back. How could you?"

With a shrug, Charles replied, "The same way you tried to *excuse* the Joint Chiefs. It's over, Barton. You might as well calm down and make yourself comfortable. You'll be here until Tanner is sworn in, minimum."

Charles turned to leave. Olstein jumped from the bed and scurried in front of him, barring his path to the door.

"You can't keep me in here against my will! Who do you think you are?"

111

Charles pushed him out of his way and rapped on the door. He looked back and in a calm, controlled voice, said, "General Charles Everley, Interim Chairman of the Joint Chiefs of Staff, Chief of Staff of the Army. And, yes, we can and will keep you here. That's how a coup works. Get some sleep. Have a good night, Barton."

The door opened and Charles stepped through it leaving Olstein gaping at him in a speechless stupor. Agent Warren looked in, then closed the door firmly. The sound of the key turning in the lock signaled the discussion was over.

~~~~~

The meeting was not going well.

President Phil Roman was looking for ideas as to what they could do to try to get control of the country again, as well as how to help the people, many of whom by then were most assuredly out of food and water.

"Communications is our biggest hindrance," General Angie Bale said. "We can communicate with our own assets out of the country, with operations that were shielded by being underground, and any bases that had hardened facilities set up. That isn't many. If we can't communicate, we can't coordinate."

"Then what do we do?" Phil asked, exasperation apparent in his tone. "How do we find out what's going on out there? We need more information!"

"What about the HAM operators?" General Carl McKenna chimed in. "Especially those prepper people. I bet they shielded their equipment, God love them."

Phil's face lit up. "Yes! Have we tried to reach any of them?"

"I doubt Olstein even considering issuing that kind of order, but we'll get on it as soon as we break here." Angie was making notes on a legal pad.

"Great! Now we're getting somewhere! What else can we do until we get more information?" Phil asked eagerly.

"Well, we could start gathering supplies together," General Anton Masters replied. "MREs, water filters and purification tabs, Mylar blankets, even generators. FEMA has that stuff stashed all over the place. As soon as we get communications, we can start spreading the word about distributions around the country. We'll need security at those locations though. National Guard is my suggestion, if we can find them. We can pay them with supplies. It will be less intimidating to the people than Marines or soldiers."

"I like that. Do we have any idea how much FEMA has stored?"

"Not that I know of. My guess is warehouses full. It will help for a little while. The problem is going to be when those supplies run out. How are people going to get food then?"

"I've put in a request to speak with the leaders of our allied countries," Phil replied. "They should start sending aid immediately. God knows we've sent plenty to them."

There were nods and murmurs of assent from around the room. Phil went on.

"About the National Guard. I really want to utilize them as much as possible for the very reason you stated, Anton. Do we have any way of finding them?"

"Apparently, some are actually at their post," Charles said. "That's who is with Sorley. He picked them up in New Jersey. Maybe we can find more doing the same. If they were on duty when it went down, they probably had more supplies there than at home. A good reason to stay put if you ask me. I mean, look at us. We all moved in here for the same reason."

"I think that's good for now. Angie, you're covering communications. Notify me the second we hear from our allies. Charles, I'll leave the rest of the assignments to you.

If you get any push back from anyone with FEMA, let me know. We don't have time for any of their bureaucratic bullshit." Phil stood up and the Chiefs did the same.

"Yeah, and it's too cold outside to be out there pissing on trees. I can handle them," Charles replied. "It's also getting late. Let's try to get at least a couple of hours of rest. We've got a country to get back."

~~~~~

The Chairman was rubbing his hands together, laughing out loud.

"Look at them! They are in total upheaval! Anarchy rules the streets! They are burning their own cities to the ground!"

The satellite images his technician had loaded on the large screen in the conference room showed the cabinet members what their leader was referring to. Cities like Los Angeles, Chicago, and Atlanta each looked like one huge conflagration. The scenes included gruesome pictures of bodies lying everywhere, with people walking past them as if it was a normal thing to see. Huge gangs could be made out combing through neighborhoods in a strong semblance of a swarm of locusts.

"It is beyond what I had hoped for! You see? Take away their luxuries and their expensive toys and they revert back to their violent beginnings. They have no self-discipline, no respect for each other. They are selfish, self-centered narcissists who care for no one but themselves, and their true nature is now bared for the world to see! They are fighting the war for us, comrades! When the time comes, we will land on their shores and scoop up whatever of the population is left to begin rebuilding the country for ourselves and our new holdings. I think we shall call it … West Korea. Yes, I like the sound of that. You may go."

The Chairman dismissed the officers with a wave of his hand and a smug smile on his face. The admirals and generals left quickly. Two of them lagged behind the others, and when they were a safe distance away from the conference room, one of them whispered to the other:

"Do you think it will be that easy? That we can just go in and the Americans will give up and follow our orders?"

The second general shook his head. "No. Not all of them anyway. There are people there who value freedom over everything. They call themselves patriots. They will fight to their last breath. We should not underestimate them. Not for one second."

Chapter 16

The group was quiet as they proceeded down the turnpike. As before, when a death had occurred, they were left to reflect on what their country was quickly devolving into and what life was going to look like for the ill-prepared. The lack of preparedness on the part of the majority of the people and the government weighed heavily on them all but perhaps on David Tanner the most. He had addressed the remaining men from the failed carjacking attempt before they got on their way.

"I'm sorry for the loss of your friend, but this is not a way to live, even now," he'd admonished them. "You can't steal from others for your own survival at the cost of someone else's. If we had just been regular people, not military, possibly with children, would you have taken food that could have fed a child? Was this your long-term plan for a new way of life?"

None of the men answered their soon-to-be president, choosing to inspect the snow on the ground in front of them rather than meet his eyes full of disapproval. Their shock at realizing who they'd tried to rob was replaced by shame at their actions.

The men had been put into service to open one of the blocked lanes by pushing the car out of the way. Their weapons were returned to them without ammo. Since Marco was going to stay on top of the camper to keep an eye on them until they were out of sight, the decision was made to give them back. As he was handing their empty guns to them, Hutch had said, "You might need these, especially if you come across anyone out here like ... well, you."

After a brief stop to bring Marco back inside the camper, they made their way down the desolate, snow-covered highway. The overcast skies meant visibility was pretty much what was right in front of them. They were again met with a road that, though not plowed, had been driven on by some other vehicle since the snow stopped, giving them a set of tracks they could stay in and make better time.

"I keep wondering what other vehicles have been out here," Damon said as he peered through the windshield. "I didn't see any that were actually running on the way up, and we haven't seen any since we left; but it's obvious something else has been on this road."

Darrell was driving, as he had switched with Hutch so he could get some sleep. "I was thinking the same thing. Pretty good-sized track width tells me either another military vehicle or a big truck or SUV. How much of the motor pools were shielded? Any idea?"

Damon shook his head. "Not really. That wasn't part of my job duties, but, if I had to guess, I'd say maybe ten percent at the most. Even that may be pushing it. Think about all the bases where everything was sitting around out in yards or on lots. We're lucky anyone was smart enough to have any of our vehicles in hardened storage. No one believed this would ever happen."

"Yet, here we are," Darrell replied. "At least we're making good time now. Good choice on the turnpike. Any guess as to when we'll get to D.C.?"

"Well, we just crossed Rancocas Creek. That puts us about one hundred and fifty miles away from Washington. If we don't run into any trouble — make that any *more* trouble — we could make it in about three to four hours."

"I'd guess it's about zero one hundred. I've never seen the sun rise from the nation's capital. For that matter, I've never seen the nation's capital. I feel like that hobbit dude.

I'm going on an adventure!" Darrell chuckled at his own joke, as did Damon and David Tanner. Melanie and Brock were asleep.

"We still have to deal with Wilmington and Baltimore. And the next thirty miles has quite a bit of suburbs close to it so keep your eyes open."

"Will do, and back to whatever has been through here, it was nice of them to clear a path for us."

Darrell pointed ahead, and Damon saw that all of the cars were indeed off to the side of the road. There was a clear avenue for them to travel.

"Somehow I get the feeling they didn't clear it for us." Damon was peering into the darkness trying to see anything off to the sides. After what they'd already been through, any abandoned car was a potential ambush point. However, they did not encounter anyone as the miles passed by. Damon's idea that it was in some way safer seemed to be a good one. There were very few ramps, and both sides of the turnpike were lined with trees for the most part. Since there was little access, it seemed to be a less than desirable area for carjackers and others who might try to do them harm.

Just as Damon was starting to relax a bit, they saw a roaring blaze ahead on the left. He leaned forward and peered through the windshield.

"What the hell is that?" Darrell asked. "It's some kind of building. Can you tell what it is, Damon? Or what it was?"

Damon was looking at his maps with a flashlight. His eyes grew wide as he looked at the inferno and said in a hushed voice, "That was the Moorestown Station for the New Jersey State Police. Somebody set it on fire!" He pulled out a small set of binoculars to get a closer look. "I see a lot of people outside, like some kind of a rally or something. Don't slow down, Darrell. In fact, speed up if you can."

Tanner was trying to see the fire as well. When they were almost beside it, he asked Damon, "Can I use those for a second, Major?"

"Absolutely, Sir."

Damon handed the binoculars back to David. He put them to his eyes and adjusted the focus. After a moment, he dropped them from in front of his face and called out, "We need to stop! We have to go over there and help them!"

"Sir? Help who?" Damon asked, confusion apparent in his tone. Melanie and Brock woke with a start at the commotion.

"See for yourself!" he barked, thrusting them toward Damon. "Sergeant, stop this vehicle!"

Darrell started to slow down as Damon took the binoculars and tried to see what Tanner saw. When he did, he looked at Darrell and said, "Don't stop! Go! Go! Go!"

"What's going on?" Agent Stephens called from the rear, tensing up in anticipation of an unknown threat.

"I said to stop! We can't just leave them like that!" Tanner was wild-eyed with anger.

Damon looked back at Tanner and said, "Sir, we have one mission. That is to get you to the White House. Nothing can interfere with that, and we cannot deviate from the plan. I'm sorry, but we can't help those men."

"They're police officers! We are going to need all the help we can get to control the lawlessness that is, quite apparently, a big issue now. How will we do that without the police?"

Damon held Tanner's gaze. "I don't know the answer to that, Sir. But then, I'm not the one who has to figure things like that out. You and your advisers will. But those men," he said, pointing toward the fire, "are beyond our help. Even if we did stop, it's too late; and we would only be putting everyone here in danger." He looked pointedly at Melanie and Brock, who were watching and listening, fear etched on their faces. "I don't think you want to do that." Tanner did not respond.

"What the hell is going *on* over there?" Stephens said again louder.

Damon turned back to face the road and replied quietly, "They hung troopers from the entry way and set them on fire."

No one spoke as they continued on their way down the turnpike. Besides the roar of the tires in the snow, the sound of Melanie's soft sobs was the only thing that could be heard.

"Momma, why are you crying?" Brock's concern for his mother was felt by all the men inside. He hadn't understood what they were talking about earlier it seemed.

Melanie patted his arm and said in a soft voice, "It's nothing, sweetie. Why don't you try to go back to sleep?"

He gave her one more worried look then closed his eyes and snuggled up next to her. She wrapped him in the blanket and looked at her husband over the top of their son's head. Tanner responded to her with only a short, almost imperceptible nod then turned back to the window. He seemed to have the weight of the world on his shoulders at that moment. Definitely the weight of the nation.

For over an hour they drove with no interaction from anyone. When they'd passed the far outskirts of Philadelphia, the sky was lit up with an orange glow, indicating that the city was burning out of control. The city of brotherly love was obviously lacking in said emotion. The closer they got to the Delaware River, though, the more animated they became.

"I never thought I'd say it, but I'm going to be glad to have Jersey in my rear-view mirror," Darrell said. After so much quiet time, his voice sounded much louder than it actually was inside the Humvee. He paused, apparently surprised at how loud he sounded even to himself.

Thankful for the distraction, Damon picked up the conversation. "I totally agree. I hope this side of the bridge is still clear. It looked pretty open from the other side when I came through the first time."

"What are we looking at timewise, Major?" Tanner asked.

Damon studied his maps again. "We're about sixty miles from Baltimore, Sir. We'll take the bypass and go around it, which will be another twenty or so miles, then about twenty-five more to Washington. Once we get to D.C., there should be a strong military presence, and we shouldn't have any problems getting to the White House. I think another two hours and we should be there."

"Then do you think it would be okay if we stopped for a few minutes? I'd like to stretch my legs, and I'm sure Agent Stephens would as well. He's folded up like a pretzel back there."

"I'm fine, Sir," Stephens replied. "I want us to get there as quickly as possible."

Tanner turned slightly so he could see his Secret Service agent. "As do I, but I don't think a five-minute stop is going to throw us off."

"As soon as we get across the Delaware, we'll find a place to pull over, Sir," Damon said. "I could use a five-minute stretch myself."

The Delaware side of the river was highly residential, so they continued on until they crossed the state line into Maryland. That area was much more rural. After crossing over Highway 279, Damon pointed to a section of road that was open and had only a couple of abandoned vehicles on it. Darrell started to pull off to the shoulder, but Damon stopped him.

"Best to not get off the path here. It's not like we have to give way to traffic."

Darrell laughed and said, "Good point. Old habits are hard to break. This spot looks good to me."

When the vehicle stopped moving, Melanie woke up. Laying Brock down in the seat, she got out with the men. The camper emptied as well. Hutch came up to them to inquire if there was a problem and to see how Darrell was doing driving. Darrell assured him he was good to go. Damon led Hutch away from the Tanners and told him what they had seen at the trooper station.

"Holy shit! What the hell, man? Is everybody going crazy?"

"I don't think we've even begun to see how bad this is going to get. You should probably station someone at the back window and one on each side to watch for trouble. That leaves only one able to sleep, but ..."

Hutch shook his head. "I doubt anybody will be doing any more sleeping until we get to the White House."

Damon looked over at David Tanner. "For some, maybe not much after we get there either."

Chapter 17

No ambient noises from appliances, electronics, or the furnace should have left the house deathly quiet.

That wasn't the case for Joel.

The lack of electricity meant that Lauri couldn't use her CPAP machine for her sleep apnea. If Lauri slept without it, Joel usually didn't sleep; not in the same room she did anyway. After about an hour of the noise, he got up with a sigh, grabbed his pillow and an afghan off a chair in Elliott's room, and headed out in search of a quieter place to sleep. He made his way to the boys' room and scooted Cameron over so he could share his pallet. Cameron grumbled in his sleep but rolled over, giving Joel the space he needed. Aaron, who was in the top bunk, woke up as Joel was trying to get comfortable.

"What are you doing, Pops?" Aaron whispered as he sat up and squinted into the darkness.

"Trying to get some sleep," Joel hissed back. "Nana without her machine is not conducive to anyone else sleeping in the same room."

Will woke as well and seeing his dad trying to get comfortable on the floor, climbed out of the bottom bunk. "Here, Dad. Take the bed. I'll sleep on the floor."

"No, it's fine. Really," Joel replied with a wave of his hand.

Aaron hopped down from the top. "No, it isn't. Uncle Will can have the top, you take the bottom, and I'll take the floor. I have younger bones."

"Yes, you do. I accept your proposal," Will said with a sleepy grin. "Come on, Dad. No arguing."

Joel nodded and the three men settled into their new locations. Joel fell asleep immediately. Just as he was about to drift off, Will heard a low growl from Lexi, who was in the living room with Ethan. After a moment, he heard Ethan and Elliott talking in whispers. He couldn't hear what they were saying, so he climbed back down to see what was going on. His movement shook the bunk beds slightly, which brought Joel awake.

"What is it? What's going on?" Joel asked.

"I heard Lexi growl. Elliott and Ethan are up. I'm going to check it out." Will had slipped his tennis shoes on by then.

"Hold up. I'll come with you," Joel said. "I don't think sleep is on the agenda tonight anyway."

The two men walked quietly down the hall. Elliott had turned the lantern up a bit, casting the room in a soft glow. He and Ethan turned at the sound of the other two men entering the room.

"I'm not sure what's going on. Lexi growled and has her hackles up. She's been staring at the back door. Maybe it's another coon trying to get to the rest of the chickens," Elliott said softly as he was lacing up his boots. "I did miss having a dog around for that, if nothing else — early warning system."

He put on his coat and grabbed his shotgun. Ethan followed suit.

"Do you want us to come with you?" Joel asked.

"No, you two stay in here. I'd grab a pistol at least," he added, noting that neither man was wearing a side arm. "Just stay by the back door and listen. I'll holler if we need you."

When the back door opened, Lexi took off like a shot. Elliott shined a light in the direction she'd headed. "She's definitely after something!" He and Ethan hurried out into the night. Will looked at his father as Joel closed the door behind them.

"Are we really living in a world where you can't go outside at night without a gun for protection anymore, Dad? It seems alien to me to automatically reach for a weapon before I walk out the door."

"It does to me too, son, but I'm sure Elliott is right. There will be a lot of desperate people out there. Some of them are bound to show up here wanting to take what we have. We have to learn to be ready for something bad to happen. We have to be ready to defend your mom, Carly, and Amanda, as well."

Will snorted a laugh. "There's a better chance that Amanda will be defending us."

Joel grinned at his son. "She is something else. I think she might be a keeper. What do you think?"

"Time will tell, Dad."

Lexi was out of sight, but Elliott and Ethan could hear her running around the outside of the barn. Elliott held his light up high to try to see farther into the darkness. Ethan did the same.

"Should I call her, Dad?" Ethan asked, concern etched in his voice.

"Wait and see if she finds whatever it is she heard," Elliott replied. "Probably another coon. Sometimes a couple of them will run together."

Suddenly, Lexi started barking in alarm, and both men hurried toward the sound. Before they could get to her, they heard something else. A yelp ... from a human.

"Ow! Get off me, dog! Get away!" the man's voice yelled out into the night.

Elliott pushed the partially opened barn door wide and shown his light in. "Who's in there? Come outta there now, and lemme see your hands!"

Ethan had his light shining as well, so Elliott pulled up his shotgun and aimed toward the spot the noise seemed to

125

be coming from. In the flashlight beam, they could see Lexi staring up the stall divider, stoic, growling, and hackles raised so high it looked like she had a Mohawk. Ethan panned the light up to the top of the stall wall.

"Taylor? What the hell are you doing in here?" Elliott said, lowering his shotgun slightly. "Get down from there! Son, call the dog off."

"Lexi, come."

Lexi backed up, then turned to join Ethan and his dad. She sat dutifully beside Ethan but stared dog daggers at the intruder. Taylor climbed off the wall and stood with his hands slightly raised.

"Uh, you can put the gun down, Elliott. I'm not armed. I told you I don't even have a gun at home."

Elliott glared at him. "No, I think I'll keep it for now. I'll ask you again: what the hell are you up to? It's the middle of the night, for cryin' out loud!"

"I was just … um … looking around," Taylor replied sheepishly. "I didn't know you had a dog."

"She's a recent addition to the family. Don't change the subject! What were you looking around for? Just because I offered you free use of my well pump doesn't mean you can come and go whenever and wherever you want on my place. You're lucky you didn't get shot!" Elliott was getting worked up and his face was turning red.

Taylor seemed to be trying to figure out what to say. Finally, he blurted out, "I'm desperate, okay? I'm trying to figure out how I'm going to take care of my family now! We need some place like this. I can't protect them at our house. Soon I won't be able to feed them. What would you do if you were in my place, Elliott?"

"Well, I wouldn't be looking around for what I could take from someone else's family, I'll tell you that!" Elliott shouted. "You said you had food to last a week, maybe two. I know you don't have anything to hunt with, but I can

126

teach you how to set snares. I was even thinking about getting you set up with a gun and teaching you how to use it for hunting and protecting your family, but now I don't think I'd trust you with it. You'd probably use it to steal at gunpoint!"

Taylor's eyes grew wide. "Oh, man, that would definitely help, but I still don't think I could protect them by myself. We need to join a group or something. We don't know anything about survival — at least, not how to survive without electricity. We need help! We could contribute here. We're willing to learn, we just —"

"I told you we don't have room," Elliott said shaking his head. He had calmed down a bit. "We have nine people here now. That's a full house. We don't have enough food to last the winter, either. You expect me to let my grandsons go hungry for your family? I never met you before this happened. I'm sorry, but you're going to have to figure this out for yourself. I'll teach you a couple of things, but I'm not gonna lie — this is going to be a tough winter for everybody who doesn't have a house full of food, a means to get water, and some way to heat their home. I can't take care of your family. I have to take care of mine. Now, I want you to get off my property. You can still come get water during the day, but I don't want to ever see you here after dark again. Do you understand me?"

Taylor's shoulders sagged in defeat. "Yes. But will you still teach me about snares? And how about that gun?"

Elliott raised his shotgun and let it rest over his shoulder. "I'm going to need to think about that now. I'll let you know what I decide."

"When do you think that will be?" Taylor asked, pushing the issue.

"When I decide! Now git!"

Taylor hurried past them, giving Lexi a wide berth. Lexi gave him a low growl in return. That got Taylor moving even faster.

When he was gone and they could no longer hear his footsteps in the crusted snow, Ethan said, "So, are you going to help them? It's kind of sad about his kids and him not knowing how to do anything."

Elliott started toward the door. "I'm sure I will at some point, but not to the extent that it takes anything away from anyone here. I plan to sit down with Lauri tomorrow and see if we can figure out how far we can stretch the food we have. I may go hunting in the next few days. If I can bag a deer, I could give that family some meat, at least."

Ethan followed him and held the flashlight so his father could see to latch the door. "You're a good man, Dad."

"As good as I can be at the moment. By the way, remind me to get a chain and padlock on this door tomorrow. I don't want to make it easy on the next person who tries to take anything from in there, especially the livestock." He looked down at Lexi who was right between them. Reaching down to rub between her ears, he said, "She's a good one. Glad to have her with us. Let me know if you need anything for her. We'll try to make sure she gets a portion of the food, as well. She'll definitely be earning her keep."

Will and Joel were watching through a window with the back door slightly ajar so they could hear if the other men called for help. When they saw a flashlight beam headed toward them, they hurried over to the door. Elliott and Ethan stamped snow off their feet on the porch and came inside.

"Was it another raccoon?" Joel asked as they were taking off their coats.

"Nope. It was a varmint, though. The two-legged kind."
Elliott hung his coat up and turned back to them. "That guy
Taylor was out in the barn skulking around."

Will piped in. "What? Why?"

"He never came right out and said, but I think he was
scoping the place out for food, or a place to squat — or
both."

"Do you think he'd steal one of the chickens or
something?" Joel asked.

Ethan snickered. "If he did, he'd have no idea how to
clean it. He's a city boy, start to finish."

Will eyed his former brother-in-law. "You know, it's
weird, but I never knew you hunted or knew anything about
that kind of stuff."

"Yeah, I haven't hunted in years, not since I was about
Aaron's age. Now that I'm back and could hunt with my
dad, I don't have much life left to do it. I didn't make time
when I should have. Don't wait, Will. If there's something
you want to do, do it. You never know when you'll run out
of time." Ethan smiled at Will, winced as if in pain, and
walked slowly into the living room. Will watched him go.

Turning to Elliott, he said, "How long does he have?"

"He said a few weeks, a month at the most. Toward the
end he'll be too tired to get out of the house anymore. He'll
pretty much stop eating and sleep a lot. It won't be long
after that. At least, that's how it was with his mother."
Elliott paused and shamelessly wiped a tear from his eye.

Joel stepped up beside him and laid an arm across his
shoulders. "Well, if there's one good thing to come out of
all this, at least you won't have to go through it alone.
We'll all be here to help and support both of you."

Elliott nodded and said, "I hate the circumstances but
I'm really glad you're here. I don't know if I could do this
on my own."

Joel gave his shoulders a squeeze. "You won't have to, buddy."

Chapter 18

Arturo Rodriguez, the Secretary-General of the United Nations, was in Austria, along with the majority of the Security Council, who had flown in from all over the globe for the emergency meeting to discuss how best to assist the United States in its time of need.

"From the reports we have gathered, the entire country is in chaos," Margaret Owens from the United Kingdom said. "There has been looting, armed thugs stealing from innocent people, others being mowed down in the streets for fun! This is what their Second Amendment has allowed to happen. All those guns they have are making it easy for the lawlessness to run unchecked!"

There were murmurs of agreement from some around the table, chuckles and shaking of heads from others. Arturo called for order. "Yes, I believe our mission will be twofold — to provide aid to the people in the form of food, water, and basic necessities, but also to provide security, particularly in the larger cities. There can be no peace when there is no law enforcement. It is going to take a long time — many years, in fact, from the experts' estimates — before the United States will be able to provide even basic resources to the populace. I foresee this will be a long, arduous road for them. We have commitments from the permanent member countries to send emergency rations and supplies, but we will need all member countries to assist, as well."

"And what of their attacker?" Li Qiang, the representative from China, spat in anger. "North Korea must be held accountable for this heinous act. They have crippled an entire country! Millions of innocent people will pay the price for his blatant hatred of America. And not just in that country. If Americans are not working, they are not paying taxes. If they are not paying taxes, the government cannot make payments on their debt — if their government could even function, which is definitely not possible now. If they do not make payments on their debt, it impacts the countries holding those debts, not the least of which are China and Japan. This is not just an attack on the United States. They must answer for this action!" Haruto Tanaka, the Japanese ambassador, was vigorously nodding in agreement.

"And they will," Rodriguez assured him. "But first, we must do what we can to help the United States regain control of the country. I'm surprised we haven't heard from them yet but having to relocate for this meeting may mean they don't know where to contact us. We should start with their assets outside the country and try to get word to President Olstein to let him know —"

He was interrupted by an aide who rushed into the meeting room. "Forgive me, Senor Rodriguez, but this couldn't wait. We have news from America!"

"Excellent! I was beginning to get worried that President Olstein hadn't reached out to us yet."

"No, Sir, not President Olstein. President Roman. Phil Roman is the president now," the aide replied, voice full of excitement. "President Olstein has been removed from office by the Joint Chiefs of Staff and Speaker Roman, who is now the acting president!"

The room erupted in chaos as everyone jumped from their seats and started shouting at once. The words *overthrown* and *coup* were used many times.

"This is unacceptable!" Margaret Owens shouted above the din. "They have no right to do this! Something must be done immediately!"

Rodriguez pounded on the table with his fist. "Everyone! Calm down! Take your seats so we can address this newest concern."

He waited for them to settle down before he spoke again. "Obviously, things are much worse there than even we were made aware. If their military leaders were behind this, then it is indeed a military coup. You are correct, Ms. Owens, their Constitution has a process for impeachment of a sitting president, which they have clearly not followed. So, we now have an obligation to not only provide humanitarian relief, but to assist President Olstein in regaining control of the country. We will have to send all available peace-keeping troops to his aid."

"Perhaps we should speak to President Roman, if that is what we are to call him for now, and find out why they chose this path," Nawaf Damji, the Kuwaiti representative, interjected. "It is clear we do not know the circumstances under which such a drastic move was made."

Rodriguez scowled and replied, "It doesn't matter. This is no time for a complete upheaval of their governing body. We will send the peacekeepers to reinstate President Olstein, and then we will get to the bottom of this whole debacle."

"And what of the Joint Chiefs and Speaker Roman?" Damji asked.

"They will be taken into custody and held until everything is sorted out. If it is found that there were valid reasons to remove Olstein from office, we will assist them in going through the proper channels according to their Constitution. They all took oaths to uphold it and to obey their president. It appears they have committed multiple violations of that oath."

Damji shook his head. "You are assuming they are guilty of treason without hearing the whole story. We know very little of what has been going on there since the power

133

grid was taken down. President Olstein has always appeared to want more power than their Constitution afforded him. At least, that is how he seemed to me. Many times, he has voiced frustration in public statements at the constraints it put on his ability to effect the changes he wanted to make. In a catastrophic situation such as they now find themselves, I can't help but think he would use this as an opportunity to begin enforcing new rules that would not be in the people's best interest, while most certainly fulfilling his. I am not comfortable with this action. I am not in favor of a military action on the part of this body."

Murmurs began anew. Damji's remarks had apparently sparked new thoughts on the situation. Rodriguez called for quiet.

"Very well. We *will* send the peacekeepers with the relief items. Let me finish," Rodriguez said, holding up his hand as he saw Damji about to voice another objection. "They will be tasked with safeguarding and distribution of the supplies. When they get there, however, they will also find out what the hell is going on. They will speak with Olstein, Roman, and the Joint Chiefs, along with anyone else in the White House, Congress, or Washington who can shed some light on this mess. Once we have the whole story, we will make a decision regarding further action. Is that acceptable to everyone?"

Nods and verbal agreements were his answer. He stood up and picked the papers up that were lying on the table in front of him.

"Then let's get the Americans some help."

~~~~~~

The bunker was quiet. Even Olstein had stopped his ranting and fallen asleep. The light footfalls of the Marine sentry

134

on guard duty were the only sound for the most part. Well, that and General Everley's snoring. It filled the barracks area. The men didn't seem to be bothered by it. General Angie Bale, on the other hand, was having a hard time dealing with the noise.

She got up and climbed out of the top bunk she had been in, trying to get some rest. She picked up her boots and padded out of the large room in her sock feet. As she passed him, she prodded Everley with her foot, causing him to roll over onto his side. The cacophony ceased. She looked around the room and whispered, "You're welcome," then went on out the doors. She stopped just outside and slipped into her boots. She was knelt down lacing them up when the sentry approached.

"Everything okay, Ma'am?"

She looked up at him with a smile and said softly, "Yes, everything is fine, Corporal. I couldn't sleep so I decided to go check on comms and see if we had any updates."

"Would you like me to escort you there, Ma'am?"

Finished with her boots, she stood up and replied, "No need. I think we may be in one of the most secure areas of the country at the moment. Carry on, Corporal."

"Yes, Ma'am."

Angie went down the hall to the communications room. As she opened the door, she heard a young ensign saying, "Yes, sir, I'll relay your message to the president immediately." At the sound of the door opening, the ensign turned around.

"Good morning, Ma'am," she said as she handed Angie some papers. "I was just speaking with Ambassador Wentz in Germany. He is working with the European countries coordinating relief efforts and supplies to be sent here ASAP. There was an emergency meeting of the U.N. in Austria and —"

135

Angie's head snapped up from the notes she was reading. "The U.N.?"

"Yes, Ma'am. They are gathering troops to send here to help re-establish order, and they will be in charge of the disbursement of the supplies coming in. The Secretary-General sounded upset when I told him President Olstein wasn't available."

"Well, this should be interesting, Ensign ..." she waited for the young officer to finish her sentence.

"Weaver, Ma'am. Debby Weaver."

Nodding, Angie went on. "When is all of this going to take place, Ensign Weaver?"

Debby checked her notes. "Mr. Wentz said within a couple of days. That could be by Christmas. It's hard to believe Christmas is just a couple of days away, isn't it, Ma'am?"

"Yes, it is, and I think it will be one to remember, Weaver. I guess I better start rousting people awake. Looks like it's going to be a busy day, and we've got a lot to go over. If anything new develops, come get me." Angie headed for the door.

"Aye, aye, Ma'am."

When Angie stepped into the corridor, Lawrence, the executive chef, was making his way to the kitchen. She stopped him.

"Excuse me, aren't you the head chef? I'm sorry, I don't think we've been introduced."

With a smile and a slight bow, he replied, "Yes, Ma'am. My name is Lawrence. Is there something you need?"

"Yes. I'm not sure what your schedule is, but I need a couple of urns of coffee as soon as possible in the conference room. We've got a long day ahead of us."

"It's already brewing. I'll have it brought in momentarily. Would you like me to go ahead and prepare breakfast, too?"

136

"That's probably a good idea. We're going to be busy and will need some protein and carbs for brain fuel."

"I'll get right on that, Ma'am," Lawrence said, giving her another slight bow.

"Thank you, Lawrence." Angie continued on to President Roman's quarters. Agent John Masters was standing by the door.

"Good morning, Agent Masters. I hate to do it, but I'm going to need to wake the president."

With a slight nod of his head, Masters turned and knocked softly on the door. From within, they heard a sleepy, "Come in."

Masters turned the knob and leaned his head in. "General Bale to see you, Sir."

Roman got up and slipped his tennis shoes on, having slept in his sweats on top of the comforter. "Send her in, John."

Masters pushed the door open for Angie. Once she was through, he closed it behind her. Roman yawned and scruffed his hair.

"You know, the least you could do is bring me a cup of coffee when you wake me up after ..." he paused and looked at the clock beside the bed. "... three hours' sleep."

She chuckled and replied, "Sorry, Mister President. It's on its way. Believe me, we're all going to need it."

At her words, his eyebrows raised. "Has something happened?"

"You could say that. Apparently, the U.N. has invited themselves in."

"What? Why?"

Angie shrugged. "I guess they are going to be escorting the relief supplies here, then they'll be in charge of distributing them. They're also going to *help* us get things back under control, so they say." She crooked her fingers in air quotes at the word "help".

"Who said we needed their help? We haven't even had a chance to get started!" Phil was pacing the room as he spoke.

"I'm not sure, Sir. But I think we need to find out, and quickly, before they get on the way here."

"Agreed. Get the other Chiefs up. Looks like our day has started without us."

Chapter 19

Outside of the occasional stop to clear the road of abandoned vehicles, Damon and his crew made good time. The closer they got to Baltimore, though, the more anxious the occupants of the Humvee became. The horrific crime and homicide statistics from a city of just over half a million people made it a particularly dangerous place to be, under the best of circumstances. Under the ones they found themselves in then, they could only imagine what they would find there.

They had discussed the route options during their break. Damon had taken the long way around on the 695 bypass for the trip up. It included a bridge across the Patapsco River. It also meant going a few miles out of the way. While they were all in a hurry to get to D.C., when David Tanner brought up staying on 95 and taking the tunnel to shorten the distance, he was quickly outvoted by the military men.

"Sorry, Mr. Tanner, but that's a choke point if there ever was one," Hutch had responded. "On the bridge, we have some options. In the tunnel, those are gone. It's narrow and might be impassable. If we have to stop to try to clear a path, we'll be sitting ducks in a pitch-black concrete cave. Better to take the longer route. Plus, it puts us further outside of Baltimore. We want to stay away from that city center, if at all possible. The way it has declined over the years is tragic. My guess is, with things the way they are now, it's extremely dangerous."

The rest of the group murmured their agreement as they discussed the possible hazards on the bridge. Hutch went on.

"Even that far outside Baltimore, there could still be thugs or just desperate people out looking to ambush somebody trying to get across. We're only about forty miles from the capital. I vote to wait for sunrise. It's probably around thirty minutes away. We'd be able to see any potential problems better."

The consensus was that Hutch's idea was sound, so they had taken their time getting back on the road. Their timing was good; they got to the interchange for 695 as the sun peeked out from the horizon.

Damon was in the passenger seat, sharing the events of his trip north with the rest of the occupants. He pointed to the Walmart parking lot and told of the looters and chaos he had seen. Now, there were just a few people milling about in the parking lot. It was clear that anything which could be used to survive had long since been cleared out of the store. Windows and glass doors were shattered, showing only a dark entry from that distance. They saw no more human activity until they crossed the Back River.

The first thing coming up on their right was a mobile home park. The ramp for Highway 150 and the entrance to the trailer park was just past an underpass. Hutch stopped the Humvee when he saw it.

"Yeah, I'm going to say that's a little suspect. What do you think, Sorley?"

"No argument from me," Damon replied. Everyone in the back leaned forward to see what they were talking about.

There were large tarps hanging from the overpass on both sides of the expressway, obscuring their ability to see the spaces underneath Diamond Point Road, which crossed over 695 there. They could see the road but not the concrete abutment that started at the street level and went to the underside of the overpass. Damon pulled out his binoculars to try to get a better look.

"I can't see anybody from here, but I'm pretty sure that's the point of the hides they've put up," he said to no one in particular. "Better send some scouts. Easy getting out though — no way to know if there's someone behind that with eyes on us already."

Hutch slowly opened his door, pausing for a moment in anticipation of an attack. When it stayed quiet, he got out, ducking his head below the top of the door, and ran, crouched down, to the back of the Humvee. A slight bend in the road where they sat and trees growing close to the shoulder gave him a bit of cover, so, after waiting a moment between the vehicle and the camper, he went on to the door. He pulled it open quickly and stepped inside.

After relating the situation to his team, Marco exited and took up his sniper position on top. Stacy climbed into the Humvee to utilize the hatch for her spot. Darrell and Liz took up positions between the Humvee and trailer, rifles trained on the hidden areas behind the tarps. Hutch went back to the driver seat.

"Light and Thompson are going to scout ahead, see if they see anything. We'll follow them slowly. Maybe whoever hung those tarps is still sleeping. Here's hoping anyway."

Dawn was coming on quickly, driving the darkness away and lighting up the world around them. Liz and Darrell had moved to the front of the Humvee and were walking toward the overpass, slightly crouched, rifles pointed in front of them. Hutch kept the armored vehicle creeping along behind them, staying close.

A movement that slightly billowed the tarp on the right grabbed their attention. The rifle barrel that came through a previously unseen slit in the material caught the glint of the rising sun.

"Gun!" Stacy shouted from above the hatch. She fired at the spot she had placed the metal reflection. Liz and

Darrell stopped, then started backing up as fast as they could toward the relative safety behind the Humvee, while keeping their eyes trained on the now visible slit in the tarp. Liz was on the right side by the passenger door trying to find a target when they heard the shot. Blood spattered the side of the vehicle. The spray hit the windows as Melanie started screaming inside, while Corporal Elizabeth Thompson fell backward onto the snow-covered highway.

Hutch burst out of the driver side leaving the door open so that Darrell and he could use it for some protection. All four remaining Guardsmen opened fire on the still unseen shooter's assumed position. More shots started coming at them from behind the tarp on the left side of the overpass.

"Thompson! Report!" Hutch called out as he and Darrell returned fire on the shooter in front of them. Liz didn't respond.

"I'm on the left!" Marco yelled. His rifle set to semi-automatic, he fired three-round bursts at the tarp, moving his shots from side to side, higher, then lower across its expanse.

What seemed like minutes was actually seconds before Hutch called out, "Cease fire!"

They waited for return fire to begin again, but none came.

"Light, pop some smoke and get to that hide on the left. I'll check on Thompson, then take the right. The Humvee stays here until we clear the road." Hutch slammed the door and Damon locked them both.

Staying low, Hutch went behind the Humvee and peered out from the right side. Liz was lying beneath the passenger door, a large circle of blood beneath her. He didn't detect any movement. Bent over to keep his profile low, he hurried to where she lay and knelt down beside her.

"Manning! Perez! Cover me!"

"Roger that," they replied one after the other.

Her eyes were closed as he stuck three fingers from his left hand against the side of her neck. He let out a breath he didn't realize he was holding. Softly, in a voice only she could hear, he whispered, "Yes! You're alive! Let's get you into some cover."

He grabbed the back of her vest and quickly dragged her to the camper door. Picking her up in a fireman's carry, he opened the door and set her on the floor inside. Leaning back out, he called up to Marco.

"Perez! I need a medic! Get in here and check her over!" Hutch had grabbed a roll of paper towels from the counter above, rolled a wad off, and was applying pressure to the wound on her shoulder right beside her vest. He lifted her off the floor enough to see her back.

"Through and through. I'll take it." He took another wad of towels and placed that against the exit wound, then laid her back down. Coming in the door and grabbing his pack from the bench, Marco squatted down beside her. Hutch moved out of his way. Just as he was about to leave to get back to the task of clearing the road, her eyes fluttered open. Seeing her commanding officer standing over her, she spoke to him.

"Cap?" she said, in a questioning tone.

Hearing her voice, he turned back. "Hey, Thompson. You're going to be fine. There's an exit hole so we just need to get you patched up."

"Okay, but Cap?"

"Yeah?"

"This getting shot business is getting old."

Marco chuckled as he was cleaning her wound. "Yeah, twice in one day is a bit of a long shot, Lizzie. What say you stay in until we get to D.C.?"

Hutch grinned at her comment and nodded at Marco's reply. "That sounds like a good idea to me. Consider yourself on leave, Corporal."

143

"Thank goodness." Liz closed her eyes again, wincing from time to time as Marco was working on her.

"Holler if you need anything, Perez," Hutch went on. "You stay in here with her for now. You can watch from the door for anything on this side." With that, he stepped out of the camper, went into a crouch and headed back to the front of the Humvee.

Darrell had worked his way to the overpass by then, confirming two dead, one on each side. After kicking their rifles away, he shouted, "Clear!" and shifted his focus to the road and exit ramp in front of them, looking for any additional threats.

Hutch joined him, shaking his head as he was inspecting the two men lying in pools of their own blood. "Idiots. If they had stepped out where we could have seen them, we could have tried to talk this through. They might still be alive."

Darrell continued to scan the area. "Yeah, and I'm surprised no one else has shown up yet. There was no missing all that gunfire noise. You think they were acting on their own?"

"I doubt it. Let's advance and see if there's any other threats ahead." Hutch slowly started walking toward the exit ramp. He hadn't taken a dozen steps before he saw a woman running toward him yelling.

"Willis! Willis! Oh my god, Willis!" she screamed as she approached. Hutch and Darrell brought their rifles to bear on her.

"Stop! Stay where you are, or we'll be forced to fire on you!" Hutch called out.

The woman came to a stop, hands trembling as she held them in front of her mouth. "Who are you? Why did you kill my husband? What's *wrong* with you?"

144

"Keep your hands where we can see them and approach slowly," Hutch said in a calmer tone. The woman complied; eyes fixed on the body behind them.

"Why? Why would you do that?" Her voice shook as tears streamed down her face.

"Because he fired on us, ma'am," Darrell replied. "We're New Jersey National Guard. He shot one of our people. A medic is working on her now."

She turned her head slightly to look at him. "Her? He shot a woman? I'm sure he didn't know it was a woman."

"It doesn't matter whether it was a female or a male. He fired on us. We defended ourselves." Hutch's matter-of-fact tone brought her attention back to him.

"No! You must have shot first. He wouldn't just shoot people like that."

"Well, he did," Hutch said. "If he had come out where we could see him and tried talking to us, this would have turned out a lot different. So, you tell me — why would he shoot first without even finding out who we are?"

Sniffling, she replied, "He probably thought you were them."

Darrell and Hutch looked at each other, confusion apparent on their faces, then turned back to the woman. "Them? Who is them?"

"Some men that have been through here. They had a vehicle like yours, were dressed like you ... said they were contractors for the government and were sent out to get supplies for their men. They took half of our food and we didn't have that much to begin with. Said they'd be back to check on us in a couple of days. Willis and Henry over there," she indicated the other dead man with her head, "decided they were gonna set up out here and try to keep them from taking what little we have left. Now, he's gone!" she stopped, her voice catching on the last word. "What's

145

going to happen to me? Who's going to help me find food? Were you coming to help us?"

Hutch shook his head. "No, we're on our way to Washington D.C. If those tarps hadn't been hanging there we wouldn't have even slowed down. I'm sorry about your husband, but we really need to get moving. Are there any other surprises, besides this one, maybe further up the road?"

Looking at her dead spouse, the tears started again. "No, not from us anyway. We have another couple of guys set up closer to the trailer park entrance. There's only one way into it. But is help coming? It's been days and we haven't seen anyone from the government, the police, nobody. What are we supposed to do?"

Darrell had grabbed the edge of the tarp and was pulling it down. Hutch went over to help. They let it fall over the dead man. Darrell proceeded to do the same with the other one as Hutch turned the woman and replied in a sad tone, "The best you can. That's all you can do. That's all any of us can do."

The woman went over to her husband's body and knelt down beside it. She whispered, "Wait for me, Willis. It shouldn't be too long now before I'm with you, because I don't think I'll make it in this crazy new world without you."

When they got back to the rest of their group, Hutch filled them in on what had happened and their interactions with the woman. They checked on Liz and once she was situated as comfortably as they could get her in one of the bunks, they loaded up to continue their trek. David Tanner offered to go talk to the woman, to reassure her that someone would be coming to help as soon as possible. Damon nixed the idea.

"I'd prefer the least amount of people know who you are, as well as where and why we're headed to D.C. I'm sorry, Sir, but I can't let you do that."

Setting his lips into a grim line, Tanner shook his head slowly. "You're right, Major. It's very frustrating though — seeing people who have no idea how to live life without the comforts they've come to know and having to stay silent when they ask for help."

"I understand, Sir, but honestly you can't give them a time frame anyway. You have no idea how long it's going to take to get aid into the country nor how or when it will be dispersed. I think it's best if we keep you under wraps until we get to the White House." Damon had climbed into the driver seat, with Hutch riding shotgun. He turned to look over his shoulder at the president-elect. "And I'd like to get there as soon as possible."

Chapter 20

"What are you guys doing up so early?" Lauri asked in a sleepy tone as she walked into the kitchen and found the four men seated around the table drinking coffee. The morning sunrise was just starting to light the large room from the window over the sink. She took a cup out of the cabinet and went to the percolator on the stove. Lifting it, she added, "And this is a fresh pot. How long have you all been up?"

"A few hours. We had some excitement in the night," Elliott replied as he got up and joined her at the stove. "I'll take another cup if you're pouring."

Lauri poured his cup full and looked into his eyes, her own filling with worry. "What kind of excitement? Is everyone alright?"

Elliott smiled and said, "Everybody's fine. Go ahead and get your coffee and sit down. We'll fill you in."

She apologized profusely to Joel when he admitted her snoring had made him leave the bed they were sharing. He shook his head with a smile, got up to get more coffee, and kissed her cheek as he went by. "We knew it would be like this. Don't fret, darlin'."

They told her about finding Taylor nosing around in the barn. Her look of alarm changed to concern as they discussed how or even if they could help the young family.

"I just don't know if I could sleep at night knowing those three children were freezing or starving. There has to be something we can do." Her voice broke, letting them know she was on the verge of tears.

"I want us to sit down and make a full list of all the food we have," Elliott said. "If I'm figuring right, I don't think there's going to be a whole lot left to share, if any, before we can get a garden producing. We should be able to keep meat in the freezer for a while, but that depends on how many other people are out there hunting, too. We've got deer, squirrels, rabbits, wild boars, even some wild turkeys. There's a lot of meat out here. That is, until everybody in the area starts needing it for food. And if people start finding their way out here from Millington, who knows? Let's just do a big pot of oatmeal for breakfast this morning then we can get to work."

They were eating their cereal when Amanda came in. With a grin, she hurried to the stove. "Yum, I love oatmeal. Morning, gang!"

Will shook his head and said to no one in particular, "She's a morning person."

"We could tell," Ethan replied with a snicker. "I'm guessing with your line of work you aren't. Well, weren't."

"Yeah, not a lot of call for a bass player now. Looks like I'm going to need to learn some new skills."

Amanda was walking over to the table with a bowl and a cup of coffee. "I think I'll make a shooter out of you. Then you can do security, hunting, critter control, all kinds of things."

Will noticed she was carrying the TIG inside the waistband of her jeans. "Looks like you're already comfortable keeping a gun on you. I guess the rest of us need to follow your lead. It's going to feel weird for a while, I'll tell you that."

She sat down across from Will and shrugged as she stirred her breakfast. "Elliott is right. You know what we saw on the way to your parents' house, then on the way here. The world is full of assholes, and it's going to hell fast. Anyone who can't defend themselves or protect their family and their supplies isn't going to make it. Survival of the fittest isn't what we have to deal with, though. It will be survival of the meanest, the sneakiest, the most desperate, the biggest groups, or the best prepared. That's our new world. Welcome to the real-life Hunger Games." She took a bite of her oatmeal and eyed him as she chewed.

Will shook his head and looked down into his coffee cup. "Well, that sucks. And I'm out of coffee. I guess we better start rationing that if we want it to last a little while. I'm pretty sure we can't grow it in Tennessee." He went to the sink and rinsed his cup from the water jug spigot. "I'll get the others up so they can eat. Sounds like we have a busy day ahead of us." He went down the hall to wake Carly and the boys.

The kitchen was quiet, as everyone was mulling over what Amanda had said. Finally, Lauri spoke in a soft, frightened voice.

"Is it really going to be like that? People fighting over scraps of food, killing each other for supplies?" Her bottom lip quivered as a tear ran down her cheek. "How can this be? We're one of the richest countries in the world. Surely the government is working on a way to fix this. They can't just leave us like this!"

Joel got up and went to squat down beside his wife. Taking her hand in his, he said, "I'm sure they're working on trying to get something done, honey. But this is a big country. Only Canada and Russia are bigger than us. That's a lot of people who need help, a lot of transformers to replace, hundreds of thousands of miles of power lines — this won't be a quick fix. I'd guess they'll work on the biggest cities first, like New York, Los Angeles, Chicago … that's like fifteen million people right there. That's also one side of the country to the other. The logistics are mind-boggling. So, we're going to have to do our best to get by for now. You're really good at making a little go a long way when it comes to food, so why don't you get started on that list for Elliott? Let us worry about the other stuff." He pulled her hand up to his mouth and kissed it softly, then laid another kiss on top of her head. She dabbed at her eyes with a tissue she had in her pocket, gave him a forced smile, and took her things to the sink.

Amanda watched her walk away and said quietly, "I'm sorry. I'm mouthy and direct. I don't always think before I spout off with whatever is in my head. I didn't mean —"

"Don't fret over it," Joel interrupted. "Most people aren't mentally or emotionally ready to deal with something like this. Plus, we were talking about Taylor and his family right before you came in, and she's upset at the thought of them going without food. I'm sure she didn't sleep well without her machine, which doesn't help any either."

"I can help with the hunting. I've been hunting since I was ten. My dad took me every year. Bagged my first buck when I was twelve." She put her hands on her hips and stuck her chest out to emphasize her pride at her accomplishment. Ethan and Elliott laughed, and she grinned at them.

"That's pretty impressive, Amanda," Ethan replied. "I didn't get my first buck until I was fourteen. Dad said it was because it took me that long to learn how to be quiet in the stand."

Laughing, she said, "Yep, that's the hardest part for a kid. Sitting still."

They were sharing hunting stories when Will came back with the rest of the family. Cameron was rubbing sleep from his eyes as he walked to the stove. Looking into the pot with a grimace, he whined, "Oatmeal? What about the biscuits, Pap?"

Elliott frowned at his youngest grandson. "I think you should be happy we have any food to eat, young man. There are going to be a lot of people going hungry real soon. We're going to have to do whatever we can to stretch what we have. There will be biscuits again, just not today. Now, be grateful, not hateful."

Cameron's shoulders slumped as he took the bowl offered to him by his grandmother, who had met them at the stove to dish out their breakfast. "Yes, sir." He shuffled over to the table and plopped down. He reached for the bottle of honey in the middle and added, "Maybe we can find some bees around here so we can still get honey, especially if we're going to run out of sugar."

Elliott raised an eyebrow and said, "Actually, there's a guy who lives about a mile up Highway 14 that raises honeybees. Maybe we can work out some kind of trade with him. My guess is there's going to be a lot of that kind of business being conducted now."

"Yes, barter immediately becomes the method of acquiring supplies in a collapse," Joel commented. "While this wasn't technically a financial collapse, no one can access their funds in the bank, and it wouldn't do them any good anyway because there's no supplies to buy. The new currency is anything you can use to survive."

Amanda stood up and headed for the sink with her dishes. "Which includes ammo. I vote we go spend some ammo money and get some training in."

Cameron started shoveling his oatmeal into his mouth. "Me, too. Wait for me!" he cried around the mushy cereal.

"Cameron! Don't talk with your mouth full," Carly barked. "That's disgusting!"

"Yeah, bro. Nobody wants to see your food." Aaron shielded his eyes and turned his back to his brother as he worked on his own breakfast.

"Sowwy," Cameron replied, still trying to talk around his food. Carly shook her head and started into the living room with her coffee.

"Aren't you going to eat, honey?" Lauri called after her.

"I'm not a breakfast person, Mom; you know that. Not until like lunchtime."

"Yeah, unless things have changed, it's pretty much don't talk to her until at least one cup of coffee has been installed. I used to tell her she needed a sticker on her forehead that said, *for full functionality, apply caffeine*." Ethan had a slight smirk on his face. The room erupted in laughter.

"Nope, still the same," Aaron replied straight-faced, looking up to see if his mother was going to come back for a rebuttal. She did.

Glaring at Ethan, hands on her hips, she scrunched up her face and growled, "I'll have you know I *can* function without caffeine. I just prefer not to. I miss Starbucks already."

"Well, you don't need to be missing breakfast, Carly girl," Elliott said. "You're going to need the calories to get your day started. We'll run out of coffee soon and —"

"*What*? No coffee? But I need it!"

Ethan cocked his head to the side. "You just said you can function without it."

Carly blurted out, "Stay out of this, mister!"

No one was even trying to hide their laughter at the exchange. Finally, Elliott got control of himself. "Just a small bowl then. For today. For me. We'll work you up to it. Seriously, our days are going to be busy and probably pretty physical, so it is important to get some food in your belly. Okay?"

Looking skyward, Carly relented. "Fine. A *small* bowl. Like three bites, four tops. Maybe six. Max."

Lauri handed her the bowl with the small spoonful of oatmeal in it. Carly looked into the bowl with a slight grimace and shuffled to the table. Cameron held the honey out to her.

"It helps."

She looked at him sullenly then took the bear-shaped bottle and squirted some onto the cereal. She spooned a small bite into her mouth and chewed it slowly.

Cameron slid the spoon around his bowl and jumped up. "Okay, I'm done. Let's go shoot!"

"Don't you have chores first thing in the morning?" Amanda said, looking at him with a sideways glance.

"Yes, he does. We all do. We need water brought in, wood split and piled on the porch, the animals need to be tended — work before play," Elliott admonished his youngest grandson.

Cameron hung his head and mumbled, "Yes, sir. I'll get ready." He headed out of the kitchen toward the bedrooms.

Everyone else who was still sitting at the table got up and took their dishes to the sink. Lauri shooed them off when they tried to wash them. Everyone went to their respective rooms to get dressed for the outdoors.

Lexi had been lying on the floor by the wood stove, seemingly asleep. She raised her head when the boys came through, receiving a pat from each of them on their way past her. She looked at Ethan when he walked in, then suddenly snapped her head around to the front door. She popped up and ran to the entryway, hackles raised and that low growl starting in her throat.

Ethan called into the kitchen. "Dad, I think there's someone out front. Lexi's hearing something."

Elliott and those left in the kitchen hurried into the living room. Elliott peered through the peephole.

"Who is it, Dad?" Ethan asked.

"I have no idea but there's at least four of them I can see, kind of rough-looking."

"What are they doing?" Joel's voice sounded a bit nervous.

"Pointing at the well and the roof, likely the smoke from the stove, and talking to each other."

154

Ethan's voice was strong. "What do you want to do, Dad?"

Elliott grabbed his shotgun in one hand and the door handle in the other. "Grab Lexi's collar and bring her out with us. I don't know who they are or what they're thinking, but I'm pretty sure it's nothing good as far as we're concerned."

"What do you want us to do, Elliott?" Amanda asked as she pulled the TIG out and checked there was a round in the chamber.

"Get someone at each window on the front. Give me a minute to get out and ask them who they are and what they're doing here. Then just slide the curtain aside so they see the movement and the barrel of a gun in the window. I want to make sure they know, without a doubt, there are people here who are willing to fight for this place."

"How do you know they aren't just looking for help, Elliott?" Lauri was standing in the kitchen doorway with a dishtowel in her hands, twisting it in agitation.

"Because they haven't come to the door to ask for help. Makes me think what they want is to take. That ain't gonna happen."

Chapter 21

General Charles Everley was stomping around the room, sloshing coffee out of his cup with every step.

"You know what's going to happen, right? They'll get here and we'll never get them out. Those peacekeeping forces are like warts. They burrow in, are hard to get rid of, and keep coming up with reasons to stay."

"Charles, please calm down. At least put your coffee on the table. You're making a mess." President Phil Roman looked from the irate general to Ensign Debby Weaver, who had taken the message. Angie brought her in at Roman's request. Noticing she was standing at attention, Phil said, "At ease, Ensign. I'd like to hear more about the Secretary-General's reaction to President Olstein not being available."

The junior officer placed her hands behind her back and moved her left foot slightly away from her right. Addressing the president, she replied, "I sensed concern in his tone, Sir, but he didn't press the issue. It was almost like he was expecting that answer."

"He was. Our earlier call to them has, no doubt, been shared throughout the Security Council. They know we removed Olstein from office. They don't know why. The fact that he didn't ask …," Phil paused, giving the ensign a chance to dispute his statement. She shook her head, so he went on. "… leads me to the conclusion that they have already made up their minds that we were in the wrong."

Phil nodded at Angie. She addressed the young lady. "That will be all, Ensign Weaver."

Snapping to attention, she replied, "Aye, aye, Ma'am." Executing a smart about-face, she went out the door, closing it behind her. Phil addressed the Chiefs.

"Charles is right. We'll be hard-pressed to get the peacekeepers out if they come in. The council has been trying to insert themselves here for some time, in an attempt to chip away at the Second Amendment, among other things. This may get ugly."

"If?" Angie asked. "Can we keep them out? How? We barely have enough boots on the ground to secure the White House."

"Oh, we have more troops," Charles replied. "We just have to get out and find them here at home or bring them back from wherever they're stationed. We have no comms with any of the bases here, but we are in communication with our people abroad. Olstein wanted to get them back here to terrorize the American people, to get them to fall into *his* line. If the peacekeepers show up uninvited, I call that an invasion, and that is more than enough reason to recall them. Once we get them here, we can send teams out to gather more."

"Don't they need our consent to come in?" General Anton Masters interjected. "We haven't asked them to assist, not with peacekeeping measures. Their claim that the troops will be here to disperse aid sounds a bit contrived to me."

"Yes, they are supposed to get consent. I'll be placing a call to the Secretary-General as soon as we finish up here to see if I can get him to admit what their true intentions are. Charles, I'd like you and General Bale to contact the bases outside the affected zone and put their commanding officers on alert that we may need our forces back here sooner rather than later. Leave all of our assets in Asia where they are, particularly the ones in South Korea, China, and Japan. In fact, let's tighten up that area and get as many boots on the ground in South Korea as we can. I'd like to see the Chairman sweat a little." President Roman looked at his notes, then went on. "Any units we can get back here in

157

twelve hours or less should be put on the highest alert, ready to move at a moment's notice. That should make for a nice welcoming party for the peacekeepers, if they do indeed show up. I intend to try to persuade the Secretary-General to rethink that strategy. I doubt it will work. The U.N. views this situation in the same light Olstein did — a chance to oppress the American people, to constrain our liberties and change the course of our future, more than this event has already done. I won't sit idly by and let that happen. I hope we are all on the same page here."

"You're damn skippy we are!" Charles blurted out. "I could have left day one with Admiral Stephens and headed off to the woods of Tennessee. I chose to stay and try to do whatever I could to stop Olstein from making this worse than it already was. I think we're doing that. I'm not giving up now!"

Calls of "Hell yeah!", "Damn right!" and other affirmations filled the room. President Roman smiled and nodded.

"Excellent. Now let's get to work."

~~~~~~

Margaret Owens was not happy. She had followed Rodriguez to his office.

"Why did you back down, Arturo? You were right in the first place. If President Olstein had a plan, then I'm sure it would have been what was best for their country. He's been in office for eight years. I can't even comprehend a scenario that would need this kind of drastic action so quickly after a catastrophe of this magnitude. He has more experience leading the country than Roman. He has never tried to act outside of the confines of his office."

"Only because Congress and their Constitution prevented him from doing so," Secretary-General

Rodriguez replied as he removed his suit coat and hung it up. "Whether or not we agree with all the aspects of it, that document was written to prevent certain things from happening no matter the circumstances. Damji wasn't wrong about Olstein. He has always had an agenda, always looking for an opening to grab more power or control. I'm pretty sure he had designs on gaining a position with the council. But Damji was also right about needing to find out what's going on over there and why these steps were taken. I may have jumped the gun assuming wrongdoing on the part of the Chiefs and Speaker Roman. We'll get to the bottom of it."

"I disagree. This was not the time to engineer a coup and create a major upheaval in their leadership! They need an experienced leader now more than ever. I can't imagine —"

"No, you can't. Neither can I," Rodriguez said, cutting her off. "I can't imagine what is going on over there or how they are dealing with life without electricity ... and in winter, no less. My guess is the larger cities are in complete chaos, with criminals running rampant in the streets. Looting, theft, rape, and murder are most assuredly widespread. When there are no consequences, the devils come out to play."

Owens threw her hands in the air. "What do you mean there are no consequences? Of course, there are! Breaking the law is still a crime whether the lights are out or not."

"And who is enforcing those laws?" he asked with a slight note of condescension. "Do you envision that the police have reported for work every day like nothing untoward has happened? How would they be able to travel to a crime scene? For that matter, how would they even know about it?"

Owens opened her mouth to respond then closed it. "Well, I ... I mean, they could ..."

"Exactly. We rely on electricity for everything. To communicate, travel, and feed ourselves; to stay warm in the winter and cool in the summer; to purify our water and make our waste disappear. We are a society dependent on technology, and without it most people wouldn't survive.

"And Li Qiang brought up a very valid point. This attack is not just on the United States. It has far-reaching effects, possibly worldwide. The American dollar is quite possibly worthless now. The monies the American government sends to foreign nations has stopped. They can't pay their debts. What countries like China and Japan will do to recoup their loans is anybody's guess. This is not going to be a quick relief effort. It will take years, if ever, for them to get back to where they were. I don't know if the nations of this body can afford to provide that kind of long-term assistance, when many of them were relying on aid from the United States."

Rodriguez paused, seemingly deep in thought. Owens pounced. "What are you saying, Arturo? We are going to send food and water and provide relief efforts, aren't we?"

"Short term, yes," Rodriguez replied with a furrowed brow. "I just don't know how long we can sustain that support."

Owens' eyebrows raised into her hairline. "They're one of the original members! Our headquarters is there, in that country. We can't just turn our backs on them."

Rodriguez looked at her. "So, how long do you think we can provide a country of millions with food and water?"

"Well, I don't know … a few months? Surely they can get back on the right track in that time."

Rodriguez laughed. "How? If the transformers are fried — and I'm talking about the big ones at the power plants — it will take years to get them replaced. They cost millions of dollars. Each. And guess where most of them are made? China. I don't see them getting in a hurry to

160

build equipment for a country that won't be able to pay for it for God knows how long, on top of the debt they already have with China that they aren't currently paying on. They're going to need a lot of help for a long time. I'm not sure the rest of the world is going to want to provide that assistance for years."

"Then what will they do? How will they live?" Owens had a look of fear on her face. "Do we just leave them to fend for themselves?"

"Why do you care so much, Margaret? I detected disdain in your voice earlier for the Americans."

"I detest their culture of guns," she replied gruffly. "All the mass shootings, especially at schools — it's unnecessary and preventable if they would put more restrictions on them. But that doesn't mean I want to stand by and watch them all die of hunger or disease or be killed for their food or shelters."

"I ask again — why do you care whether or not we help them?"

Owens looked down at her hands for a moment, then back up at the Secretary-General. "What if it was my country that had been attacked by that crazy little git? Or yours? Could we so nonchalantly deny our own people their basic needs? The United States has always answered the call of any nation that asked for their help. How can we turn our backs on them in *their* hour of need?"

Rodriguez sat heavily in the chair behind his desk. He put his head in his hands and mumbled through them, "Unless someone figures a way out of this for them, how can we not?"

Chapter 22

The roadblock consisted of a Humvee sitting at an angle with a car on either side. They had already crossed Bear Creek and were on the Francis Scott Key Bridge, crossing the Patapsco River. They couldn't turn around. There was no way to get past it.

"I think we're about to find out who *them* is," Damon said as he slowed to a stop.

"Son of a bitch," Hutch grumbled as he checked his rifle, making sure he had a round chambered. Manning had stayed in the Humvee and was in the back with Agent Stephens. She started toward the turret opening. Stephens laid a hand on her arm.

"I'll take it. You protect them." He motioned with his head toward the Tanners, then proceeded to the spot between them. He pushed the lid up quickly and dropped back down. Stephens waited for incoming fire. It was quiet. He rose into the turret and trained his rifle on the man in fatigues who had risen behind the roadblock. He directed his voice quietly into the cabin.

"Okay to find out what they want, Major?"

"I've got a feeling we already know what they want but, yeah, go ahead and ask," Damon replied. "And be careful."

With a quick nod, Stephens directed his raised voice in front of them. "We're going to need you to move that vehicle. We're on official business."

The man behind the other Humvee smiled. "Our business is official, too. We're gonna need you to vacate that vehicle nice and slow. Leave your weapons inside and come out with your hands up."

"And what agency are you with?" Stephens said calmly.

"Homeland Security." The man's smile never wavered.

Stephens shook his head slightly. "I don't think so. Homeland doesn't wear fatigues. They wear police uniforms."

The man's smile changed to a smirk. "Well, we're the new Homeland Security. We wear whatever the hell we want to."

Stephens continued his line of questioning. "I see. And who issued your orders and assigned you to this location?"

"We're what you might call a fringe unit." At that, five more men's heads showed up from behind the vehicles, rifles pointed at Stephens and various points on the Humvee. "We decide where we're working. And another Humvee will help us continue our work."

"And what work would that be?" Stephens asked, seemingly unfazed by the additional men.

"It's classified." The man and his cohorts laughed loudly. "I could tell ya, but then I'd have to kill ya."

"Good luck with that." Stephens put his eye to the scope of his rifle. "I'm done talking now. Move or this gets ugly."

The man crouched down so that just his head was visible when Stephens leaned into the scope. "I don't think you understand the situation here. This is our area. This is our bridge. We say who comes and goes. We don't take orders from nobody! I got five guys here. Who do you think you are?"

"I'm a Secret Service agent. I have military personnel with me. They're trained for fighting assholes like you who think they can take advantage of other people when something catastrophic happens. We're under orders from the Joint Chiefs, and we will carry out those orders, even if it means going through you. This is your last warning.

163

Move that vehicle!" He shouted the last words for all to hear.

The door to the camper opened and Darrell and Marco exited. Darrell moved up between the Humvee and camper, while Marco hurried to the rear to climb the ladder to the roof, assuming his regular position of overwatch. Hutch climbed out of the passenger door and, with his rifle trained on the roadblock, walked backward to join Darrell behind it. The man's eyes widened, but he didn't speak again.

Hutch yelled out, "Call your mark!"

"Left!" Darrell replied.

"Right!" Hutch followed.

"Left!" Marco answered from the top of the camper.

"Right!"

The female voice got everyone's attention.

"Thompson?" Hutch asked over his shoulder, not taking his eyes off the roadblock.

"I'm good, Cap. Far right is mine." Her voice was tinged with pain, but strong, nonetheless. Hutch let a slight grin touch his lips, then focused his attention on the business at hand.

The movement of the soldiers into tactical positions had the desired effect on the bandits. The cocky attitudes were replaced with more subdued facial expressions on men who were quickly exposing much less of their vital organ areas to anyone who might want to use them for targets. The spokesman and assumed leader's face had changed from a self-assured smirk to an uncertain scowl.

"We're not moving!" he shouted to Stephens. "I hope whoever is driving that thing is good at backing a trailer, because it's a long way off this bridge. Or, we can make a deal. Leave us some of your supplies — food, guns, ammo — and we'll call it a toll. Oh, and we'll take the girl, too."

164

"We don't make deals." Stephens still had his eye on the scope with the man in his sight. "But ... I'll make an exception just this once."

The man's face changed to a leering grin. Stephens went on.

"The deal is you move that Humvee and let us pass, and we'll let you live. Otherwise, this won't end well for you. The deal expires in thirty seconds."

The man's face changed again, this time to rage. "*You* don't make the deal! *We* do! And I'm done talking now!" The man began to crouch as he started raising his own rifle. His men followed suit. That is, until they saw their leader's head snap back from the impact of the bullet. The spray from the exploding hole in the back of his skull splattered the men on either side of him with blood and brain matter. Their eyes grew wide as all of them tried to make themselves as small as possible behind the cover of the cars.

Stephens had ejected his spent shell casing and chambered a new cartridge. In a calm voice devoid of emotion, he called out, "Okay, *now* who's in charge over there?"

None of the remaining men spoke or even showed their faces. Stephens waited just a moment and continued. "Well, if none of you want to take over for your idiot former spokesman, then I'd suggest you come out with your hands up where we can see them. Nice and slow. No sudden or stupid moves like your dead buddy. Do it now!"

The first thing Stephens and the soldiers saw were five pairs of hands rising from behind the cars. The remaining men stood slowly, almost tentatively, eyes wide and full of fear. They weren't fully upright — more of a crouching stance — as if they wanted to keep their options open to drop back behind cover, if needed.

"Good boys. I'm going to need you to come on out in front of those cars and kneel down and keep your hands where we can see them." Stephens watched them through the scope as he delivered the instructions. When they had all complied, Hutch took over, stepping out from behind the Humvee.

"Is that everybody? Because if I see any movement from behind those cars, it won't end well for any of you." Hutch eyed the men waiting for an answer. When none came, he shouted, "Speak up! Is there anybody else out here?"

The men looked at each other. It seemed none of them wanted to draw attention to themselves. Finally, one of them spoke in a timid voice.

"N-no … sir. There's nobody else." Hutch could see his body trembling. Whether it was from fear or the snow he was kneeling in wearing only jeans, he wasn't sure — and didn't really care. He started toward the men, eyes darting in all directions, watching for threats. Darrell proceeded along with him from the other side. When they reached the men, Hutch slung his rifle.

"I'm going to pat them down, Light. Watch them."

Darrell gave a slight nod and Hutch proceeded to search the men. He found a couple of pocketknives, which he tossed aside into the snow. Finding nothing else that could be used against them, he stepped back and pulled his rifle back around in front of him.

"Okay, you can stand up now." The men did as they were told. Without taking his eyes off them, he spoke to Darrell. "Light, check the other side of that roadblock. Just in case these fellas weren't entirely truthful."

Darrell headed to the cars blocking the road. Keeping one of them in front of him, he scoped out the area behind them. The only person he saw was the dead man, lying in a pool of his own blood. He turned back to Hutch.

166

"All clear, Cap. Want me to make a hole here?"

"Yes. Get the road opened up so we can get back under way. And gather those weapons they left and throw them over the side of the bridge."

The men's eyes grew wide. The one who had answered earlier became animated. "Aw, man! You don't have to do that. We won't use them on you, I swear! We need those guns for self-defense. It's dangerous out here already, and it's gotta get worse!"

"Especially with ass wipes like you terrorizing folks who are just trying to get by. No, I think you need to get a taste of what you've been putting other people through. Maybe it will help you find a different path in this crazy new world we're in. I just hope you don't run into anyone like you while you're searching for it."

The wannabe road agents flinched every time they heard a splash from their guns hitting the water. With the lack of other noises, the sound carried well. Once he had dispatched the weapons to the river, Darrell climbed in the other Humvee and fired it up. He backed it up and parked it along the safety rail. The opening was more than wide enough for them to drive through. He climbed out and tossed the keys behind the vehicle onto the snow-covered road. He smiled as they landed, sending up a little puff of snow and turned back to his team.

"Good to go, Cap," he said as he walked back through the opening.

Hutch looked at the men standing before him. "Alright, you guys line up over there." He indicated the railing to his right. The men didn't move right away, seeming hesitant to leave the relative safety of the center of the bridge.

"Wh-what are you going to do to us?" the one who had spoken earlier asked in a voice laced with fear and uncertainty.

167

"Nothing, as long as you stand over there and be quiet," Hutch snapped at him. He scowled at the men until they complied with his directive.

"What are we going to do with them, Cap?" Darrell said under his breath when he reached Hutch. "We take off so they can start being douches again and terrorizing the people in this area?"

"We don't have much choice," Hutch replied. "It's not like we can take them in, and we can't shoot unarmed men no matter how much they deserve it."

"Then what? We just leave them here?"

"No other option." Hutch turned to the men standing by the railing. "We're going to be on our way now. If I come back through here and hear one word, one little whisper that you idiots have been bothering people again, I will hunt you down and take every one of you out. You got that?"

With a vigorous nodding of his head, the one who had taken on the role of spokesman replied, "Y-yes, sir. I swear on my mother's life you won't hear another thing about us."

Squinting at the man, Hutch said, "Is your mother alive?"

"Yes. Well … um … she was up until this happened. She lives in upstate New York, so I don't know." Hutch's scrunched up face had the man hurrying on. "B-but I hope she is. I mean, my dad's there, so yeah … I'm pretty sure they're okay."

"Well, maybe you should do something decent for a change. Climb in that Humvee and go find out."

The man nodded again. "Yeah. Yeah, I can do that."

With a soft sigh and a shake of his head, Hutch headed for Damon and the rest of his people. He stopped and looked over his shoulder at them. "Stay there until we're out of sight. Don't make me order somebody to shoot your dumb asses."

The men looked like a line of bobblehead dolls with all of their heads bobbing up and down. The one on the end had a big grin on his face and was giving them a thumb's up. Hutch walked back to their Humvee, with Darrell walking backwards behind him, never taking his eyes off the men. When they got back to the vehicle, Hutch pulled the door open to a cab full of curious faces.

"Well, Captain? What's the situation now?" Tanner asked after a moment.

"All good, Sir," Hutch replied. "Let's move out. Stephens, I'm going to pull Perez off that roof back there. You stay put until we can't see them anymore."

"Roger that." Stephens hadn't moved through the whole confrontation. He still had the scope to his eye.

Hutch leaned back and called out to his people. "Load up! We're burning daylight."

Marco scrambled off the roof as Darrell and Liz climbed back in the camper. Marco nudged her at the doorway.

"Good job, Lizzie! You didn't get shot that time."

Liz turned and shot him a look that could freeze water, if it weren't all frozen already. "Shut up, Perez, before *you* get shot — by me."

Marco's eyebrows shot up as his eyes widened. "Hey now, is that any way to talk to the guy that saved your life?"

Liz rolled her eyes. "You did *not* save my life. You patched me up. Big difference."

Marco shrugged. "Pah-tay-to, pah-tah-to. Speaking of potatoes ..." He leaned back so that he could see around the door. "Cap, okay if we grab a bite while we're riding?"

"Yeah, bring seven protein bars and water bottles up here before we head out," Hutch replied. "That should tide us over until we reach D.C. One bar each. We need to keep rationing until we know what the situation is there."

169

Marco groaned as he climbed into the camper. "One protein bar? I can eat three in one sitting."

Darrell chuckled. "You and me both, brother. I guess we're going to find our lean bodies again real soon."

With the bars and water in his hands, Marco stepped out the door. "I wasn't looking for mine."

Chapter 23

At the sound of the door opening, the four men in the yard looked up. Their eyebrows raised a bit when they saw two men and a large dog step out of the house.

"Can I help you fellas?" Elliott asked in a calm, firm voice. Ethan kept a tight grip on Lexi's collar. Lexi stared at the men, seeming to be waiting for something. Her body was tensed like a coiled spring waiting for release.

One of the men back by the pump started to reach inside his jacket. Elliott pulled the shotgun up and pointed it at them as Ethan put his free hand on the pistol at his waist.

"Keep those hands where we can see them!" Elliott said, voice now raised. The man stopped his movement and raised his hands slightly in front of him. The other three men did the same as the one closest to the house smiled and took a slight step forward. Elliott tipped the barrel of the shotgun down and pointed it at him. The man stopped but continued to smile.

"Easy, buddy, no cause for alarm," the man said. "My friends and I are just checking the area out to see if we might be able to stay around here somewhere. You've got a nice setup here. Water, heat, looks like you guys are eating okay. We'd be willing to share the workload and share the wealth, so to speak. That's a big house; should be plenty of room for a few more people."

"We're full up," Elliott said, never taking his eyes off the man.

"Well, that ain't very neighborly of ya," the man replied, his smile turning to a sneer. "We've got more people than this —" he motioned toward the other men, "— and we need places for them. This one looks damn near perfect for our needs. Folks are going to have to help each other out to get through this mess. I mean, it's almost Christmas. You wouldn't want ole Santa to leave ya coal in your stocking, now would ya?" His companions snickered behind his back.

In his peripheral vision, Elliott saw the curtains move in the living room window to his left. His eyes darted back to the men in front of him, and he could see that their attention had been drawn to the windows across the front of the house. With a thin-lipped smile, he replied, "We ain't neighbors. Like I said — we're full up. Y'all need to move on now. Maybe you'll find some abandoned homes on down the road, or even down the highway. There's nothing for you here."

His gaze shifting from Elliott to Ethan to Lexi, the man took a step back and said, "Oh, I think there's plenty here. I'm sure we'll be seeing each other again, old man. C'mon, boys, let's go."

Elliott and Ethan watched the men walk away, talking amongst themselves and turning back to look at the house frequently. When they were out of sight, Elliott finally loosened his grip on the shotgun and let the barrel drop. He turned his head and looked at Ethan.

"Damn it, this is bad. They'll be back. We need to get these people trained to defend themselves, each other, and this place. We've got work to do, son."

~~~~~~

Carly wasn't good at shooting. At all.

Her fear of the gun was glaringly apparent in the way she held it, as well as her stance and attitude. Her hands shook, and her shoulders were hunched, no matter how many times she was told to stand up straight. When she pulled the trigger, her whole body went rigid and her eyes were closed. The Walther PK380 she was trying to master, which Amanda had shot first and deemed an easy-to-use, accurate pistol after shooting the center out of a target, looked foreign and uncomfortable in Carly's hands. Having swung the barrel around causing everyone in attendance to duck for the third time, Elliott held his hand out and took the pistol from her.

Sighing, he said, "Okay, Carly girl, we're going to try something different with you. Amanda, Ethan, y'all continue with the lessons and the practice. Carly, you come with me."

Carly crossed her arms over her chest and stomped off after Elliott. "I still don't understand why I have to know how to shoot! If there's nine people here and eight of them can shoot, that should let me off the hook. I can pass out bullets or something. We're lucky I didn't shoot somebody already. I suck at it! And I chipped one of my nails, which I have no way of getting repaired now."

Elliott rolled his eyes then pasted a smile on his face as he turned to his daughter-in-law. "Honey, think about this. What if, God forbid, you were outside by yourself and those men came back. By the time you could scream for help, if they hadn't already grabbed you, it'd be too late. You could be dead before anyone could even get to you. You need to know how to protect yourself."

"I couldn't shoot a person, Elliott! I mean, I can't even hit a paper target and you think I could manage to fend off an attacker with that thing? I'd probably shoot myself and save them the trouble. I just won't go outside by myself. I'll make sure one of the boys, or Annie Oakley over there, is with me." She pointed behind her to where Amanda was working with Lauri, who wasn't much better than Carly. From where they stood, they could see her hands shaking as she pointed the pistol at the target. "Not Mom, though. She's as bad as me."

173

"You just need to get comfortable with it, Carly." Elliott dropped the magazine out into his hand and stuck it in his coat pocket. He checked to make sure the gun wasn't loaded and held it out to her. She looked at the pistol then at Elliott.

"What?" she asked in an unveiled attempt to delay the inevitable.

"Take it. It's not loaded." He pushed it into her hand. "I want you to carry this with you all the time. If you don't have something in your right hand, I want to see this pistol there. Inside, outside, lying next to your plate at the dinner table and beside your bed at night. When it's not in your hand, I want to see it in your back pocket. I want you to get comfortable handling it."

He positioned all but her index finger on the grip. She immediately placed that finger on the trigger.

"No! I never want to see your finger anywhere near the trigger unless I tell you. Hold it like this." He pulled his own sidearm out of his pocket and showed her how to hold it. "Keep your index finger laid along the side of gun right above the trigger. Always. Unless you are actually about to shoot, stay away from the trigger!"

She modeled her hold to match his. "Now see? This is okay. This doesn't scare me. Am I doing it right now?" She started to pull the gun up in Elliott's direction. His hand shot out and pushed the barrel down toward the ground.

"Carly! Never point the barrel of a gun at anything you don't plan to shoot!" The exasperation in his voice was quite apparent.

"But you said it's not loaded," she replied in a confused tone.

"What if I was wrong? What if I thought I had cleared it but didn't? Treat every gun like it's loaded, even if you unloaded it yourself!"

"But if I know I unloaded it, why would I think it was loaded?"

Elliott blew out a breath with a huff. He seemed to be struggling for the right words. Finally, he blurted out, "Just do what I say! That's how it is! That's the rule! Treat every gun like it's loaded. End of discussion!"

Carly scowled at the older man. "So that's where it came from."

"Where what came from?" Elliott asked, exasperation still apparent in his tone.

"*End of discussion.* Your son used to use that on me all the time, especially when he knew he was wrong and didn't want to admit it. He'd say, 'End of discussion' and walk away."

With a bit more patience, Elliott replied, "Well, that's not why I said it, honey. But this subject — this point of contention — is not open for debate. It is the only way to be around guns and not get yourself or someone else hurt. And in our current situation, they are now a necessity of life. Bad people were here today, and I doubt they'll be the last ones we see. Folks are going to get desperate when their food runs out. We'll be lucky if we have enough for us to get through the winter. There won't be any extra to hand out.

"If you assume all guns you handle are loaded, you will always be conscious of *how* you handle them. I know this is not a life you're used to. Hell, none of us are ready for this. But we have to do the best we can with what we have to work with, and we have to watch out for each other. We have to be able to defend this place and what we have, or we'll be the ones out looking for supplies. I'll do whatever I have to do to keep you and the boys and the rest of your family safe, but I can't do it by myself. I need help. We all have to help each other; protect each other. Do you understand?"

Carly had been looking down at the pistol in her hands. When she raised her head to look at Elliott, a lone tear ran down her cheek. "I'm scared. This thing terrifies me," she said softly, indicating the gun with a slight raise of her hand. "But I'm more scared of someone I love getting hurt because I couldn't do anything to stop it. And that includes you, Elliott."

Elliott looked at her with an unspoken question on his face. She didn't wait for him to ask it.

"You said the rest of *your* family. You should have said the rest of *our* family. You are as much a part of my family as anyone else here. I've known you since I was sixteen years old. I can barely remember a time you weren't there. We, all of us, are a family."

With a sheepish grin, Elliott asked, "Even Ethan?"

Carly raised an eyebrow at him. "Yes, even that one. Although he's more like a stepchild. You know, like I have to accept him because you two are a package deal."

With a chuckle, Elliott wrapped an arm around Carly and steered her back toward the rest of the group. "Yep, you can't pick your relatives, Carly girl. But his time is likely pretty short. I hope you can make peace with him before it's too late."

"I'm trying, I really am. At least I'm getting past the feeling of wanting to smash his face in every time I look at him."

He nodded, smiled, and patted her shoulder. "That's definitely a start."

~~~~~

The four men walked down the road to an old van they'd left waiting for them around the bend, close to Highway 14. The one who had done the talking at Elliott's flipped a

176

cigarette butt to the ground as he reached for the door handle.

"How many people you think they have, Wayne?" he asked the one who had started to reach inside his coat while they were in the yard.

"Two at the windows in the living room, two more at what I'd guess were bedrooms. At least six counting the old man and the other guy on the porch. One of the ones in the living room was a chick, from the long blond hair I saw. Could be more, Cody." Wayne Mitchell was reaching for the passenger door. "What do you want to do, man? Keep looking for a place?"

"Hell no!" Cody Randolph replied. "That house, the well with the hand pump on it, that whole layout is exactly what we need to get through this mess. That's the one we've been looking for. It's the golden egg."

"But if there's six of them and only four of us, how can we take it from them?" one of the other men asked. "We don't have no more people like you told that old man, Cody."

"Well, Dougie, I guess we need to go find some more people," Cody said in a snide tone. "Wouldn't want that old geezer to think I was lying, now, would we? Get in the van. You too, Bo."

When all four men had climbed inside, Cody started the engine. The old Chevy van grumbled a bit before roaring to life. Cody grinned at his companions as he slowly stepped on the gas to keep the tires from spinning on the slick road.

"I tried to get my old man to sell this thing for years. Didn't think it was worth anything. It's gold now. Let's go find some more guys who are willing to do what needs to be done for a decent place to live. We found it. We just need to take it."

177

Chapter 24

"I think there might be a misunderstanding here, Mister Roman."

"That's Mister President. And I think we understand perfectly." Roman had U.N. Secretary-General Rodriguez on the speaker in the radio room. General Everley was with him. Everley stuck his tongue out and bit it. Roman chuckled quietly. When Rodriguez could be heard talking again, they both turned their attention to the radio.

"Oh. Well … yes. Yes, of course. I apologize, Mister President."

Everley pantomimed hitting a baseball then raised his hand above his eyes as if shielding them from the sun, simulating hitting a home run. Roman covered his mouth to stifle a laugh. He pasted a serious expression on his face before speaking.

"We have no desire for peacekeepers to be here. We don't need them. We have our own troops who will handle what needs to be done. If you want them to escort the supplies here, that's fine; but we'll take over once the shipments arrive." Roman's tone left no room for argument — or so he thought.

"Well, I'm afraid without more information about what has gone on there, the council is not comfortable sending supplies to be controlled by a military force that, quite frankly, has apparently executed a coup against your country's duly elected leader. We'd like to know exactly what happened."

Roman looked at Everley, who shrugged his shoulders and mouthed, *Go for it.* With a nod, Roman began.

"Let me give you the short version, Mr. Secretary. Our duly elected president was planning to usurp the authority of his position. He planned to suspend the rights of the citizens — rights guaranteed by our Constitution — and to set himself up as an oligarch. He tried to dismiss the Joint Chiefs. His idea was to bring all of our troops home and have them steal from the American people for the greater good. He wanted to repeal the Second Amendment, among other unconstitutional edicts, and was planning to stay in office indefinitely, even though we have a new president waiting to take his spot in less than thirty days. The very fact that he was not going to step down for the incoming president is a treasonous offense. We felt it was in the country's best interest to stop him and try to keep things under control as much as we can until president-elect Tanner is sworn in. Does that make the council more comfortable with our actions?"

The room was silent as they waited for a reply from Rodriguez. After a few moments, he responded.

"Are you sure those were his intentions? Perhaps you misunderstood —"

Roman cut him off. "I can read you the list of ridiculous executive orders he wanted to implement. It's all there."

Another moment of silence. Finally, Rodriguez replied hesitantly, "Well … if he put it in writing … I guess that's a different matter."

Everley leaned over and whispered in Roman's ear, "Ya think?"

Roman smirked as he spoke. "So, when can we expect to start seeing some relief supplies show up, Mr. Secretary? Things are getting bad fast. Reports tell us looters have already cleaned out the grocery stores, and we're going to have a lot of cold and hungry people here. We were hoping we'd start seeing shipments by the weekend."

The pregnant pause from Rodriguez was felt over the radio lines and filled the small room. Roman looked at Everley, whose face was contorting in anger. He had held

179

his tongue to that point, but, apparently, his patience had waned. He stepped toward the microphone and bellowed, "General Charles Everley, Chairman of the Joint Chiefs speaking! You *are* sending supplies, right? You *do* intend to come to the aid of a fellow *original* member country, correct? We've provided aid to almost every country in the world when it was needed for over a hundred years! Some of them damn well better be stepping up to reciprocate now that *we* are the ones in need!"

"We are looking into what can be done, General," Rodriguez said in a soft voice. "The scope of the damage to your technological infrastructure is massive, and it's almost unimaginable that it can be corrected any time in the near future. If we send supplies now, how much will be needed for the over three hundred million people who live there? The numbers are staggering. How long would that amount of support be needed to sustain the population? We are looking at years, many years, until you are able to bring new transformers online and regain some semblance of your former lifestyles. I don't think the member countries have the resources to assist for years — not without creating a hardship in their own countries, anyway. This event has caused worldwide chaos. We need to —"

"*Event*? Did you just call this catastrophe an *event*? This was an attack! A blatant attack on our country by a little weasel of a dictator who deserves to have a nuke dropped on his head! And I intend to do everything in my power to see to it that that's exactly what happens to that wormy little bastard!" Everley stormed out of the room and slammed the door behind him.

Roman waited a moment to see if Rodriguez would respond. When he didn't, he picked up the mantle. "You dare make the excuse that helping us, when we find ourselves in the direst of circumstances we have ever seen, would put a hardship on the contributing countries? Let me give you a little history lesson, Mister Rodriguez. World War I. It wasn't our fight, but we answered the call of our fellow human beings without hesitation, because that's what decent people do. The cost of that war was more than any previous war in our history. And ten years after it was over, our economy had still not recovered, which caused the Great Depression. That lasted ten more years.

"Just as we were finally getting back on track, we were dragged into World War II, when our base on Pearl Harbor was attacked. We declared war on Japan, and then Germany, Japan's ally at the time, declared war on us. We had done nothing to antagonize either country; yet, both were hell-bent on taking us down. We waged a war on both fronts and emerged victorious. And then we helped rebuild the war-torn countries. Because that's what decent people do.

"We've fought other people's wars for the past sixty years, including one against the country that blatantly attacked us a few days ago without provocation. When someone asks for help, we go. Now *we* need the help. So, you and the council better figure out how to provide it — now and for however long we damn well need it!"

Roman made a slashing motion across his neck, signaling the radio operator to disconnect the call. He turned on his heel and headed for the door, muttering, "I've got a feeling we're on our own."

~~~~~~

"The nerve of that man! History lesson indeed!" Margaret Owens shouted in outrage to the assembled council members. They had listened to the conversation between Rodriguez and Roman in a conference room outside the Secretary-General's office. The microphone on their end had been muted.

181

"He spoke the truth. When Saddam Hussein invaded my country, the United States was the first to call for action to remove the Iraqi forces from Kuwait. The Americans came to the aid of your country, Ms. Owens, when Germany was trying to take over Europe. Who made the decision not to extend aid to the Americans?" Nawaf Damji, the Kuwaiti representative, asked in an agitated tone. Multiple conversations were ensuing around the room.

Rodriguez walked in and joined them. "No decisions have been made," he said, voice raised above the din. The room grew quiet. "We are weighing our options. Their recovery will take years. Are you all committed to long-term aid, no matter how long —"

"Yes!" Damji cried out. "Whatever they need for as long as they need it. And if any of you would refuse to do the same, I would remind you that Americans do not walk away in the face of adversity. When they are back to full strength — and don't think for a second they won't get there, with or without our help — they will remember who helped them and who turned their back on them. I have already spoken to my country's leaders, and we will do whatever we can for the United States. We are loading oil onto ships as we speak. The rest of you must decide whether you want to be America's ally or something else."

"Of course, we're allies! What else would we be?" Margaret said sarcastically.

Damji shrugged. "The opposite of ally is foe. If you abandon them in their hour of need, how else are they to view your actions?"

Margaret's eyes grew wide. Damji didn't wait for her response. "Better yet, try to imagine if your country were the one that had been attacked. What would your expectation of support from the U.N. be?"

"Well, we would expect assistance, of course, but the United Kingdom has a much smaller population than the United States. It wouldn't take nearly as much to sustain our people as it will to sustain the Americans."

"If the attack had been on your country, it would affect others close by. A bomb detonated above the English Channel would reach into France and Belgium, as well. Would those countries be any less worthy of aid?"

"That's ridiculous!" Margaret fumed. "Of course not! Every affected country would be offered assistance."

"As should the United States," Damji said with a nod. "They will need everything we send. They would be the first to offer help to any of our countrymen if the situation were reversed. They should expect the same. I vote we start shipments immediately to Washington D.C., as that is where their leaders are. I also think we should offer troops if they want them, but on their terms, not ours. Treat them as you would want your country to be treated in the same circumstances. Will it be a hardship? Probably. But we should all act like ... how did President Roman put it ... *decent people* and do the right thing."

The room was silent as each member seemed to be pondering the words of the ambassador from the small country of Kuwait.

Rodriguez sighed. "You are correct, Ambassador Damji. Of course, we must help the Americans. The task is so daunting ... yet, it must be done. We also need to deal with their attackers. North Korea must be punished."

"How?" Li Qiang, the ambassador from China, said and snorted a laugh. "They are already sanctioned in every way! It means nothing. They have declared war on the United States and, by crippling their economy, on China as well. China will reciprocate!"

"In what manner?" Margaret asked in a voice tinged with fear.

183

Qiang slammed his fist on the table. "My government's leaders are meeting right now. War will be declared on North Korea by China!"

Haruto Tanaka, the Japanese ambassador, stood up. "Japan will join China in the war on North Korea."

Rodriguez hung his head and clasped his hands in front of him. "I think we should take a moment and pray, if you are so inclined, for all of us. I believe we are about to enter World War III."

Chapter 25

Damon's entourage continued across the bridge and into Hawkins Point. Damon considered stopping in at the Coast Guard station and checking on Captain Jeanna Rogers, but he had no way of knowing if she was still there and, honestly, hoped she wasn't. There were no orders coming down, and he didn't know if there would be any time soon. Besides, he was within a couple of hours of completing his mission, and he really wanted to be out of the Humvee for a while. A long while.

The little island didn't really offer anything in the way of supplies for hungry, cold, desperate people, so there was no activity around them as they passed through. However, after crossing Curtis Creek, they ran into a surprise.

Troops.

Rounding a corner in the Baltimore Beltway, they came upon a team of about a dozen soldiers walking up the highway. They were geared up as if they were on a hike. At the sound of the vehicle, they came to a stop and turned to face it. They were already carrying their rifles in a low ready position; and, while they were attentive, they did not seem overly alarmed, probably because they recognized the Humvee as military like them. Damon pegged them as Army from their ACUs.

"Huh. Wonder what's up with this?" Hutch commented as he peered out the windshield.

"I'm going to guess reservists," Damon replied. "There's a reserve center just off the interstate up ahead. But I am curious as to what they're doing out here. Let's ask."

"Okay, but stay sharp. Things aren't always what they appear to be. You want me to go with you?" Hutch asked.

"Sure. You got this, Stephens?" Damon looked into the rear-view mirror at the agent in the back.

Stephens, who was squatting between the Tanners just under the hatch, nodded. "Got it. I'm curious to know what the deal is myself."

Damon climbed out the driver side door while Hutch exited the passenger side. They started toward the soldiers, who were now headed in Damon and Hutch's direction. The man in the front spied the gold leaf insignia on Damon's collar and snapped to attention with a salute. His team followed suit. Damon smiled as he reached them, returned the salute and said, "At ease, gentlemen."

The men relaxed and the one in front, wearing captain's bars, stepped forward. "Captain Roy Dorn, Major. I must say it was a surprise to hear that Humvee. I haven't heard a running vehicle since the lights went out. I'm guessing it was in hardened storage."

Damon stuck his hand out to Roy. "Major Damon Sorley. Yes, and a good thing it was. Where are you and your men headed?"

Roy shook Damon's hand and replied, "D.C., Sir. We can't get orders at the base so we're going to see what we can do to help."

Damon looked the men over. "You were planning to walk there?"

"Yes, Sir. We didn't have anything else going on, so we figured why not?"

Hutch stepped up and extended his hand. "Captain Chris Hutchinson, New Jersey National Guard. Friends call me Hutch."

"Nice to meet you, Hutch," Roy said shaking his hand. "Like Starsky and Hutch?"

Hutch chuckled. "Yeah, I guess so. So, you were going to walk forty miles to check in for work?"

"Yeah, we'll probably miss a roll call or two," Roy said with a slight smirk. "Can I ask what you guys are doing out here? I'm guessing you're heading the same place we are."

"You guessed right. And I think we can give you guys a lift if the camper can carry the load. What do you think, Hutch?" He turned to his companion, an unasked question in his eye.

Hutch grinned. "I think it will be just fine for them to join us. He'd never let us leave them to walk anyway."

Roy looked back and forth between the two men, sensing there was a silent conversation going on between them. "Um, he? He who?"

With a smile on his face, Damon jerked his head toward the Humvee. "Come see."

All the men followed Damon and Hutch to the passenger side door. Hutch opened it and Damon leaned in.

"Sir? Could you step out here for a minute?"

David Tanner climbed out and watched as the new arrivals' eyes grew wide in recognition.

Damon turned to the men and said, "Gentlemen, may I present Mr. David Tanner, your soon-to-be Commander-in-Chief. We are on a mission to get him to Washington as quickly as possible. Sir, these men are reservists from 1SG Brandt, I assume?" Damon looked to Roy for confirmation. Roy nodded slowly as he stared at Tanner.

"Good morning, men. It's a pleasure to meet you." He proceeded to walk to each man, shook his hand and asked his name. When he had greeted them all, he went back to stand beside Damon. "Where might you all be going this chilly morning?"

"The same place you are, Sir. Looks like there's some kind of command structure still at work if you're on an assignment, Major."

"Yes, most of the Joint Chiefs are there and we have comms with our bases outside the affected areas. Right

187

now, we need to get back on the road." He turned to face Tanner. "Sir, I figured you'd want —"

"You figured right, Major," Tanner cut in. "We will absolutely be taking these men with us. I have no doubt we're going to need every enlisted man and woman we can find. I wouldn't dream of leaving them out here when we're all going to the same place."

"Roger that. Captain ..." Damon paused when both Hutch and Dorn turned to him. "Er, Captain Dorn, I'd like you to ride in the Humvee for now so we can fill you in on what's happened to this point. I'm sure you've got some ideas, but we'll give you the details that we have so far."

"Sounds good, Major. Men, follow Captain Hutchinson. Looks like we just scored a ride to D.C."

The men shouted in unison, "Hooah!"

Roy Dorn's eyes grew wide as Damon relayed the facts of what had transpired at the White House. When Damon paused for a moment, Roy spoke up.

"Wow. That's just crazy! He was really planning to do all of that? The president, that is."

Damon nodded slowly as he drove. "Yep. I'm glad there were people in the capitol that put a halt to that real quick."

"No kidding! So, Speaker Roman is the president now?" Roy asked.

"Interim president," Tanner interjected from the back seat. "He'll hold the position until my swearing in day. But we'll be working together between now and then to start getting things back in order while we figure out how to fix this mess."

Roy turned slightly in the passenger seat to face Tanner. "Can it be fixed, Sir? I mean, this thing is huge. The whole country without power, cars and trucks don't work, machines don't run — it won't be easy."

188

"No, it won't, Captain. It is a daunting task when you think about everything and everyone that has been affected. But then something happens, like us running into you and your men. You didn't let the fact that you had no car to drive keep you from trying to do something to help. You adapted to the situation and overcame the obstacle. That's what Americans do. That's how this country came to be. It won't happen overnight. But rest assured — we *will* get our country back."

Roy smiled at Tanner. "Yes, Sir. I believe we will."

They had passed I-895 and were coming up on a residential area. The highway they were traveling had been lined with concrete walls to dampen the sound of hundreds of thousands of cars passing by daily from the homes behind them. That turned out to be a blessing because the walls weren't easily scaled by the average person. They did see a large white banner of some sort hanging from the wall. It was billowing in the breeze of the chilly late December morning. Roy leaned forward trying to see what it was.

"Damn."

The single word he uttered was laced with concern, enough that the rest of the occupants were trying to see for themselves what he had seen. As they passed it, they could tell what it was. The banner was actually a large white sheet that had been painted with red letters. It read simply:

HELP US!

The passengers of the Humvee were quiet as they drove past the silent plea that spoke so loudly.

Finally, Roy said softly, "How can we help everyone? There're so many people in this country. They're probably out of food by now and the water stopped running yesterday. We have a lot to do and not much time to do it before ..."

His voice trailed off, the unfinished thought hanging in the air of the cab like cigarette smoke in a crowded bar.

Never taking his eyes off the road, Damon replied, "We can't save them all. We just have to do what we can where we can and when we can. The rest is up to God."

"There's probably a lot of people talking to Him right now," Stacy commented from the back. Her statement hung in the air of the small space as each of them seemed lost in his or her own thoughts.

The underpass for Baltimore Annapolis Boulevard appeared, and Roy watched as Damon visibly tensed up. He turned his attention to the road, his curiosity piqued.

"Is something wrong, Major? Did you see something ahead?"

Damon shook his head and replied, "No, it looks okay. We had a run-in a few miles back with some residents who had set up an ambush site at an underpass, but this one looks clear."

"Oh, man. Was anybody hurt?"

"Liz got shot," Stacy blurted out. "Through and through. Perez patched her up."

"And the men who were trying to ambush us were killed," Damon said in a quiet voice. "They shot at us and we had to return fire."

"Holy sh—" Roy stopped, eyeing the child sitting on his father's lap in the back seat. "Er, cow. A firefight, right in the street?"

"Yes, and it's only going to get worse as time goes on. Desperate people are dangerous. They aren't thinking clearly and make rash decisions without considering the consequences. We are just a few days into this catastrophe. I can't imagine what it will be like in a few weeks." Damon was scowling yet breathed a sigh of relief when they got through the underpass unmolested.

190

They went through another residential area they couldn't see due to the concrete walls lining the interstate. They were approaching the underpass for I-895. Damon was scanning the area with a confused look on his face.

"We've got a slight problem," he said to no one in particular.

Roy sat up straighter and looked ahead. "What's wrong?"

"I want to get on 895 so we can bypass as much residential area as possible then take 95 on into D.C. But there's no off-ramp."

"No, there's not one on this side," Roy replied. "Only on the other side and going the opposite direction."

"Well, I guess we're going to have to make one." Damon went around a stalled car in the outer lane they were using and stayed in the one closest to the median strip. Once they had passed under 895, he stopped and parked the Humvee. Turning to face the Tanners, he said, "I'm going to get out and see if there's anything that can hurt us or the camper hidden under the snow. Sit tight."

"I'll help," Roy added, climbing out the passenger door. He was met by Hutch and a couple of his men who had exited the camper to see what was going on.

"Problem?" Hutch queried, scanning for anything untoward around them.

Damon met him between the two conveyances. "For once, no. We need to get up there," he turned, pointing to the elevated highway behind them, "with no ramp. I should be able to make a wide enough turn to go up the off ramp here, then another turn to get us going the right direction. I just want to make sure there is nothing we can't see under the snow. You know how they love putting concrete things on the side of the road. We just need something to poke around the ground."

"Let me check the camper. There may be something in there we can use." Hutch went back to the open door. He could be heard relaying the update to the occupants inside it. After a moment, he came back out with a few things, followed by Marco and some of the reservists.

"These should work." He laid out a couple of hiking poles and some long plastic legs, possibly from a canopy or screen room attachment.

Damon nodded and smiled. "Excellent. Yes, that should do the trick. Everybody grab one and start working your way up to the ramp. Let's get the shovels and scrape out a path to follow while we're at it."

"Great, more shoveling," Marco grumbled from the rear of the group. "That one protein bar ain't gonna cut it."

Chapter 26

Lauri begged to be released from firearms training with the excuse she needed to be putting the food inventory together. Amanda seemed relieved to accommodate her request. She hurried back to the house with Will along for protection. When they got inside, she hung her coat by the door and heaved a sigh.

"Thank goodness that's over. I've never been so scared in my life." Lauri hurried into the living room to warm her hands by the wood stove. Will followed. "I just don't think I'll be able to do that. Handle a gun, I mean."

"I think you're going to have to figure out how to get past that, Mom," he said as he extended his own hands toward the stove. "You didn't see those guys that were outside. I think one of them was about to pull a gun on Elliott. It's getting bad already, and it hasn't even been a week. We have to learn how to defend ourselves."

Lauri was wringing her hands anxiously. "I don't know if I can, Will. Guns are so dangerous. All I can think is I might accidentally shoot one of you ... one of us. I could never live with myself if something like that happened."

"That's why we're training, so nothing like that happens." Will turned around so his backside was toward the stove. "No one is going to hand you a gun and say, *Here, good luck with that.* But you need to learn, Mom. The world is changing — fast. We have to get ready for what's coming."

"I don't think I'll ever be ready to shoot someone, Will. I don't think I could."

"What if someone was pointing a gun at Carly or one of the boys? What if you were the only one that could stop them?"

Lauri didn't answer. She was shaking her head and had tears streaming down her face. Will stepped over and wrapped his arms around her. "It's okay, Mom. We'll figure it out. Honestly, I don't know if I can shoot someone either. I hope neither one of us has to find out."

Lauri wiped her eyes and took a deep breath. "I think I'll go start working on that inventory. Do you want to help?"

"Sure thing. If we have to work, inside work on a cold day like this is my choice." Will grinned in an attempt to lighten the mood. It worked. Lauri smiled at her son.

"Amen, honey."

"Focus on your breathing, Carly," Amanda said from behind her. "Don't think about anything but steady breathing."

Carly's finger twitched on the side of the barrel.

"No, keep your finger away from the trigger. We're just breathing and getting used to holding the gun." Amanda was speaking in a calm, even tone. There was almost a cadence to it.

Carly relaxed a bit, closed her eyes and stood there holding the pistol in front of her and breathing in and out slowly.

Amanda went on. "Okay, now open your eyes and focus on the front sight of your pistol. Don't worry about anything else."

Carly opened her eyes. "I see it."

"Good. Now, slowly move the barrel until the front sight dot is in line with the back-sight dots."

Carly closed her right eye. Amanda saw this and said, "Wait, stop. Hand me the gun — safely."

Carly knew what she meant after being admonished multiple times about watching the barrel. She pointed the pistol down at the ground and passed it to Amanda. "Did I

194

do something wrong again? I'm never going to get this right."

"No, no you didn't do anything wrong. Elliott, I think I figured out what's going on here." Amanda had turned to Elliott with a big grin on her face.

"What is it?" Elliott asked, looking confused. "Is the weapon faulty?"

"Nope. Carly, hold your hand out like it's a gun and line up on your fingertip."

Confused herself, Carly did as instructed. She pointed her right finger and closed her eye. Her right eye.

Elliott's face lit into a smile. "Holy cow! Now I know what's wrong. Why didn't I see that before?"

In an exasperated tone, Carly blurted out, "What? I'm hopeless, right? I suck at this."

Elliott laughed. "No, Carly girl. You're not hopeless. You're right-handed and left eye dominant."

Completely clueless, Carly replied, "Come again?"

"Watch me." Amanda handed Elliott the gun Carly had been working with and simulated holding one using her hand as the gun. Closing her left eye, she said, "Do you see which eye I close automatically?"

Carly nodded. "Your left."

"Right. Er, correct. Right-handed people are usually right eye dominant. But you automatically closed your right eye. That means you're left eye dominant. It's not that common but it is a thing. We just have to help you make your right eye dominant for shooting."

"Or teach her to shoot left-handed," Elliott added.

"I wonder which would be easier and faster?" Amanda queried thoughtfully.

"Let's get her to try shooting lefty first. The problem is the brass ejecting in front of her eye is going to be distracting. Hang on a sec." Elliott went to the bag they had

195

brought and pulled out a small revolver. "Okay, Carly, try shooting this one with your left hand."

Carly's eyes grew wide. "Are you nuts? I can't do anything with my left hand. Something as simple as stirring my coffee with that hand feels clumsy. I'm pretty sure trying to shoot with it is more dangerous than I already am."

"Humor me." Elliott handed her the Ruger LCR .38 special, after making sure it was loaded. "Just use your right hand to hold it steady."

Doubt written on her face, Carly took the pistol in her left hand. "It feels weird."

Elliott nodded. "It will at first. Take your time, line up on the target and give it a go."

Carly hesitantly took the pistol, mindful of her trigger finger position, in her right hand. She switched to her left and lined up on the paper target. She looked at the gun for a moment then let it drop.

"There's no back dots." She raised it again to show them.

"There won't be on that gun, honey. Just line that front sight up on the target. Let the sight cover what you're aiming at." Elliott pointed to the front sight. "Actually, this is an updated sight. That's a night vision sight. Very helpful under low light conditions."

Carly turned her attention back to the gun and the target in front of it. She took a deep breath, blew it out slowly, moved her trigger finger in place and squeezed. The recoil pitched the gun up in front of her. "Wow! That's got a kick. A lot more power than the other one."

She turned to look at the rest of the group. Everyone was smiling at her.

"What? What are you all grinning about? What'd I miss?" she asked suspiciously.

"Not the target," Ethan said with a grin. He pointed down range to a pristine target save one hole a bit high and to the right. The body silhouette placed her shot squarely on the left shoulder.

"Oh. My. God. I hit it. I freakin' hit it!" Carly started jumping up and down with her finger still on the trigger. Elliott quickly stepped over to her and grabbed the gun.

"No celebrating with a loaded weapon!" he barked at her. She calmed down but couldn't hide her giddiness.

"I can't believe it. All this time I thought I sucked at it. I was just doing it wrong for my brain."

Aaron snickered. "Yeah, Mom, if anyone tells you you aren't right in the head, you can tell them that actually you are."

"Huh?" Cameron looked at his older brother. "What do you mean?"

"The left side of your brain controls the right side of your body and vice versa. So, if Mom is left eye dominant, the right side of her brain controls that."

"No sh— um, I mean … wow. That's amazing." Cameron blushed as the almost verbalized expletive was quickly covered up. Not quite quick enough, though, from the scowls on the faces of his mother and both grandfathers. His father and brother, along with Amanda, were trying to hide their smiles and giggles.

"Well, I for one am tickled for you, darlin'," Joel said as he draped an arm over Carly's shoulders. It seemed a somewhat subtle attempt to take the focus off Cameron's slip. "How did it feel?"

"Strangely, it felt right, Dad. Not weird like I thought it would. How come I shot to the right, Elliott? I was aiming for the middle."

Elliott paused for a moment, then replied, "My guess is because you are, in fact, right-handed. Your dominant hand was trying to take over. Fortunately, you don't have a lot of experience shooting yet so you haven't built up muscle memory for this task. I think your left hand can do what it needs to do without interference from the right with a little practice. Great job, Carly girl! I knew you could do it."

The right corner of Carly's mouth turned up. "I didn't. Can I try again, just to make sure it wasn't a fluke?"

Everyone standing there looked around the group in awe.

"You actually want to shoot again?" Amanda asked, a look of surprise on her face.

Carly shrugged. "It felt better than before. And I actually hit the target. That was kind of ... cool. There, I said it. I liked it."

Elliott nodded. "Absolutely. Just take your time and get a little bit firmer grip on the gun with your left hand."

Carly stepped up to the makeshift shooter's bench. Concentration etched into her face, she chewed the edge of her bottom lip as she lined up her shot. She fired and barely flinched. She stared at the target. Perfect center mass shot.

She laid the revolver on the bench and turned to the shocked group. Hands on her hips, she boasted, "Okay. I think I've got this. I'm trained now."

Elliott laughed as he shook his head. "Not by a long shot, missy. You're going to have to hit that target consistently a lot more times than this and learn proper safe gun handling. But it is a good start. Okay, everybody, let's get this stuff packed up and get back to the house. Plenty of work to be done yet today."

"Aw, man, I wanted to shoot some more," Cameron said in a whiny voice.

"The apocalypse isn't going anywhere, Cam," Joel replied. "You'll have plenty of time to practice, too."

They were heading back to the house when they heard an unfamiliar sound — unfamiliar to their current reality anyway. They all stopped in their tracks to listen.

It was a running vehicle.

~~~~~

After stumbling upon Elliott's place, Cody Randolph was determined to get his hands on it. Not knowing for sure how many people they had, he thought doubling the number of his own men was a good and achievable goal.

They had driven down Highway 14 for a while but the further they got from Memphis, the less densely populated they found the surrounding area. He turned around and headed back the way they had come.

"Change your mind?" Wayne Mitchell asked from the passenger seat.

"Only about where I'm going to look for people. I think I want to stick closer to the place we're going to take so we can keep an eye on it. I don't want anybody else coming in and thinking it's up for grabs. Maybe some of his neighbors know how many people are staying there. No matter what — that place is ours." Cody was increasing his speed slowly, since the road was still covered in snow, but it seemed to be getting slushy. He eased back the other direction. "And we're keeping the blond and any other chicks they have in there."

An evil gleam in their eyes, Bo Carver and Doug Hartman bumped fists in the back of the van.

"Warmth, water, and women," Bo said with a leering grin. "That place is a triple win."

Chapter 27

General Everley's mood had not improved.

"I can't believe they would even consider leaving us to fend for ourselves!" He was pacing the conference room, face red with anger, alternating between yelling out loud to no one in particular and mumbling expletives under his breath to himself. President-elect Roman tried to calm him down.

"Charles, please sit down and try to relax for a bit. You're going to give yourself a heart attack or a stroke if you don't, and I'm not sure what we have for medical personnel at the moment."

Everley plopped down in one of the black leather chairs. "What are we going to do? How do we feed millions of people long-term, in the middle of winter, with no factories, no trucks or trains running, no communications — I don't see how we can do it."

"If the theories are to be believed, it won't be that many for long," Phil Roman replied solemnly. "Everyone on life support is gone by now. Everyone on oxygen will suffocate when the supply they have on hand is gone. Those who depend on dialysis or prescriptions to regulate their heart or blood pressure ... it will truly become survival of the fittest."

The room was quiet. The sound of pills rattling was heard, and all heads turned to it. General Anton Drysdale had emptied a prescription bottle into his hand. He looked down at the pills then up to the faces looking at him.

"Looks like I'm good for at least a month. Depending on the stress level, who knows after that with my blood pressure," he replied with a shrug of his shoulders.

Roman nodded. "The next phase is starvation and disease. Without sanitation, waste won't be dealt with properly. What food and water we have now can easily become contaminated, and most people don't know how to safely handle those things when conditions are not necessarily clean. Couple that with not being able to get to a doctor or hospital for treatment — and even if they could, there's no power there either — and we'll end up with a dysentery or typhoid epidemic, both of which need strong antibiotics to treat them. It's going to get ugly, and it's going to last for a while."

"There's nothing we can do to help or stop the spread of disease?" General Angie Bale asked, voice laced with despair. "I mean, people lived a long time before electricity. Some people still live without it today. If our ancestors made it ..." She let the statement hang in the air.

"The problem is people today — most people anyway — have never lived without it," Roman replied. "They never knew a time when water didn't come out of a faucet or when food came from the local farmer, not the local grocery store. Very few know how to hunt or how to grow a vegetable garden; most of them are clueless about things like that. On top of that, winter is just beginning. We'll have a long few months before crops can go in the ground. How many people will starve to death before spring? For them to learn those things, we need people who know how to do it to teach them.

"Then there's logistics. How do we get word to the people with no communications? Everything we do is centered around electricity. If we tried to use word of mouth, how long would it take to reach the people? A hundred and fifty years ago, horses were the mode of transportation and everybody had them. We're dependent on cars and trucks that no longer run. The last I heard, about seventy percent of the population of this country was overweight and out of shape. They won't be walking far. I'm completely open to suggestions here, people."

The room was quiet. Everyone seemed lost in their own thoughts at the enormity of the situation. Finally, General Carl McKenna spoke up.

"I can't even begin to fathom how we will feed millions of people nor how we can reach them. What do we have in hardened storage, maybe a hundred trucks? Hell, that's enough for … what, a couple of hundred miles around D.C.? Maybe if we had some kind of centralized location like Kansas to act as a hub. We transport the supplies there and disperse them."

"How do we get the supplies there?" Angie asked. "And what supplies are we talking about? We don't have any large caches that I'm aware of."

"Those bastards at the U.N. are going to send us aid or wish they had later." Everley had a resolute look on his face. "They can send us some more vehicles and semis to haul the stuff with while they're at it. If they don't, things will be a whole lot different when we get back on our feet. And we *will* get back on our feet."

"Charles is right," Roman added. "The discussion with the Security Council is not over, not by a long shot. We may wait to contact them again until Mr. Tanner arrives. He's really good at negotiations. Any update on when that will be, Charles?"

"I talked to Sorley at daybreak. They're in Maryland. Had a run-in on a bridge with some locals. It didn't end well for the locals."

Everley gave them a short version of the episode. Eyes wide, Angie asked, "Is it that bad already? I thought we'd have at least a week before we saw that kind of thing."

"It's that bad," Charles said quietly. "That wasn't the first altercation they've had either. One of the guardsmen is already wounded."

202

Roman's head shot up. "Wounded? What happened?"

"She's fine. Took a round, through and through. I'll let them tell everyone about it when they get here. They should be past Baltimore by now and well on their way down 95. I think they'll be okay until they start getting close to Washington. I told Sorley to call me when they hit the outskirts. We'll send an escort to get them the rest of the way safely and without interruption. I expect to hear from him any time now."

"Good Lord — shooting at the National Guard? Who does something like that?" Angie's tone reflected the expressions on the faces of the other chiefs.

"Desperate people." Roman's solemn tone bespoke his feelings on the matter. "It's started, sooner than I hoped, but not completely unexpected. We will definitely need to muster as many National Guard members as we can find. This is spinning out of control already."

Everley looked at General McKenna. "Carl, I think you should take on finding our National Guardsmen. I suggest we offer to pay them in supplies. Any of them with families will probably jump at the chance to get their hands on food."

"Yeah, I can do that," McKenna replied. "And that should be a great incentive for them to report in. Everybody's going to be looking for ways to feed their families. We just have to figure out how to find them with no way to contact them."

"I think I can help with that." Vanessa Jackson, Olstein's former chief of staff, came in, followed by David Strain. "President Olstein had us load a database with all active military members onto servers down here. It was updated and backed up daily. I wasn't sure why he wanted it, but I think it's exactly what you need to find them."

The men stood when she entered the room. She shook hands with Phil Roman and General Everley, who were

203

closest to the door, then took a seat, nodding to each of the chiefs in turn as she greeted them. When she was seated, everyone else sat down again.

"I'm so glad you're here, Vanessa," Roman said with a smile. "You know more about what we have to work with than probably anyone else in Washington at the moment. I assume David brought you up to speed on the way?"

She smiled in return. "Yes, and I must say none of it surprised me. I commend you for taking over before things got too far gone. Just tell me what I can do to help."

"Getting us on that database is a great start," Charles replied. "What if we take the people we have here and start sending them out in small squads to round up the troops? When they get enough for another squad, we send that one a bit further out. They can set up a base of operations at the closest guard post."

"But how do we stay in contact?" Angie asked. "We don't have enough satphones."

"There are other lists ..." Vanessa paused. "Bulk purchases of food and medical supplies made by people online, gun and ammunition purchases from states where those things are recorded ... and people with ham radio licenses."

"He was tracking all of that? Why?" Roman asked, incredulously.

Vanessa shrugged. "He never said why, but my guess is in case something like this actually happened. Even though he blew off the report from the EMP commission publicly, I think deep down he believed it to be a real possibility. I think he was hedging his bets."

"That sounds about right," Everley said gruffly. "But the ham radios won't work either. They use electricity. They'll be fried like everything else."

"Maybe not," Anton Drysdale interjected. "If he was tracking the people I think he was tracking, they may have taken precautions against a situation like this."

"He was, General." Vanessa had a knowing look on her face. "He was monitoring preppers."

Drysdale nodded. "Then there could definitely be working radios out there. And not just ham radios. There may be two-ways that work as well."

Angie looked at him, confusion apparent on her face. "How can that be if everything electronic is toast?"

"Simple. Faraday cages," Drysdale replied nonchalantly. "If they shielded the equipment, it should be good to go."

"I've heard of those. Do they really work?" Angie asked, intrigued.

Drysdale grinned. "I guess we're going to find out."

"And the sooner the better," Roman added. "Vanessa, I hate to put you to work as soon as you walk in the door —"

Vanessa waved a hand in the air. "I've been bored out of my skull since I left. It's not like Netflix is working."

Roman chuckled. "Good. Angie, if you'll go with Vanessa and get the database loaded, I'd like to start printing off lists of people to find. Start within a thirty-mile radius of D.C. Vanessa, if you can provide us with lists of all the National Guard post locations in the same area, we can check there for personnel and supplies."

"Personnel? Do you think there are guardsmen there?" Vanessa asked, cocking her head to the side.

Everley commented, "There could be. Major Sorley found some in New Jersey. They can't be the only ones to have holed up in their post."

"Great. That would save some time and resources." Vanessa stood up and headed for the door. "Right this way, General."

"Angie, please," Angie replied. "I think we're all going to get to know each really well in the coming days and weeks."

Vanessa reached for the door handle and turned back to Angie. "Yes, ma'am, I believe you're right."

Chapter 28

Damon called General Everley when they were about twenty miles outside of D.C. He figured they'd run into their escort just as they reached the bigger residential areas, and he was correct. Just after crossing the Patuxent River they found the two Humvees that would be their escorts at a cross-through on I-95. Roy Dorn had offered to drive, and Damon had taken him up on it so that he could coordinate the meet-up.

Roy came to a stop in the center lane. Everyone climbed out of all the vehicles to greet the escort and stretch their legs. Damon walked around the front of the Humvee; a slight limp apparent in his gait. Hutch went to him, concern etched on his face.

"You okay, Damon?"

Damon nodded as he rubbed the old wound. "Yeah, just stiff. I'm not used to sitting for two days straight."

"Hopefully, that's about to end," Hutch replied. "I think you're due for some leave, Major."

"If General Everley offers it, I'll take him up on it," Damon said with a grin.

The soldiers from the escort reached them, came to attention and snapped a salute. "Captain Steve Bird, Major. Honored to escort you and your people to the White House. This is Lieutenant Frank Horton," he indicated the man to his left, "and Master Chief John Lundy."

Damon returned the salute and inspected the servicemen's uniforms. "At ease, gentlemen. I see we're representing pretty much all the branches, guys. Army, Air Force, Marines and Navy. Good to see you. Any signs of trouble on your way through town?"

Steve relaxed and addressed Damon. "Yes, Sir, they've been scrounging military personnel from all over the city. It kind of feels like the branches are going to merge. As far as the city goes, it isn't pretty, but no one tried to accost us. The looters have taken pretty much anything of value, especially food, water, blankets, those kinds of things. Military facilities are secure for now."

"For now?" Hutch chimed in. "Is that subject to change, Captain?"

"We're expecting it to get worse as the hoarded supplies dwindle," Steve said. "It won't take the people long to figure out there are other options besides Safeway and Walmart for food."

Damon crossed his arms. "I would think a line of armed soldiers would be a deterrent."

"Normally it would, but desperate people do desperate things," Steve replied. "Starving people do crazy things."

"Indeed, they do, as we've seen already on our trip here." David Tanner approached the group of military men. They seemed to be standing a bit taller when he reached them. "Our country is in disarray and it's getting worse by the minute. If you gentlemen are ready, I think we should make our way to our destination. There's no time to spare."

"Right you are, Sir. Steve, one of your vehicles in front of us and one behind, okay? Let's finish this trip. Lead the way." Damon reached out to shake Steve's hand. They shook hands and headed to their respective rides.

"I'll take over driving, Roy. You can hang with your men in the camper." Hutch followed Damon to the Humvee.

"Works for me," Roy said as he changed direction and went toward the trailer.

When everyone was back in their respective vehicles, the convoy headed out. Hutch grinned. "It's nice to have some more warm bodies. I may be able to let my puckered sphincter relax now."

Those inside the Humvee chuckled. Brock looked up at his father and said, "Dad, what's a sphincter?"

"It's a muscle in your ... um, behind." He didn't elaborate.

"The one that helps you poop?" the child asked innocently.

"Yes, son, that one."

"Maybe mine will unpucker, too, then. This was a scary trip."

The occupants burst out in laughter. The mood of the travelers was definitely lifted having more support.

Hutch looked up into the rear-view mirror. "Sorry, Sir. I don't have kids, so I forget we have little ears in here with us."

Tanner smiled back at him. "It's fine, Captain. You could have chosen a much worse phrase."

"Roger that, Sir. It was on the tip of my tongue." Hutch glanced over at Damon. "How far to the White House?"

Damon was checking the map and measuring. "Looks like about twenty miles if we take the shortest route through town. I'm not sure what route Bird is going to take."

Hutch pointed to Damon's phone. "He's got a satphone, right? Call him and find out."

"I must be tired. It didn't even dawn on me to use the phone." Damon reached for his phone and called the Air Force captain. They talked for a few minutes. When Damon shut the phone off, he turned to Hutch. "He said we're going right down New Hampshire Avenue to Sherman, then Euclid to 16th. That's how they came out to meet us and they've already cleared a path."

"Residential or commercial areas?"

Damon looked at his maps again. "Mixed bag. I'm not too worried about the residential neighborhoods with a convoy of three Humvees though."

Tanner leaned forward. "Isn't Lafayette Square going to be between us and the White House?"

Damon turned and nodded. "Yes, Sir. They said we'll be driving around it. They've manually dropped the barriers on Madison and have it barricaded until we get there."

Tanner sat back, and they rode in relative silence for a while, the only sound coming from the large tires pushing through the deep snow.

Their trip was uneventful until they exited onto New Hampshire and reached Silver Spring. A large housing complex was on the right and they could see residents out milling about. The sound of the engines of the three military vehicles turned heads, and people were hurrying toward the street. They were shouting something, but between the thick windows and the roar of the tires, those inside the Humvee couldn't hear what it was.

"Uh oh." Hutch was watching the crowd making its way to the road. The hatch of the front Humvee opened, and a head popped up with a rifle. The voice over a loudspeaker could be heard.

"Stay back! Do not approach the vehicles. We have no supplies for you at this time. If you do not comply, you will be fired upon!"

The shooter in the hatch brought his weapon to bear. The crowd hesitated. Damon looked into the side-view mirror and saw that the Humvee in the rear had moved over a lane, closer to the right side of the road, and had its own shooter aiming at the restless group of people. The mob stopped, apparently unwilling to test the threat. They were still yelling and flipping off the caravan as it passed.

As the convoy continued on its way, people from houses on both sides of the street who had obviously heard the vehicles or the loudspeaker, or both, were lining the sides of it shaking their fists and throwing things at the vehicles, holding swaddled babies aloft as if they could somehow elicit sympathy for the children's plights. Melanie had silent tears running down her face as she watched them go by, helpless to do anything. Her husband reached over and took her hand, gently squeezing it.

"As soon as we can, we'll send people out to help," he told her resolutely.

"What if it's too late for those babies?" she asked, heartbreak apparent in her voice.

"We'll just have to pray it isn't," Tanner replied as he released her hand and patted it before turning back to watch the crowd.

They were working their way nearer to the city itself, going through residential areas where the speed limit was thirty-five miles per hour. They were moving along at close to fifty.

"Looks like Bird is trying to fly," Hutch grumbled, as he struggled to keep the Humvee in the ruts being left by the front vehicle.

"Funny," Damon replied. "He probably figures no one will try to accost us at this speed."

"I wouldn't. Oof!" Stephens called out from the back as he was thrown into the side. "Nothing to hang on to back here, Hutch."

"Sorry, man. Cowboy up cuz this bronc is a buckin'!"

Careening down the street through abandoned cars which had been pushed aside, as evidenced by the large dents in them, they saw the sign telling them they had entered the District of Columbia. There was a renewed sense of urgency among them. They were getting close.

The satphone rang. Damon answered it almost immediately. "Sorley."

He listened to the caller on the other end for a moment then with a grim nod replied, "Understood. We're on your six." He clicked the phone off and turned to Hutch. "We're coming up on a place where New Hampshire heading south makes a jog. We're going to cross over into the northbound lanes, so we don't have to slow down. Just stay behind them."

"Roger that." Hutch's hands were gripping the steering wheel tightly.

They were approaching Grant Circle. Bird wasn't slowing down.

Hutch's eyes got wide. "He does remember we're hauling a camper, right? I can't make that turn at this speed."

"Slow down to whatever speed you need to make the turn safely. If he doesn't reduce his speed and gets too far ahead, I'll call him." Damon had the phone in his hand ready to dial.

There were townhouses extremely close to the street in the circle. Some of the residents were out on their stoops talking to each other. The first Humvee barreling around the circle caught their attention.

"Shit." Hutch watched as two women started toward the street then ran out into the street, frantically waving their arms for attention. They were standing directly in the path the first Humvee had left as it passed them.

"I'm gonna need someone in that hatch, pronto!" Hutch yelled. "Manning!"

"On it, Cap!" she called out. She had been sitting directly under it and only had to stand up to open it. Damon was dialing the phone when it rang.

"This is Lundy. We're coming around. Get Bird to make the circle and take our spot."

The second Humvee passed them on the left and pulled in front of them. Hutch slowed down but stayed close to their new escort. With the hatch open, they could clearly hear the loudspeaker in Lundy's vehicle.

"Move aside! We will not stop! You will be run down if you don't comply! This is your only warning!"

Hutch and Damon could no longer see the two women as they were hidden by the Humvee. They heard a scream then saw the women dive to either side of the advancing vehicle. Lundy went on and Hutch followed. Bird had made the loop and was behind them.

Shutting off the phone, Damon commented, "Bird said he was sorry for flying the coop."

"Funny." Hutch shook his head. "Did I hear you say we're keeping this convoy a little tighter from here on in?"

"Yes, and a bit slower. We've got wide streets right now on down Sherman, but Euclid is narrow. It's an upper middle-class area but desperate people ..." Damon let the sentence dangle.

Hutch heaved a big sigh. "Great. Can't wait."

As they drove on, they saw people out everywhere. The temperature outside was right at freezing but the sun was shining, and it seemed the people preferred the cold sunshine to the not quite as cold and dark interiors of their homes.

"Man, there's people everywhere. What's the population anyway?" Hutch was staring ahead but using his peripheral vision to keep an eye on potential threats.

Damon was trying to keep eyes on everyone he could. "Over six hundred thousand last I heard. The District of Columbia has the highest population density of all U.S. states, with over eleven thousand people per square mile."

"I'm thinking it's not going to be the place to be real soon," Hutch said. "I think I'm starting to pucker again."

"Your sphincter, Mr. Hutch?" Brock chimed in from the back seat. Damon and Stephens stifled a laugh. Tanner chuckled and Melanie covered her face with her hand.

Hutch looked up into the rear-view mirror and gave him a nervous grin. "Exactly, buddy. But don't you worry. You're going to be safe in the White House."

The boy smiled. Hutch shot Damon a look. Damon gave him a curt nod and replied under his breath, "I hope so, too."

Chapter 29

They stood listening until the vehicle had passed the house. The sound coming from the muffler faded into the distance.

"Was that a car?" Cameron asked of no one in particular.

"Yes. Let's get this stuff packed up and get back to the house pronto." Elliott was handing guns and ammo to Amanda, who was filling the duffel bag as fast as she could.

"Why? What's going on?" Carly asked as she hurried over with the pistol which she tried to hand to Amanda as well. Amanda raised her hand to take it, but Elliott laid his own hand on hers.

"You keep that, Carly girl. Put it in your pocket. That goes for the rest of you, too. Keep a side arm on you." Elliott went back to what he was doing. "We'll talk about it when we get inside where it's warm."

When the bag was loaded, Aaron picked it up and they all headed toward the house. Lauri met them on the back porch.

"Did you hear that? Another car that runs! Maybe it's not as bad as we thought it was going to be," she said excitedly. Upon seeing the grim looks on the faces of her family, she wrapped her arms around herself and added, "… or not. What's wrong?"

Elliott was directing traffic from the steps. "Come on, everybody. Inside, quickly." He turned to Lauri. "We'll talk about it inside, okay?"

She nodded, worry etched on her face, and went through the door Joel was holding open for her. When they were all in the house, coats hung up, and snowy shoes and boots left by the door, Lauri went on. "Well? Why is another car that works bad, Elliott?"

Elliott motioned with his hand for her to follow him into the living room where the family had gathered to warm themselves by the wood stove. He said nothing while he stretched his hands out toward the heat source. Everyone looked at him expectantly until Carly blurted out, "For God's sake, Elliott, spill it! What's so bad about hearing another car on the road?"

Elliott looked up at her then took in each of the rest of them in turn. Finally, he said, "Have you heard any other vehicles since this mess started? Besides the one that brought you here, that is."

Everyone slowly shook their heads and waited for him to go on. "Me, neither. I'm pretty sure that if any of the neighbors around here had one, we would have seen or heard it by now. That means that car or whatever it was we heard is carrying people who don't live in this area. They're out here looking for something, like those guys that were here earlier. We need to start thinking about security."

"Like guard duty, Pap? I can stand guard. Just tell me when and where. Oh, and how. Will we have a password? I'm sure I'll need to carry a gun. Which one is best for guard duty?" Cameron peppered his grandfather with questions, bouncing in excitement. Amanda laughed along with Will, Ethan grinned, and Aaron rolled his eyes.

"This isn't a game, Cameron," Carly replied sternly. "Teenagers do *not* stand guard. Tell him, Elliott." She crossed her arms in a huff.

"Well ..." Elliott drew the word out before he went on. "We'll probably need everybody to take a shift. There's ten of us here and twenty-four hours in a day. If we went with two per shift, that's going to be almost five hours per team to cover the place the whole time."

216

"No, Elliott, I'm putting my foot down on this," Carly shot back at him. "Aaron and Cameron are not soldiers, or policemen. What if those guys come back? No, it's too dangerous."

"Car, everything is dangerous now. What if those guys came back and we didn't know until they'd busted down the door because we weren't watching?" Will spoke softly to his sister as he looked at his nephews. "Aaron is almost eighteen. That's old enough to enlist if he wanted to — without your permission. During the Revolutionary War, there were kids as young as fifteen fighting for our freedom. They aren't babies anymore, sis. They aren't little boys. You can't protect them forever, and you sure can't protect them from what we're facing now."

Carly's face was beet red as she turned on her brother. "Are you actually agreeing to this, Will? You only have two nephews. Are you willing to risk their lives? Because I'm not! I'm their mother and what I say goes!"

"All of our lives are at risk now," Ethan interjected. "Were you at the window this morning? Did you see that one of those guys was about to pull a gun out on Dad and me?"

"You don't know that for sure!" Carly screeched. "He could have been just trying to keep his hand warm. And this is none of your business anyway, Ethan. You have no say in what these kids can or can't do. You gave up that right when you left us!" She turned on her heel and stomped back to the kitchen. Lauri went after her.

There was an awkward silence hanging heavily in the room. It was broken by Cameron.

"I think she's warming up to you a little bit, Dad," he said with a sly grin. Aaron snickered behind his hand.

Ethan's grim face changed to just the hint of a smile. "What makes you say that, Cam?"

217

"Well, she didn't shoot you. She is armed, you know. And she's figured out how to use it."

The room erupted in much needed laughter.

Ethan laid a hand on Cameron's shoulder. "You may be right about that, son."

"I wouldn't test that theory," Joel said with a hint of mirth. "She may have forgotten she had it on her."

Ethan's eyes grew wide. "Good point."

"The nerve of him thinking he has any right to tell me anything about how to raise my boys!" Carly was pacing like a caged animal around the large country kitchen, hissing the words through her teeth in a loud whisper. "He shows up after ten years and wants to play daddy now? It's too late for that."

Lauri was wringing her hands. "Honey, please calm down. I don't think that's what he was doing or is trying to do."

Carly stopped just short of the open doorway to the living room and put her hand on her hips. "Then what it is, Mom? What am I missing?"

Lauri looked at her daughter with a tear running down her cheek. "I think he's trying to make amends. I think he just wants to spend some time with them, get to know them before he ... you know ... dies."

Carly opened her mouth then closed it. She leaned around the door jamb and peeked into the living room. Ethan's hand was on Cameron's shoulder and they were all laughing at something she hadn't heard. As if sensing she was watching, Ethan turned and looked at her. With the laughter still in his eyes, he gave her an almost imperceptible nod of his head. He then turned back to the conversation.

"Yeah, I guess," Carly replied with less venom in her tone. "I keep forgetting he's not going to be here much

218

longer. In some ways, he's still the Ethan I knew when we were younger. Charming when he wants to be, defensive and stubborn at other times. But he's also calmer, not so easy to lose his temper. He seems more … I don't know … peaceful maybe. The old Ethan would have been raging against the world right now, saying it wasn't fair that this was happening to him, what had he done to deserve this, blah, blah, blah. We all know what he did to deserve it. But still —"

"No one deserves what he's got coming, Carly girl," Elliott said as he joined them in the kitchen. "Yes, he was a bad husband and father and son. But without meds for the pain, he's going to die —" Elliott's voice caught in his throat as a tear formed in the corner of his eye. He reached up and wiped it away. "I'm sorry. I didn't mean to interrupt. Just looking for a cup of joe."

Lauri hurried to the stove and turned the burner on under the cold percolator. "I'll have this heated up in just a few minutes, Elliott. Can I get you anything else?" Lauri seemed embarrassed, busying herself with wiping off the counter next to the sink.

"No, the coffee will be fine. Were you able to get a good inventory on our food stores?" Elliott's attempt to change the subject did not go unnoticed by either woman.

Lauri heaved a relieved sigh. "Yes, I did. I think we'll be okay for two to three months. We can make soups and stews with meat from the freezer and the pasta you seem to have a lot of. I don't know anything about these freeze-dried foods you have. Do we just add them to the broth?"

"For the most part, yes," Elliott replied. "We may need to add a bit more liquid but then I'm pretty sure the soup will get more and more watery as the food stores dwindle. If we can make it three months and the weather isn't too harsh, we'll be able to plant some early spring crops before it's all gone. I'll do some hunting to supplement the meat, but the weather seems to be warming up already and we're probably going to have to start pulling stuff out of the freezer and get busy canning it soon, so we don't lose it. I think the extended forecast had us back up around fifty next week. Even with the makeshift generator, I don't want to take any chances on losing any food."

"I'm good with water bath canning but I don't know anything about pressure canning," Lauri said. "I hope you do."

"I do. I haven't done it in a while because it was just easier to put meat in the freezer, but I can still do it. We'll sit down together tomorrow and go over it, maybe pull some meat out and give it a go."

Lauri smiled. "That sounds great. Let me check that coffee." She touched the side of the pot and picked up a potholder, grabbing a cup off the draining rack at the same time. "I think this is hot enough now. Here you go, Elliott."

She filled the cup and handed it to him. He took a tentative sip. "Perfect. How much coffee did we have?"

Lauri checked her list. "Five three-pound canisters and a dozen jars of instant. I didn't know you liked instant coffee."

"I don't, but it's better than no coffee and it keeps forever. I mean, technically it's coffee, but it tastes different." Elliott seemed lost in thought for a moment. "That should last us a few months, at least. Then we'll be drinking dandelion root coffee."

"Gah! Weeds?" Carly's grimace was comical and caused Elliott to chuckle and Lauri to giggle.

"We'll see how you feel about that *weed* a week or so after the coffee runs out," Elliott said with a smirk. "I know how you are about your coffee."

"Did someone say coffee?" Amanda asked as she strolled into the kitchen. "I could use some if we have it."

"Enjoy it while you can," Carly remarked offhandedly. "Apparently, we're going to drink a weed-based, coffee-like substance when it's gone."

Amanda looked confused, Carly shrugged, and Lauri and Elliott laughed again. Lauri handed Amanda her cup. Amanda took a sip and looked at Elliott. "I can work up a patrol schedule if you want, Elliott. You've got a ton on your plate, and I know who the strong shooters are. We can pair strong and not so strong together until everybody gets their shooting skills up to snuff."

At the mention of the need for security, the mood in the room grew more solemn.

"That would be a big help, Amanda. I'd appreciate it," Elliott replied.

"It's the least I can do. You offered me a port in this crazy storm. I'm not sure where I'd be right now if I hadn't run into Will, which led us here — a safe place — well as safe as any place can be right now." She paused and chewed the edge of her bottom lip. "This place is sustainable if we can hang on to it."

"We'll do whatever we have to, because I'm not going down without a fight." Elliott set his jaw in determination.

The words were no sooner out of his mouth than Cameron burst into the kitchen. "Pap! There's a van coming up the driveway!"

Elliott hurried over to don his boots and grabbed his coat, along with the shotgun he had left by the back door, as the kitchen and living room became a flurry of activity. Lexi was running back and forth between both rooms barking and growling at the windows and doors. As he reached for the doorknob, Elliott said over his shoulder, "I guess the fight is here."

~~~~~

Cody, Wayne, Bo, and Doug hadn't had to go too far down the road before they found Taylor Livingston and his friends, Devon Brown and Jason Caton. The three were trying to chop wood with a hatchet. The sound of the van had all three men looking up in excitement. Cody pulled into the driveway and the three hurried over to the driver side door.

"Oh, man, are we glad to see you!" Taylor exclaimed. "Your van still works. That's awesome! Hey, any chance you can give us a ride into Millington? We're almost out of food and we have no running water. I need to pick up a bunch of stuff for my wife and kids. I'm Taylor, by the way. Taylor Livingston. These are my buddies, Devon Brown and Jason Caton. They live a few houses down."

"Dude, there's no food or water left in Millington," Cody said casually. "I don't think there's anything left in any stores. So, you guys are out, too, huh?"

Dejectedly, Taylor replied, "Yes. I don't know what we're going to do. I can't just sit and watch my kids starve to death. But if the stores are empty ..." His voice trailed off with a silent sob.

Cody saw an opportunity. "Well, what about your neighbors? Maybe they can lend a hand."

"I've tried," Taylor lamented. "Either they don't have any to spare, or they do, but won't help anybody else."

Cody pressed on. "Well, that doesn't sound very neighborly. Who was it that wouldn't help?"

Taylor pointed back in the direction of Elliott's place. "There's an old guy that lives on the other side of the Harrisons. His name is Elliott Marshall. I know he has food and water. He let us get some water from his well pump, and there was a plate of biscuits on the table the first time I was there. He's got a wood stove, too. It was so warm inside. I asked him to let us stay there but he said no, that he had a house full. I all but begged him, told him we'd help with chores, whatever we had to do, but he wouldn't budge."

"A houseful, huh? Did he say how many was there?" Cody asked innocently.

"Nine or ten, I think," Taylor replied. "Why?"

Cody ignored his question. "What would you do to get a place like that for your family?"

"Are you kidding me? I'd do anything!" Taylor's eyes lit up. "Do you know of a place?"

Cody looked at the other two men. "How about you fellas? You looking for a place like that, too?"

Jason spoke up first. "Hell yeah. I got a pregnant wife at home. She's freezing and our food is getting low, too."

Devon added, "No wife or kids for me but I definitely need a place better than mine. All I had was frozen pizzas, and I've been cooking them on the grill. It feels like it's warming back up, so they won't be frozen much longer."

Cody looked back at the occupants of the van and smiled. He turned around to the three men and said, "I think we need to talk."

Chapter 30

Damon and crew made it through D.C. There were a few skirmishes with some of the people out milling about who thought they could take on three Humvees filled with military personnel. They found out they were mistaken.

Gun laws in the District of Columbia are some of the strictest in the United States. The laws within the district that kept citizens from possessing firearms, or made it almost impossible for them to obtain the licenses and registrations required, put the residents at a distinct disadvantage. They had no handguns — not legally, anyway — and with the police department being the final say as to whether or not a rifle or shotgun registration would be approved, the people's Second Amendment rights were all but non-existent. Of course, none of those restrictions kept weapons out of the hands of the criminals.

The criminal element was emboldened by the lack of police presence and had been making its way through the city terrorizing and killing the unarmed for whatever supplies and valuables they had. As Hutch drove down Euclid, a nice area with neat houses side by side and late-model sedans parked on the street, Damon and his fellow travelers could see that the area had been under attack. Doors hung open, windows were broken out, and they saw more than one body lying on a porch or in a yard. Melanie tried to shield her son from seeing the carnage as the rest of them stared open-mouthed at the devastation.

"Dear God," David Tanner said from the back seat. "Is there nothing that can be done to protect these people?"

"I guess that's going to be one of the things you have to figure out, Sir," Damon replied quietly. "This is why conservatives fight so hard against infringement on the

Second Amendment. All it does is make the good people helpless, because the bad ones can and do still get guns. And at a time like this, good people need to be able to protect themselves from the bad people, because right now there's no one else to do it."

"I don't think the lawmakers who came up with all those restrictions thought something like this could happen," Tanner said.

Damon set his mouth to a grim line. "Yet here we are. And the people who those politicians were legislating so hard to *protect*," he made air quotes on the last word, "are suffering the most."

"Well, it's clear to me that instituting martial law would have no effect," Tanner replied. "As you said, criminals don't care about laws. I'm just not sure how we can protect the citizens without a police presence. I don't want to use the military. I don't want to militarize this country. But I'm not sure what other options we'll have in the immediate future."

"That's above my pay grade, Sir, but I hope you and those waiting for us at the White House can figure it out." Damon's phone rang just then. "Sorley." After a moment, he said, "Yes, General, we're almost there. We're heading down 16th right now. It looks like there's been quite a bit of criminal activity around town. If you have the people to spare, you might want to send some out to meet us. I'm not sure what we're going to run into when we get there, but I imagine there will be people outside looking for answers." Another few seconds passed. "Yes, Sir. I'd say we're ten minutes out. See you then."

As he was ending the call, Tanner asked from the back, "Were they aware of what's going on out here?"

Damon shook his head. "No, Sir, I don't think so. They've got a pretty wide perimeter around the White House secured, but they aren't sending teams out for intel. I think they're waiting for your arrival to determine what the next steps will be."

Tanner was writing in a small notepad. Without looking up, he replied, "If nothing else, this trip has shown me we have a lot of work to do and it needs to happen sooner rather than later."

They weren't expecting what they saw when they reached the entrance to Lafayette Square. Marines were lined up, weapons at the ready, along the H Street side. There was a line of Capitol police in front of the troops in riot gear holding shields. Citizens were facing them, shouting and throwing trash, rocks, bricks — pretty much whatever they could get their hands on.

"Not good." Hutch slowed down when the Humvee in front of them did. They heard Lundy's voice come over the loudspeaker.

"Clear the road! If you do not make way, you will be run down. This is your only warning. We are coming through!"

The rioters turned their attention to the Humvee issuing threats. They rushed the vehicle and were pounding on its windows and body. The Humvee moved slowly, but it kept moving. A man standing by the front quarter panel screamed when one of the Humvee's tires ran over his foot. The sound quieted the crowd as they took a step back. The lead vehicle pushed through the mob.

Seeing the camper behind the center Humvee, the irate citizens converged on it. They started pushing it from both sides, rocking it back and forth, which, since it was hitched to the Humvee, rocked it and its occupants as well. Damon watched in the side-view mirror as one of the windows was broken from the inside of the camper and a rifle barrel appeared. He couldn't hear what was going on. He didn't know exactly what lead up to it. But he saw the aftermath.

One of the people in the street tried to grab the barrel protruding from the window. In the struggle for control of the gun, a shot was fired — point blank into the face of the man trying to take it. Blood and brain matter splattered the people around him, and the crowd pulled back, many running away. Those who stayed retreated to the sidewalk, grumbling loudly amongst themselves.

The Marines and police took advantage of the mayhem and advanced to the caravan, pushing the mob back with their riot shields. As the three military vehicles came through the opening that had been created, the men on foot closed ranks behind them. They walked backward, keeping their eyes on the crowd until the caravan was inside the perimeter, then went back to their posts at the entrance to the square.

Once they got on the other side of Lafayette Square, the lead vehicle stopped just past the entrance to Executive Avenue. Hutch pulled up behind them and the follow vehicle came around beside the lead. Bird and Lundy walked back to Damon's Humvee. Damon rolled the window down.

"You should be good now, Major," Bird said. "Just go straight and use the side entrance. I think General Everley is waiting for you there. And I just wanted to say again how sorry I am I left you back there. It didn't register you wouldn't be able to maneuver as well with the load."

"It's fine. We're here. Thank you for the help, guys. I'm sure we'll see each other again." Damon saw that they were about to snap to and salute him. He waved them off. "No need for that. I'm pretty sure a bunch of the rules are about to change." He gave them a nod and rolled the window up. They headed for the East Wing.

General Everley was indeed waiting for them. When he saw the Humvee's approach, he pushed the door open and walked out onto the landing. The Marines, who had been standing guard at the entrance, fanned out to either side of him. His face broke into a huge grin when Damon climbed out and walked the two steps back to open the rear door. David Tanner emerged with his son in tow. Agent Stephens helped Melanie out on the other side. Once she had joined her husband and son, Damon escorted them up the walk. When he reached Everley he stood at attention and saluted him. The Guardsmen did the same.

"Major Damon Sorley, reporting as ordered with the incoming Commander-in-Chief."

Everley returned his salute. "At ease, Major, and well done. Mr. Tanner, welcome to the White House. The rest of the Joint Chiefs and President Roman are awaiting your arrival in the bunker. We'll take you there immediately."

"Thank you, General. Excuse me for one moment." Tanner turned to Damon. "Major, I want to thank you for all you've done to bring me and my family here safely. Well, as safely as you could." He had a mischievous grin on his face. "You faced adversity getting to us and more getting us here. The two hundred miles or so we've traveled together have been frightening and enlightening, and I can't help but think that without your bravery and dedication, as well as that of those here in Washington, this country's liberty was in jeopardy. We came two hundred miles for liberty. I believe it was worth the trip. Again, thank you." He shook Damon's hand then turned to Everley. "Lead the way, General. We have a lot of work to do, and we need to get started."

Everley stood to the side of the open door. "Right this way, Sir." He waited for the small family to get through the entrance, then looked back at Damon and the Guardsmen. "Outstanding job, men. Follow us down. We have barracks you can get some rest in, and we saved some chow for you."

Marco rushed forward. "Food, Sir? Real food?" The group chuckled at his actions.

Everley squinted at him. "Yes, Sergeant, real food. Enjoy it while you can. We may be eating MREs and protein bars three times a day in a month or so."

With a cheeky grin, Marco replied, "We're good with that too, Sir. And we'll definitely enjoy it while it lasts."

Chapter 31

Taylor and his friends stared open-mouthed at Cody.

"So, what do you guys think of my plan?" Cody asked nonchalantly. He and his associates had gotten out of the van and were standing beside it.

"Um ... I don't think I can do that," Taylor finally replied. "I mean, you want us to go over there and kick them out of their house? Where would they go?"

Cody shrugged. "Who cares? Your family would have everything you need to survive this mess. That's what you want, right? You said you'd do anything to take care of them. Life is going to get messy real fast. Hell, it already has. You said you don't know what you're going to do for food and water. You're going to have to be willing to do some things you might not necessarily *like* to do but *need* to in order to survive. You can't worry about other people. You have to put your family first. It's survival of the fittest time ... or the strongest anyway."

Jason stepped in. "And just how do you propose to get them to vacate the premises?"

"Well, we could ask them to leave nicely. But I don't think that's going to work. Looks like we're going to have to force them out." Cody leaned back a bit and crossed his arms over his chest. "I know there's some chicks in there and, according to you, a couple of kids, so I think with you three and us four we should be able to persuade them that it's best for everybody and safest for their women and kids to give it up. That way no one gets hurt."

"I'm out," Devon said as he turned to walk away. Taylor grabbed his arm.

"Wait, Devon! Where are you going? We need to talk this through."

Devon snatched his arm out of Taylor's grasp. "No, we don't. I'm not going to be a part of forcing someone out of their home, stealing their supplies, and God knows what else just because they have more than me. That's not how I roll. I'm surprised you'd even consider it, Tay."

Taylor's face turned red with either anger or embarrassment — or both. "It's easy for you, Devon! You don't have anyone depending on you. I've got a family to take care of. What do I do, let Wendy and the kids starve or freeze to death? You tell me — what am I supposed to do here?"

"Not this," Devon said shaking his head. "You staying, Jay?"

Jason hesitated. "I don't know. I need some place safe for Megan and the baby."

"What makes this guy's place any safer than your own?" Devon shot back.

"Well, for one thing, they have guns." Taylor's statement hung in the air.

Cody grinned. "Oh, yeah? How many?"

"I'm not sure but the old guy, Elliott, he said he was thinking about giving me one and teaching me how to shoot and hunt. So, I bet they have a bunch. Maybe we could keep some of them."

"Or we could keep all of them." Cody's grin had turned to a sneer. "We keep the guns; we keep our new place."

"So, how would that work?" Taylor asked tentatively. "Like, how would we split up the living space? I'm pretty sure Wendy is going to want us to have a room of our own. It'd be nice if the kids could have one ..."

Cody waved a hand at him. "We'll work all that out when we get in there. One step at a time."

"Well, good luck with that." Devon started to walk away. The sound of a hammer being cocked stopped him.

"Afraid I can't let you leave, friend," Cody said as he pointed the revolver in his hand at Devon. "What with you knowing our plan and all. You're going to have to come with us whether you want to or not."

Devon turned around and stared at Cody, his gaze flitting from the man's cold eyes to the weapon in his hand. He shifted his line of sight to Taylor, who was standing off to the side staring wide-eyed at the gun. "Is this what you want, Taylor? Is this who you're willing to become?"

Taylor stammered, "I didn't think ... I can't ..."

"It doesn't matter what he wants or what you want," Cody interrupted. "This is the way it is. The three of you are going to help us take that place. Now, everybody get in the van."

"You can't make us shoot at people!" Taylor lamented. "I've never shot a gun before. I might shoot one of you, for God's sake!"

"Don't worry. Your guns won't have bullets in them, just in case anyone gets any cute ideas." Cody looked into the rear-view mirror to meet eyes with Devon. "You're just for show ... a show of force. We'll handle the rest."

"But they have guns, too — loaded guns! What if they shoot us because we threaten them?" Taylor sounded like he was on the verge of tears.

"Well, I'd suggest you stay behind a tree or something." Cody looked over at Wayne with a smirk on his face.

Wayne chuckled. "Yeah, y'all best duck and cover," he added.

Devon shook his head. "You guys are insane. What's the plan? You think you can just drive up, point a gun at them and say, *get out,* and they'll do it? They have the upper hand, morons. It's their place. They're inside. Who knows what kind of fire power they have?"

"What, are you some kind of tactical expert?" Bo countered. "How do you know so much about ... what do they call it ... oh yeah. Urban warfare. I bet you learned all that from playing Call of Duty, huh?" Cody, Wayne, and Doug joined Carl in laughing at his own remarks.

"No, I'm just not stupid like you. You're going to get yourselves killed, and us along with you." Devon turned away and looked out the back window.

"Well, I'm not planning on dying today," Cody replied with a derisive snort. "I can't speak for the rest of you."

"I can't die! I have to get back to my family!" Taylor was shouting in a panic-filled voice. "Just stop the van. I won't tell anybody anything. I can walk from here, no problem. Please, just let me out!"

"Shut up!" Cody barked at him. "You're staying. Besides, we're here."

Cody turned into the driveway and sped up, tires spinning in the slushy snow. The back end of the van fishtailed, sending the occupants careening into the sides and each other.

"Damn, dude, chill!" Doug yelled from the rear. "Aren't you afraid they'll hear us coming?"

"They're going to hear us coming no matter what, Dougie," Cody said snidely. "This beast ain't exactly quiet. Just hang on."

He barreled up the driveway, sliding to a stop as the house came into view. He threw the van into park, shut it off, then turned to the rest of the men.

"Wayne, hand those three the old guns we found. We'll take the rest. Let's rock and roll, fellas. Heads down, guns high."

"No! I can't do this. I won't!" Taylor replied as he crossed his arms defiantly across his chest when Wayne tried to press the empty pistol into his hand.

Cody pulled his gun out and pointed it at Taylor. "You either do what I say, or I'll take you out myself then go back and find that wife of yours and ... well, use your imagination." He paused for effect and, with a sneer on his lips, added, "What'll it be?"

Wayne proffered the gun again. Taylor slowly reached out a trembling hand. Holding the strange weapon out in front of him, Taylor whispered, "O-okay. Just p-p-please don't hurt my wife or my kids."

"You do what I say, and they'll be fine. Now I want you three to hang out behind the van. We'll take the side. This shouldn't take long. They've got women in there to protect too, so —"

"How do you know they have women in there?" Jason cut in. "In fact, how did you know which house it was? Taylor didn't point it out."

With a sheepish grin, Cody replied, "Ha! You busted me. We were here earlier. We had an idea this would be a sweet score, but your man there sealed it. Anyway, it doesn't matter. We're here now. Let's do this. Everybody out."

Everyone climbed out, Cody and Wayne exiting the driver side, the rest out the back. When Bo and Doug had joined their buddies, Devon grabbed Taylor and Jason by the arm and pulled them close to him.

"Stay back. Lay those guns down. If the people inside come out, I'm going to let them know we aren't a part of this. We have to stop this before someone gets killed."

Vigorously nodding his head, Taylor added, "Especially us."

~~~~~~

Elliott was at the door with Ethan and Lexi. Aaron was right behind them, as was Amanda. Joel and Cameron were set up at the living room windows. Will was in the bedroom closest to the driveway.

Carly went to Aaron and hissed in his ear, "You are *not* going out there, young man! It's too dangerous. Go help your Uncle Will."

Aaron turned to his anxious mother. "Mom, I'll be eighteen in a few days. You're going to have to accept I'm not a little kid anymore. I'm not letting Pap go out there with just Da — um, Ethan. You stay here and protect Nana. I have to do this."

"No, you don't! Amanda will go. She's a better shot than you anyway." Carly had tears running down her face. "I'm supposed to protect *you*. That's how it works."

Aaron wrapped his free arm around her and squeezed. "Things change, Mom. Our world has turned upside down. We have to change, too. I'm doing this. Stay safe." He kissed the top of her head as Elliott opened the door. The four of them stepped out onto the porch. Amanda turned back to close the door behind them and caught Carly's eye.

"I'll watch out for him, Carly. You watch out for your mom." She pulled the door to behind her.

Elliott stopped at the top of the steps. Ethan was on his right, Aaron to his left. Amanda was left of Aaron, her rifle trained on the engine area of the van.

"Not sure who you are or what you're after, but y'all need to get off my property," Elliott called out calmly. Lexi had her hackles up as high as they would go, growling and straining against the hold Ethan had on her.

Cody peeked over the hood. "Hey there, Elliott. We weren't properly introduced earlier because you were kinda rude, like you're being now. But we found someone who knows you and knows all about how nice your place is. He didn't tell us you had anyone as hot as the gal on your porch there, though. Yeah, this place is damn near perfect for our needs."

Laughter could be heard from behind the engine block. Elliott was unfazed.

"Unfortunately for you all, it isn't available. I'll say again — get off my property now before someone gets hurt."

"Well, things are a little different now. We've got some more people with us who need a place like this, too. Step out and say hi fellas." Cody leaned back so that he could see the other three men. None of them moved. "I said, step out and say hi! Don't be rude like Elliott there."

Taylor, Jason, and Devon leaned around the back end of the van. Elliott peered at them.

"Taylor? Are you the one who told them about our place? And to think, I was going to help you."

"I-I'm sorry, Elliott! I didn't know what they were planning to do! I don't want to be a part of this, but they threatened my wife and kids. I just —"

"Shut up, Taylor!" Cody yelled. "Get back behind the van and keep your trap shut!"

Before they moved back, Devon called out, "We're not part of this, Mr. Marshall! They made us come at gun point. Our guns aren't even loaded. We aren't a threat."

Cody stood up. "All of you shut the hell up! He's lying, Elliott. They're just as a much a part of this as we are. Now, drop those guns and come on down before this gets ugly."

"It's already ugly," Amanda replied. "You, the situation, all of it."

Aaron laughed nervously, which enraged Cody. "You think this is funny, bud? Let's see who laughs now!"

Cody raised his handgun and aimed it at Aaron. He pulled the trigger and all hell broke loose.

Watching the scene unfold, Ethan released his hold on Lexi. Lexi took off like she had been fired from a gun herself toward the men hiding behind the front of the van.

Ethan pushed Elliott out of the way as he dove in front of the oncoming bullet that was headed for Aaron. Shielding his son from the round, it hit Ethan in the back just below his heart. He fell against Aaron and they both went down on the wooden porch.

At the same time, Amanda crouched as she raised her rifle and aimed it at Cody. Her shot was true and hit him between the eyes. He dropped out of sight. She lined up to the right of where he had been standing, knowing his cohorts were in that vicinity. One of them rose enough for her to see the top of his head. She hit him but had no idea if the shot was fatal. He disappeared.

Elliott righted himself and scurried over to the corner of the house where the porch connected to it. Bracing himself against the wall, he aimed his shotgun at the van. Someone was screaming unintelligibly on the other side. He could hear Lexi growling and snarling, as well as the sound of material being shredded. Finally, he could make out what was being said.

"Get this dog off me! She already killed Bo! Please, help me!"

"Lexi! Come!" Elliott called out. He waited a moment then yelled again, "Lexi! *Come!*"

Lexi came around the front of the van with blood covering her muzzle. She went up the steps past Elliott and straight to Ethan, who was still lying on top of Aaron. She stuck her nose against his face and nudged. Ethan didn't move.

Adrenalin running high, Elliott raised his voice again. "Whoever is left over there better come out now with your hands up! I ain't gonna tell ya twice!"

Taylor, Jason, and Devon hurried out from behind the van, hands raised as high as they could get them. The man responded, "I can't raise my left arm. Your damn dog 'bout ripped it off!"

"Then come out with your right one up and don't make any sudden moves." Elliott watched as the man rose slowly, his right hand held up.

"Elliott." Amanda said quietly.

Without taking his eyes off the man, Elliott replied, "Yeah?"

"I've got this. You need to check on them."

"Huh?" Elliott turned around and looked behind him. "Who?" Noticing the blood pooling beneath them he dropped his shotgun and rushed over to his son and grandson as Carly and the rest of the family spilled out the front door.

"Aaron!" Carly screamed. "Oh my god! He's dead! No, no, no!"

She reached them at the same time Elliott did. Will stepped in. Together, he and Elliott lifted Ethan's still form off of Aaron. They were both covered in blood.

"Nooooo!" Carly's mournful wail filled the winter air as she placed her son's head into her lap. His eyes were closed, and he wasn't moving. Carly brushed his hair out of his eyes as she rocked back and forth, her tears falling on his face. "Who did this? Who killed my son? Was it one of *them*?" She pointed an accusatory finger at Taylor and his friends.

"No, Carly. The one who did that is dead." Amanda made the statement very matter of fact, never taking her eyes off the men in the yard. "Those three said they were coerced. That one," she pointed the barrel of her rifle, indicating the man with the mangled arm, "was with the dead one. Whether or not he lives is still up in the air."

As they were talking, Aaron stirred in Carly's arms. She gasped as his eyes fluttered open.

"Mom? What happened?"

"He's alive! You're alive! Dear Lord, thank you! Where are you hurt? There's so much blood!"

"I don't know about anything else, but my head is killing me. I think I hit it on the porch when Dad ... wait ... where's Ethan?"

Aaron struggled to sit up. As he did, they all heard a strangled cry. It was Elliott. He was kneeling beside Ethan's blood-soaked body, Lexi at his side whining softly. Ethan was still alive though blood was streaming from his mouth. He seemed to be trying to speak. Elliott leaned over to his face.

"A ... A ... Aa ... ron?" he managed to whisper.

Elliott patted his cheek. "He's alive, son. You saved his life. You saved your boy."

Ethan's blood-stained lips turned up at the edges. He closed his eyes as he smiled. Elliott's body was wracked with sobs as he watched the life slip from his only child.

"Nooooo!" Cameron rushed to his father's side and grasped his hand. "You can't die now! We just found each other! Don't leave, Dad!"

Aaron crawled to his father's side, wrapping his arms around his little brother. Carly joined them, and all three of them held each other. Ethan's eyes fluttered open again. He looked at them with a tear running down the side of his face.

"So ... sorry ... left ... you ... hurt ... you. Always ... loved ... you ..." He closed his eyes again, trying to take a breath that never came. His hand went slack in Cameron's grasp.

Cameron fell atop Ethan's body, his tears mixing with the blood. Lauri tried to comfort Carly and the boys while Joel knelt beside Elliott, who was consumed in the grief of a father's loss. Elliott leaned into his friend and wept.

Will had joined Amanda. "What do we do with these guys?" he asked hesitantly, seeming afraid of the answer. He looked at her and saw that she had tears streaming

239

silently down her face as well. He laid an arm across her shoulders. "Are you okay?"

She swiped the tears away and said gruffly, "Yeah, I'm fine. I can tell you what I'd like to do with them. It's not like we can call the cops or the sheriff."

Devon, overhearing their conversation, took a step toward them. Amanda pointed her rifle at him.

"Stay where you are! One more step and —"

"I just want to talk," Devon said, cutting her off. "I think we can help each other."

"We don't need any more of your *help*!" Carly yelled across the heads of her sons. "You murdered this man. He was the father of my children. He was a son. He was a person!"

"That wasn't us, ma'am," Devon said, shaking his head. "We weren't able to stop them. We didn't have the tools or the numbers. But I believe we can work together and make everyone safer, especially from people like them."

Elliott had been listening to the conversation. He slowly stood up, pulled a handkerchief out of his pocket and wiped his face. He walked out into the yard and approached Devon, Lexi at his side. Devon held his hand out for the dog to sniff. She did and started wagging her tail. She then turned to look at Doug who was now cradling his mangled arm in his good one and raised her hackles, emitting a growl deep in her throat. Elliott stared into the stranger's eyes for a moment, then extended his hand.

"Lexi's a pretty good judge of character. If she says you're okay, you must be. I'm Elliott Marshall. This is my place."

Devon shook the elder man's hand and smiled. "Devon Brown. I'm very sorry for your loss, sir. These are my friends, Jason Caton, and I think you've met Taylor."

Elliott furrowed his brow as he glared at Taylor. "I have. Wasn't impressed."

Jason faked a cough to cover a laugh and Devon didn't try to hide his. "Yes, sir, I get that. But he really is a good guy. He just doesn't always use his brain in the manner in which God intended."

"Hey! Standing right here," Taylor said with a pout.

"We've got some things to take care of today. I've got to bury my son," Elliott paused, a hitch in his voice. When he had composed himself, he went on. "But I'd like to hear your idea, son, because we surely aren't safe. How about you boys come back tomorrow, and we'll talk?"

"That'd be great, sir. Thank you."

"Call me Elliott. This here is the rest of my family." Elliott stood and pointed to each one giving their names. Joel joined them and shook the men's hands. No one else left the porch.

"We'll help you bury these guys if you tell us where you want them," Devon went on. "If it's okay, we'd like to take the van with us. We'll take Doug, too." He indicated the man standing off by himself.

Elliott shook his head. "I don't want those thugs on my land, dead or alive. Take 'em with you. I don't care what you do with their carcasses."

"What are you going to do with him?" Joel asked as he eyed Doug.

Devon stood thinking for a moment, then said, "I'm not sure yet. I'll let you know tomorrow."

Acknowledgments

First, let me say thank you all so much for sticking with me. I know this one took a while, much longer than I intended. I hope it was worth the wait.

My life is different now from where I was this time last year. Any of you who follow my personal page on Facebook know I made a big change in my health this past year. In doing that, I found a new passion I didn't know I had. I lost over sixty pounds — the first fifty of that in five months — and have drastically improved my health. Now, I help other people do the same. The reason is simple: if SHTF, how long could you live in your current state of health without medications? If you rely on prescriptions to keep your blood pressure or blood sugar in check, how would you fare when you could no longer get those drugs? If there was a collapse and you had to leave your home, how far could you get on foot? For me, those answers were not well and not far. At almost two hundred pounds, I couldn't walk the short distance to my mailbox without taking a break. Now, I walk twelve thousand steps a day. I feel fantastic, and I want everybody I know to feel as good as I do. If you'd like to know more about this amazing program, message me on Facebook. I'd love to share it with you!

If I got any of the military actions wrong, please forgive me. I never served, though many in my family have. I try to research as much as I can, and I don't claim to be an expert. I don't know if, in a situation like I have created, our military and its leadership would behave this way. I just hope and pray they would.

The names I gave the politicians were meant to be tongue-in-cheek. It was supposed to be funny. Some people didn't take it that way, according to some reviews I've gotten. Seriously, people — it's fiction. They are characters in a story I made up. They don't exist. If this were a real-life situation, would politicians act this way? Probably not. Again, I hope and pray they would put we, the people, first. I hope we never have to find out whether or not they would.

I know my thank you list seems redundant, but when you have a great tribe, why change it? My husband, Jim, blew me away with this cover. I've been told my covers don't look like others in the genre. That's my goal and that's what I like about them. I want them to stand out in the crowd. Thank you for taking my idea and making it beautiful. I love you, Baby.

My Aunt Carol continues to keep my scattered brain's rambling looking like a professional did it. She goes through the books multiple times to help me deliver quality work. Her editing is amazing! Thank you, sweet aunt.

My advanced reader team comes through every time. They read so fast I can send the book to them and hear back in as little as twenty-four hours. They're reading machines and I know my books are better because of them. You guys rock. Thank you so much for taking the time to help me tell my stories better!

And then there's the rest of you. The ones who heap praise on me on Facebook, in emails, and the thing that helps the most – reviews. You guys and gals are the ones who make all of this possible. You devour the words and beg for more. You call me out on situations that you don't think are plausible. Even if we don't agree, you're still there, waiting impatiently for the next installment. I never thought my books could or would reach so many people, and I am humbled by your love of my work. I hope I can continue to entertain you for many more years.

There will be a book five. It may be the last in this series, but I won't know until it's written. I don't want to drag the story out until it gets boring, but I don't want to leave anything unsaid either. I don't plan the story out ahead of time. It takes me where it wants to go. We'll see where it leads. I'll be starting on it about a month after this one launches, and fingers crossed it gets done in a lot less time. I wish I could give you a time frame, but my brain just doesn't work like that. As soon as I can is the best I can do.

Last, and most important, I give the glory to God that He blessed me with this gift to tell stories people want to read. I placed my life in His hands and all I have is because of Him. Thank you, Lord, for the many blessings you bestow upon me every day.

Please take a moment and leave a review for any of my books you've read. Reviews are written gold for indie authors. Thank you in advance!

Find P.A. Glaspy on the web!

http://paglaspy.com/add-me/ – direct link to be added to the mailing list. Never miss a launch!

http://paglaspy.com/ – the website, always updating, so keep coming back for more info. Want to stay up to date on all our latest news? Join our mailing list for updates, giveaways, and events! You'll find a spot to sign up on the right side of the website. We don't spam, ever.

https://www.facebook.com/paglaspy/ – Facebook Fan Page. Funnies, prepper info, bargain books, review begging …

https://twitter.com/paglaspy – Follow on Twitter. Total slacker here, folks.

https://amzn.to/32X9i5w – Amazon Author Page

https://www.goodreads.com/author/show/15338867.P_A_GLASPY – Goodreads Author Page

https://www.bookbub.com/authors/p-a-glaspy –BookBub Author Page

Made in the USA
Las Vegas, NV
06 October 2021

31787862R00152